Beth Reekles is the bestselling author of the sensational YA series *The Kissing Booth*, now a major Netflix hit. She lives in Wales, and is a self-confessed nerd. *The Layover* is her sixteenth book, and she now publishes both YA and adult romcoms. You can follow her on TikTok @bethreekles and Instagram @authorbethreekles.

Also by Beth Reekles

BETH REEKLES
THE LAYOVER

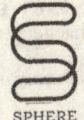

SPHERE

SPHERE

First published in Great Britain in 2025 by Sphere

3 5 7 9 10 8 6 4 2

A CIP catalogue record for this book is available from the British Library.

ISBN 978-1-4087-3027-0

Typeset in Caslon 540 LT Std by Palimpsest Book Production Limited,
Falkirk, Stirlingshire

Printed and bound in Great Britain by Clays Ltd, Elcograf S.p.A.

Papers used by Sphere are from well-managed forests
and other responsible sources.

MIX
Paper | Supporting
responsible forestry
FSC® C104740

Sphere
An imprint of
Little, Brown Book Group
Carmelite House
50 Victoria Embankment
London EC4Y 0DZ

The authorised representative
in the EEA is
Hachette Ireland
8 Castlecourt Centre
Dublin 15, D15 YF6A, Ireland
(email: info@hbgi.ie)

An Hachette UK Company
www.hachette.co.uk

www.littlebrown.co.uk

For Katie V – we'll always have Paris!
(And, more specifically, Orly Airport Terminal 3)

You're invited to celebrate the wedding of

Kayleigh Louise Michaels
&
Marcus Nicholson

Saturday 24 May
10.30 a.m.

La Villa Laguna Azul
Barcelona, Spain

Dinner and dancing to follow

*Formal attire (NO turquoise to be worn, but all
other colours are welcome!)*

Strictly NO children allowed

Accommodation and travel suggestions at kaycuswedding.com

*In lieu of gifts, please make a donation to the
honeymoon fund via our website!*

Chapter One

Gemma

Picture it: the perfect life. The one you just *know* you're supposed to be living.

It starts with the perfect man: handsome, with a great smile – one that wins everybody over, always, and makes you melt a bit when you see it. His great hair and sense of humour and the fact he pitches in with the cooking. It's a low bar, but God, does he surpass it by *miles*.

Then the perfect home: an apartment you managed to snag for a steal when the interest rates were miraculously low enough to actually get a mortgage, which you've tastefully decorated after scouring Pinterest for months for inspiration to make sure you bought the perfect pieces to suit your style. The one that, when you post pictures on Instagram or host your friends for dinner, you *know* everybody is gawking at the exposed beams and natural lighting and the parquet flooring you unearthed beneath a ratty old carpet.

And the perfect job: the promotion you've been grafting for, the chunky pay rise and swanky title, a reward for all the years you've spent working yourself to the bone. The sleep deprivation to meet 'urgent' deadlines, the hair loss from stress, the eye-twitch you've developed in response to a new message popping up on Teams – it's all worth it now.

And now, the icing on the cake: the perfect wedding.

A destination wedding, no less, at *the* most idyllic beach-side resort on the outskirts of Barcelona, all sprawling villa and white-sand beaches. The perfect dress, the perfect venue, the perfect cake . . .

It is going to be the perfect day. Sometimes, even I can't believe it's real; that anybody could achieve all this outside of a Hallmark movie.

The perfect beginning to the rest of a perfect life.

And God, do I hate the bitch who stole it from me.

My 'best friend'. The *bride*.

Standing in the airport, waiting for my flight to said destination wedding, my phone is burning a hole in my pocket. Or, more specifically, one particular video from the hen do is.

It's enough to destroy it all, I know.

I should have deleted it. As her best friend and maid of honour, I *definitely* should have deleted it.

Should have, but didn't.

And I can't help but think – in a very Carrie Bradshaw-sounding inner monologue – what a shame it would be, if that video accidentally got leaked right in the middle of such a perfect, perfect wedding.

Time Until 'I Do'

19 1/2 hours

Chapter Two

Leon

It's not a sign, that I'm late to the airport.

It's also not a sign that: I had to double back because I forgot my passport, then got a flat tyre, *then* was somehow double-charged for my Uber here, *and* spilled my cup of coffee all over my jeans. It was touch and go for a while whether the flight would even go ahead, the torrential downpour and bad winds having already delayed other flights this afternoon.

The truth, of course, is that I'm *looking* for a sign.

This wedding is a bad idea.

Which isn't a new thought, by any stretch. And I know I'm not the only one who thinks it. But what are you supposed to do when your sister claims she's met the love of her life? When she's absolutely *giddy* with it, doesn't even stop to consider that the engagement and wedding and moving in together all seems a bit rushed, because she's so completely happy?

You can't just look her in the eye and tell her she's wrong.

I was almost praying the flight *would* be cancelled. I agreed to do a speech in Dad's place, and that empty notebook I've been carrying around with me for months waiting

3

for inspiration to strike is haunting me. At least if the flight *had* been cancelled, I wouldn't have to go to the wedding at all, and wouldn't have to stand up there and lie through my teeth about how happy I am – how happy we *all* are – for Kayleigh.

When I think of this wedding, instead of conjuring up images of my sister glowing with happiness, all I can think of is the strain around the edges of Mum's smile, how Dad blinked several times before quietly saying, 'Of course,' when Kayleigh said she didn't think he was well enough to walk her down the aisle . . .

That never would've been the case before Marcus.

The beginnings of a speech swirl around in my head. I did enough googling to get an idea of how it's supposed to start.

The first time we met Marcus, I think, and my brain skids to a halt.

The first time we met Marcus . . .

I can think of a dozen empty pleasantries that would work here. The way he and Kay looked at each other lit up the room, you could tell they were meant to be, we all knew we'd be celebrating their marriage soon enough . . .

The first time we met Marcus, I think bitterly, *we hoped that'd be the last time we ever saw that pretentious, preening arsehole.*

And then I think: *There's got to be a way to stop this wedding.*

Chapter Three

Francesca

It's entirely possible that I've lost the plot a little bit, and I'm all too aware of that, but the truth is – I've never felt so alive!

I can see why they do it – all the heroines in romance movies. I can see why they throw caution to the wind and put it all on the line, do something so wildly out of character just for the *chance* to make it work with the one they're meant to be with. I'm practically fizzing with excitement; this is my very own main-character moment.

Hopefully, I think, the first of many.

I can't let myself consider what will happen if none of this works out. I'd surely just retreat into the shadows, humiliated, but . . . Well, I'm not going to be the side-character in someone else's story any longer.

This is *my* story; this is *my* great romance.

My stomach flips just thinking about Marcus. His smile, his hugs, his sharp wit and no-nonsense attitude. His lovely, amazing laugh. Every time *I've* made him laugh like that, and it's the best sound in the world, all rich and deep and infectiously charming.

The stomach-flip turns into a full-on series of Olympic-level somersaults when I think back to that night. That kiss. It's been eighteen months, but I can still remember the warmth of his palm on my cheek and the taste of his tongue like it was yesterday.

It was the kind of kiss that people write songs about; the stuff of poetry, the epic scene in a fairy tale. After months of flirting and dancing around each other in the office, it was just the two of us, alone outside a party, in the drizzle and beneath the lamplight, my body tucked into his as I stood on tiptoes and he bent to reach me, held me close, the hand he anchored in the small of my back that made me shiver . . .

We kissed for *ages*.

We fell into bed together after the party ended, cuddled close and whispering until sleep pulled us under.

But then he met Kayleigh, and we let what we had together get away from us. Ships passing in the night, a chance of something truly wonderful lost forever. Dissolved into a close friendship — but the possibility of something more glimmering in those smiles he gives me, in those long hugs and all the text messages we exchange every day . . .

It's still there. That feeling. That tension. That *spark*. I know it.

And Marcus knows it, too.

I have to speak to him.

I have to tell him how I feel.

I have to stop this wedding.

Chapter Four

Gemma

An announcement chimes through the airport Tannoy – '. . . *flight to Barcelona is now boarding . . .*' – and there's a flurry of movement inside the gate: people gathering bags, getting to their feet, patting pockets to check their phones and passports are secure.

I should be one of them. I should be elbowing my way to the front of that queue, actually, because I'm on my way to my best friend's wedding, and what's more important or exciting than that?

Instead, I'm stood frozen, phone clutched tight to my face, my boss's words ringing in my ear. 'I'm sorry, it's a bit noisy in here. Do you mind saying that again?'

So she does. And somehow, it isn't magically different to what she said before. I'm not hallucinating after all. This is *real*.

They've given *my* promotion to Kayleigh. The one *I* suggested because we were both taking on more than we ought to, the one *I* found money in the budget for, the one *I* presented on and petitioned to make happen.

I didn't even know they were interviewing for it! They didn't post a job advert anywhere. I'd made it clear in my

9

pitch for the role how I'd be the best fit, and I thought they'd agreed. So for them to have hired Kayleigh instead . . .

She had to have gone behind my back and *asked* them about it.

The perfect job, and they've given it to *her*.

She's taken everything else from me – and now this, too. The one thing that felt truly *mine*. I deserved that promotion. I fucking *earned it*. And she's taken it.

I wait for my stomach to drop, for tears to flood my eyes, but it never happens – probably because, deep down, I've known this was coming all along. The little side-chats between Kayleigh and our boss Janet, all, 'Kayleigh, can I just grab a quick minute?' and the two of them returning to the office with matching Starbucks cups looking all pally while I've been chained to my desk and flooded with work *she'd* begged me to help with. I should've known.

'Does Kayleigh already know about this?' I ask. She's been off all week – already in Barcelona luxuriating in the sun before her wedding, but she must know.

There's a beat before Janet says, 'We discussed this with her last week. I'm sorry it's taken us a little while to get back to you—'

'I was *in the office* earlier,' I snap – snarl – because God, I know things are hectic right now but it's not like she couldn't have found two minutes to call me on Teams. It's not like we weren't both *in the same meeting*, *in person*, *today*.

Clearly, Janet was too much of a coward to tell me to my face, but thought Friday afternoon when I'm headed to the airport was just the right time. I wouldn't be surprised if she'd clean forgotten about me and had a last-minute panic

10

because she knew I'd be seeing Kayleigh and should've heard the news by now.

I'm *seething*.

She's still talking in a gentle, steady cadence, as if to a child. 'We want you to know how much we appreciate all the work you put into making the case for this role, Gemma. It really showcased your willingness to go above and beyond; maybe if you continue to apply yourself this way there will be future opportunities for progression, but we've made our decision . . .'

I roll my eyes at the buzzword-filled banality of Janet's little speech, until she says –

'And Kayleigh mentioned that you've been struggling a lot with your workload lately, which was obvious to us all in your pitch for creating the new position . . .'

Hang on. She did *what?!*

'It just wouldn't have been the right fit for you at this time. And of course, we'd encourage you to seek out our mental wellbeing services if you find you are a bit burnt out.'

I hiss, 'I'm *burnt out* because you keep overloading us with work, which is exactly what I explained when I pitched the need for this new role. I'm *more* than capable of doing this job and you know it. It's what I already do—'

I'm interrupted by a gentle, patronising sigh.

'We appreciate how hard you work, Gemma, but you have a real follow-through problem. It's been made very clear to us that you struggle to complete tasks and need additional support, which Kayleigh has already proved she provides . . .'

Now, I'm seeing red.

The airport around me has become a hazy, scarlet blur, and my whole body is vibrating with white-hot fury. My mind throws up a quick montage of all the times Kayleigh has asked me for help at work, only to take it back at the last minute when her schedule has miraculously cleared. The work she's oh-so-kindly suggested helping me with because she has the contacts or the time, and I'm just glad to have something taken off my overflowing plate . . .

Fuck. She's Vultured me. Exactly like that arsehole from *Brooklyn Nine-Nine*. She's *The Vulture*.

How didn't I see it before?

The worst part is that I've always known what she's like, and I *still* didn't see it happening. I thought we were just . . . being collaborative. Helping each other out. Doing what friends do. If I never noticed, how can I expect our boss to?

But I still snap, 'This is way out of order and you know it. You *know* I deserve that promotion. You *know* I put the time in, the effort. So what, just because I'm not the smiley, bubbly one who doesn't actually get shit done, then—'

The sigh this time is *definitely* short-tempered. Janet mutters, 'This is exactly the sort of attitude problem we were concerned about, Gemma . . . Look, we've made our decision. That's that. Now, enjoy the long weekend away, and we'll see you back here bright and early Tuesday morning, yes?'

Attitude problem? She thinks *I've* got an *attitude problem*?

What the hell has Kayleigh been saying about me behind my back?

I think I say something at least halfway polite before hanging up.

I want to scream. I don't, obviously, because I think that's the kind of shit they'll arrest you for in an airport, but my knuckles go white around the handle of my wheelie carry-on bag, and bile rises in my throat.

I let it happen, ride out this wave of angst and jealousy and (fully justified) righteous indignation, because I'm going to have to bury it way, *way* down for the next couple of days.

I'll have to spend the entire time smiling and prettily crying happy tears (I've been practising, for the photographs) and gushing over how lovely everything is and how well it's all come together and what a gorgeous, stunning, lovely, *perfect* couple the two of them make, being the model maid of honour.

I hope to God some cow has the gall to wear a white dress so I can throw a glass of red wine on her. And picture Kayleigh's smug face as I do it.

I could blame it all on the promotion she stole from me, but this runs a *lot* deeper than that.

As I join the shuffle from the gate to the plane, I'm equal parts dread and impatience. Once I'm on that plane, it's real, it's all happening. On the other hand, the sooner this is over, the better.

I've been sucking it up for *months*, planning the hen do, going dress shopping and then for fittings, trawling through websites looking for venues and chasing up emails asking for quotes, discussing bouquets and catering . . . I spent *hours* finding the perfect insoles for Kayleigh's shoes. Nobody can say I've been anything less than an outstanding maid of honour.

As if she'd let me live it down if I'd been anything but.

So I gave it my all, and we both pretended I was happy

13

to do it, and every so often Kayleigh gushed how *grateful* she was.

I grit my teeth thinking about last weekend, when I took her and Marcus to the airport so they could 'settle in' ahead of the wedding. Kayleigh gave me the biggest hug, squeezing tight.

'You're the actual best, Gem, love you *so* much! It's going to be the most amazing time!'

'Yeah.' I wondered if she could hear the tightness in my voice, the edge to my words. 'So amazing.'

Kayleigh laughed. She tossed her hair as she drew away, and the ends smacked me in the face, and neither of us mentioned it. 'You *have* to say that. It was all your idea! I'm just so glad you didn't mind me borrowing it.'

She beamed at me, and I smiled back, and wanted to punch her in the face. Because she was right: she stole *my* dream wedding, and I helped her do it.

She'd never even *considered* a destination wedding before Marcus proposed. She wanted something in the countryside, in summer. But as soon as *I* mentioned the sunny springtime wedding abroad I'd always pictured for myself – well, that was that.

She's always had to one-up me.

She got the flat. She got the man. She's getting the wedding. And now, she's got the promotion, too.

It's not *fair*.

But I'm the only person who seems to see that.

And what was I *supposed* to do? We've been best friends since secondary school, when I moved and was the awkward new girl who didn't know anybody. Thick as thieves, practically our entire lives. My whole friendship group, I adopted from Kayleigh at school – even if I supplanted them quickly as her bestie. We were housemates for ages, too. We've always shared clothes and gossip and a Netflix account, so why not weddings, too?

I shove my bag into the overhead cabin with more force than strictly necessary, the wheels punching the plastic edge with a loud noise that makes a stewardess look over with a raised eyebrow.

She comes over, all smiles, and gestures at the garment bag I've dumped on the seats while I put my luggage away. 'Would you like me to take that for you?'

'Yes, please.'

Get it out of my sight. Lose it, if you have any compassion at all. Burn it.

'Special occasion?'

'Wedding,' I say through gritted teeth, then remember I'm meant to be *happy* about it. 'My best friend's getting married. That's my bridesmaid dress.'

'Oh, how lovely! Don't worry, we'll take good care of it.'

'Thanks so much.'

Don't trouble yourself, really.

If that frilly turquoise monstrosity just happened to fall on the tarmac and get run over and rained on, it could only be improved.

Also to file under things Kayleigh *absolutely* knew she was doing: putting me in that grotesque 'boho classic-romantic' dress in a colour that does nothing but wash me out, with all its tiered frills, while the other bridesmaids get to wear something sleek and flattering with a cute little ruffle just around the neckline. I'd have looked better wearing Katherine Heigl's Bo Peep look from *27 Dresses*, honestly.

15

I settle into my window seat and pull on my headphones, burying myself in my phone. I have some last-minute maid of honour duties to triple-check.

There's a text waiting on my screen from Kayleigh, from just two minutes ago.

> Just checked and looks like your flight is all on time – let's hope it stays that way with the bad weather coming in! Wish you'd gotten here yesterday, could have done with you this morning to help deal with the caterers lol, ended up late to my massage because of it. Safe trip hon! See you soooon! xxxxx

I bite my tongue, hard, and feel nothing except the rage boiling in my veins.

Oh, sure, like I should've been the one running around arguing with people because Kayleigh pitched a fit, when she had much more important things to do – like get a massage.

Kiss kiss!

I hate her, I hate her, I hate her.

But she's my best friend. She's all I've got. What else am I supposed to do?

I send back an equally trite text, unable to resist a dig about her massage when I couldn't get the time off work because we're in the middle of a project rollout, and open the Photos app.

I stare for a long while at the little thumbnail of the video from the hen do. The one I should've deleted.

God, won't it be such a shame when – *if*, of course, *if* – it played during my speech, instead of the adorable slideshow I've painstakingly put together? What a totally diabolical accident that would be. How totally furious I'd be on her behalf, her staunchest defender, so she could never blame me for being at fault.

God, wouldn't it feel so *good* to give her a taste of her own medicine?

Just this once.

Chapter Five

Leon

Unfortunately for me and my non-existent speech, the flight to Barcelona is on time. Not cancelled due to poor weather conditions, not even delayed.

I'm sweating and breathless as I get on the plane, so flustered it takes me a couple of minutes to find my seat.

It's *also* not a sign that the space overhead is full, and two air stewards have to come and rearrange other people's things to make my suitcase fit. It might as well be flashing at me in neon letters: *You're not supposed to be here! The universe is trying to tell you; why won't you listen!*

And, typically enough, I've got the window seat, so two people have to get up and shuffle out so I can get in. The strap of my bag snags on something and the lady in the aisle seat yelps.

'Ow!'

I turn and realise that I've caught one of the myriad enamel pins on her denim jacket. It's too big on her frame, looks more like a man's coat. Her long brown hair is drawn back in two French braids, then left loose over each shoulder. She's got huge eyes, framed by long, thick, lashes.

She's pretty – *very* pretty – and I'm staring, which makes this whole thing feel a thousand times more awkward.

'Sorry—'

'No, no, it's my fault!' she says, trying to disentangle us.

'No, my bad, I wasn't—'

'*Excuse me*,' huffs the man in the middle seat, currently cramped between us. 'Can we hurry this along a bit?'

She frees my bag strap, both of us blushing and apologising, and that neon sign over my head screaming *YOU'RE NOT SUPPOSED TO BE HERE!* flashes even brighter.

None of this, of course, is an omen.

Except I can't shake the feeling that it *is*.

Some great, glaring, cosmic sign from the universe hammering home that this is all wrong and shouldn't be happening. I can practically hear Nana hollering at me from beyond the grave: *Do something already! What are you waiting for?*

I buckle my seatbelt, rest my palms on my thighs – one leg is still damp and gross from the coffee spillage earlier – and take several long, deep breaths to ground myself.

I'm not even the superstitious sort. It's all bloody ridiculous, if you ask me. But Kay's been harping on about something blue this and something old that, all these wedding traditions that are meant to be good or bad luck, so I shouldn't be surprised that it's rubbing off on me.

I feel eyes on me, but determinedly don't look over at the girl in the aisle seat; I can't afford any distractions. This flight to Barcelona is my last-chance saloon: I need to write my speech, suffocate my own doubts, and get on with my sister's wedding.

It comes to something when you have to 'get on with' a wedding.

We're all to blame, I know. Me and the rest of the family. None of us really took to Marcus when Kayleigh first introduced him to the family – but bloody hell, she brought him home at *Christmas*, what were we meant to do? Of course we welcomed him in and made him feel right at home. 'Tis the season, and all that crap. We all kept our mouths shut about how rushed it seemed, that they were already talking about moving in together when they'd just met two months ago.

And when they showed up to Mum's sixtieth with that sparkling new engagement ring on Kay's finger – what was anybody meant to say, except 'congratulations'?

Mum got swept up in all the wedding planning, but I *know* she has doubts. She'll tut sometimes and say things like, 'Well, at least she's happy,' or, 'I'm sure there's a side of him we're not seeing. Maybe he's just a bit nervous around us all.'

She'll deny it profusely if Dad tries to bring it up, of course, and claim the pair of them are in love and that Marcus is family now, but we all know.

We all know that we don't like Marcus and don't think he's right for Kay, and maybe we could get past that if he hadn't turned her into someone we hardly recognise anymore, but *none of us have told her*, and now . . . Now she's marrying him, and it's too late.

We should've stepped in earlier. Should've just *said* something – taken her aside in the kitchen that Christmas and said, 'God, he's a bit up himself, isn't he? Not sure I'm keen on him, did you notice him interrupting all the time, like

20

he's got something more important to say?' We should've had a quiet word with her on the phone after the engagement, said, 'Are you sure about this, Kay? He's so arrogant and standoffish, is this really what you want? You're not just falling for all the nice gifts and expensive dates, are you?'

Mum will keep her mouth shut. She'll pretend to buy into the fairy-tale romance of it all, and not want to upset the balance for the sake of Dad's health, wanting to spare him stress that might trigger his MS. Dad will keep his mouth shut, because Mum is. And God knows my youngest sister Myleene won't say anything: she's just a kid, she's too excited to see the romance unfold to stop and think too hard about it.

Nana would've said something.

She *did*, actually. Plenty, and loudly, until Kayleigh told her, 'But Nana, I really think he's the one!' and she decided it wasn't worth wasting her breath. Not that it mattered anyway, because Kay didn't exactly bother to visit in Nana's last few months.

The whole thing is a shitshow.

And I wish I knew what to do about it.

I half listen to the safety announcements as we taxi down the runway, and wait until my ears pop after take-off before I reach into my rucksack for the little notebook that's supposed to contain my speech.

Dad *hates* public speaking. He's dreaded this day, I know, when he'll have to give a father-of-the-bride speech. He's a man of few words at the best of times, but pandering to a crowd is his idea of hell. Kay took pity on him and suggested I do it instead. A brother-of-the-bride speech.

Which should be easy enough. Talk about her childhood,

how she always wanted to play dress-up and made me play Barbies with her where they were doing impressive, girl-bossy jobs like she has now, and what a romantic at heart Kay's always been, how she told us she knew with Marcus from the very start . . .

I can write something formulaic, bland and nice and just sentimental enough. Hell, I can ask ChatGPT to churn out something for me, and then tweak a couple of bits and call it a day. This doesn't need to be Shakespeare.

I open the notebook, smooth the blank pages flat.

We've got drinks and dinner tonight, and then tomorrow . . . Tomorrow, I'm supposed to stand up and give this speech. I have to write *something*. Anything.

The first time we met Marcus, I write, *we hoped that'd be the last time we ever saw that pretentious, preening arsehole.*

Which is exactly the thing you *don't* put in a speech for your sister's wedding, but is exactly what I wish one of us had said to her, and it's all it takes for it to all come pouring out.

I'll rip the pages out later and write the proper speech, but right now . . .

It's cathartic, so I let it happen.

Putting it all on paper, shaping these feelings with words – it makes a thought snake out from the back of my mind, one that says, *But what if you told her all this? What if you took her aside before the wedding, and laid it all out for her to see?*

We all feel like we lost Kayleigh to her new relationship. Nana was the only one who might've had the spirit to say it to her face this late in the game, but she's gone now, and . . .

I remember what she said to me, when Dad first got sick.

I remember what she said to me, a couple of days before she passed.

And I know what I have to do.

So, I keep writing.

I'm not aware of the turbulence until the plane jolts so hard that my pen scrawls a rogue line all the way across the page in the middle of a word, and I look up in time to see the seatbelt signs ping on.

There's a slight crackle as the PA system comes on, and a sinking feeling in my stomach that has nothing to do with the turbulence.

'Hi, everybody, this is your captain speaking. Unfortunately, the weather conditions have worsened and we're going to have to make an unscheduled stop for safety reasons. We'll be landing shortly at Orly Airport, and ground crew will be waiting to assist you on your onward journeys. We apologise for this change in circumstances.'

The PA turns off, and leaves a ringing in my ears.

I can just hear Nana cackling in my ears. *What was that you were saying about no such thing as bad omens, boy? How's this for a sign?*

Really, I can't argue with that.

Chapter Six

Francesca

It's okay, I tell myself. *Breathe.* This sort of thing is practically expected on such a momentous occasion. It happens in all the great romances. It was bound to happen to me today. It's a *sign*!

I keep telling myself that, even as I try to calm my racing heart and wipe my sweaty palms on my jacket. The cabin is full of noise, and the crew are doing their best to make their way down the aisle to check seatbelts are fastened and to tell people to put their tray tables up. The cute guy in the window seat of my row still has his down. I wonder if he's a writer, or some kind of artist; he hasn't looked up once from that little green notebook.

When an air stewardess makes it to our row, I wait for her to tell him to put the tray table up before stealing her attention. Everybody on this flight is currently in the same situation, I know, but – but I have a *predicament*. This is life or death!

Well. Life or till death do us part . . .

'Excuse me,' I blurt before she can move away, 'but I have to get to Barcelona *tonight*. I'm on my way to a wedding. Well, I'm actually . . .' The nervous excitement that I've

24

been carrying for weeks fizzes over, and a giggle spills out of my lips. 'See, there's this guy . . .'

She gives me a deadpan look. 'Honey, there's *always* a guy.'

'He's not just any guy, though, he's—'

He's my guy, and he's marrying the wrong girl!

I've never said that out loud before, and I don't get the chance to now, either.

The stewardess's smile is tight, but she's patient as she says, 'Ma'am, everything will be sorted by the ground crew. Make them aware of your situation when you're at the terminal; I'm sure they'll be able to help.'

The window-seat guy whose bag caught on my jacket earlier leans over, then. 'Wait, I have to get to a wedding too.'

Now, the stewardess loses her composure a bit, and lifts an eyebrow at him, her polite smile all but vanished. 'I suppose there's *a guy* in your story, too?'

His face twists. 'Sort of, yeah . . .'

'Well, whatever you two need to be in Barcelona for, I can only advise that you speak to someone at the terminal. I'm sorry.'

'Wait, no, I'm serious—' he exclaims, but she has already moved on, checking seatbelts and armrests and tray tables and trying not to get waylaid by more questions she can't answer. I turn to window-seat guy. He's dragging a hand back and forth through a thick set of sandy-brown curls, muttering to himself and bent with his elbows on his knees. The middle-aged man between us gives him a withering look he doesn't notice, then huffs a sigh and puts his headphones back on.

There's bound to be more than *one* wedding happening in Barcelona this weekend, but . . .

I study the guy's profile, the squat nose and solid, square jaw accentuated by a neatly trimmed beard, scanning through my mental repertoire of people seen through long hours of Instagram stalking.

I can't place him, though, and I'm still staring – *frowning*, too, I'm mortified to realise – when he looks up and catches me.

'What?' he snaps. 'Sorry, am I bothering you?'

'Just a bit, actually,' the man in the middle seat mutters.

'No, I'm sorry, I didn't mean . . .' I'd be a bit peeved if some stranger was frowning at me, too, in all fairness, but I fumble the explanation, not sure where to start. If he *is* going to the same wedding, I can hardly let him know I'm on my way to confess my love for the groom, can I?

Window-seat tells me defensively, 'Some of us have bigger problems to deal with than meeting up with some *guy*, alright? I've actually got somewhere I *need* to be – this is a nightmare. So you don't have to look at me like that.'

Finally composing myself, I say, 'A wedding. Yes, I heard you. I was just wondering if I knew you. If we're going to the same wedding. I thought maybe you looked a bit familiar,' I add, just a little white lie, to hopefully excuse my weird staring.

He blinks, and stares back at me, eyes tracking over my features in a way that leaves me feeling – exposed.

I can see why he didn't like it. I sit up a bit straighter.

'I don't think so,' he mutters, and goes back to the little notebook he was scribbling in.

'You know, there's no need to be *rude*,' I tell him, leaning around the poor irritated man in the middle seat to scowl at him better. 'You're not the only one stressing out right now.'

He looks a little chastened and can't quite meet my eye. 'Sorry. Sorry, you're . . . you're right. I've just . . . got a lot on my plate.'

'With the wedding?' I ask more softly. The odds are near impossible that he's stressed for the same reason I am, but I can at least empathise with the wedding-related problems.

'Yeah. I have to be in Barcelona tonight, too. I have to talk to my sister before her wedding. About . . .' He fidgets with his notebook. 'Some stuff.'

'Sounds heavy.'

His *sister's* wedding, he said. Does Kayleigh have a brother? I don't remember seeing anything about her family on her socials, and she's never talked about them whenever I have seen her . . . He's certainly standoffish enough to be related to Kayleigh, though.

'Well, good luck with whatever it is you need to talk to her about.'

'Thanks,' he mumbles. 'Good, uh, good luck with your . . . guy.'

I beam, though he doesn't notice. I'm still smiling as I settle back into my seat, fidgeting with the pins on my jacket.

Good luck with your guy.

It's hardly much of a well-wish, but it's more than I've had so far.

It's not as if I can admit to my friends what's really going on with Marcus – which is a bit of a red flag in itself, I know . . . But they'll be happy for me when it all works out, and they'd only try to stop me otherwise!

They don't know him; not like I do.

27

And my family have no idea the guy from work I have such a crush on is the one whose wedding I'm going to this weekend . . .

I'm bolstered a little by this total stranger in the window seat.

I just sort of hope he *isn't* going to the same wedding as me, after all.

The crush of people clamouring to leave the plane as soon as it lands is immediate. The doors aren't even open, and despite the aisle on my left-hand side already being packed with impatient people, both the man in the middle seat and window-seat guy are standing and trying to squish past me to join the fray.

It takes far too long to get off the plane, followed by an even longer queue at customs, before – finally – we're spat out into the main terminal of Orly Airport, the hubbub of French voices and announcements jarring when I was braced for a trip to Spain.

I'm not panicking. Yet.

There's still *plenty* of time to get to the wedding. Maybe I'll be on my way to Barcelona within the hour! It's barely five thirty – I might miss dinner, but I could absolutely still make the drinks afterwards.

I let myself envisage it for a moment: arriving at the hotel bar where Marcus has plans with his friends, and the way he'll look up to see me, a gaze that will make me feel like Cinderella at the ball, how he'll walk towards me with that megawatt smile, how we'll slip away to talk – to confess – to kiss . . .

Really, this diversion is doing me a favour. Otherwise, I

would've had to sit through dinner waiting for my chance to speak to him, surrounded by people who think they're there to celebrate him and Kayleigh.

There's rain lashing down against the windows of the airport entrance, and the wind is positively *howling*. There are bits of rubbish being whipped about, umbrellas getting turned inside out, people hunkered down as they push forward against the storm to get inside.

I'll be on my way soon enough; I'm sure it'll be fine. The weather wasn't even forecast to be *this* bad, so it'll blow over.

Won't it?

But even if I'm not panicking right now, I *am* on a mission.

I brace myself as I cut through swathes of people looking for their check-in counter, tracking down the desk we were directed to over the in-flight announcements.

There's already quite a queue ahead of me, but I think I've managed to beat most of the families and couples who were waylaid juggling passports and collecting luggage. I join the line, knowing I'll be in for a bit of a wait. I can only imagine how stressful it must be for the staff to have to coordinate re-routing all those passengers, plus whatever other flight delays and issues they might have to deal with this afternoon.

I'll just have to be patient. Everything will work itself out.

'Excuse me, sorry, excuse me . . .' A man behind me leans over the rope barrier to the people ahead of us. 'Sorry, do you mind if I cut in front? It's just that I'm on a real time crunch, here. I've got to get to Barcelona tonight – my sister's getting married.'

It's window-seat guy from the plane!

He sees me looking, and when he does a double take, recognising me, too, I realise that I'm gawping at him; I'm just so surprised anyone would try to queue-jump. I try to rearrange my features into something more neutral, but I'm not entirely sure it works.

'That's hardly fair,' I point out. 'I'm on a time crunch trying to get to a wedding, too.'

'I'm the bride's brother,' he points out.

'And I'm the groom's best friend.' *Ha, take that!*

He opens his mouth to retort, but there's already a cascade of sympathetic noises going through the queue ahead of us, and then we're both being ushered underneath the rope so we can cut in.

I don't turn it down, even if it *does* feel cheeky. I look down the line as I thank everyone, but window-seat guy is too busy on his phone to say more than a quick, 'Cheers, mate.'

We're standing a bit too close, given the space we've both just squashed into wasn't really a *space* to begin with, so I can hear the dial tone on his phone as he rings somebody going to voicemail.

'Shit,' he mutters, then leaves a message: 'Kay, hi, it's me. The bloody flight's been re-routed, I'm stuck in Orly. In France. I know your geography's shite,' he adds with a laugh. 'Anyway, I'll figure things out and get there as soon as I can. I might miss all the festivities tonight, but *I'll be there*, okay? And . . . and let's find some time before everything kicks off, yeah? There's stuff I need to talk to you about. Anyway, um, I'll let you know. See ya.'

He hangs up, a long breath rushing out of him.

I say, 'Kay? As in Kayleigh Michaels?'

We're standing so close that I notice how much taller he is than me. That's not really difficult – most people are – but I have to tip my head back to make eye contact.

Window-seat guy doesn't say anything, so I continue, 'You're Kayleigh Michaels's brother? That's the wedding you're going to?'

'You're . . .' It's obviously an effort for him to remember the brief conversation we had not two minutes ago. 'Marcus's friend.'

'I'm his *best* friend.'

He laughs. 'No, you're not.'

I bristle, my shoulders squaring. I don't tend to think of myself as someone who's easily affronted, but this man seems to have a knack for getting my hackles up. '*Excuse me?*'

'I know Marcus's best man. And it's not you.'

'I didn't say I was his *best man*.' I roll my eyes. 'As if he would've wanted *me* organising the stag weekend! But we're very close.'

'Right . . .' he says, not sounding the least bit like he believes me – or even really cares. He eyes me up and down, but it's more curious than anything else, like he's trying to place me. I'm about to introduce myself properly when he says, 'Listen, whatever boy drama you've got going on with one of the groomsmen, or whatever, keep a lid on it, okay? I don't need them thinking this is some bid to get on a flight sooner, like that stewardess on the plane did.'

I flush, if only because he *does* sort of have a point, but I'm loath to let him have the last word so I say, 'What's so important you need to talk to Kayleigh about before the wedding?'

'What?'

31

'You just said, in your voicemail. You mentioned it on the plane, too. What do you need to talk to her about? Must be something *really* important if it was getting you that worked up.'

He looks at me with a face like thunder, dark enough to match the storm outside. His eyebrows pull low, and his mouth sets into a grim line.

'Nothing,' he mutters. 'That's none of your business.'

'Ooh, a top-secret important something. Colour me intrigued.'

Alright, now *I'm* being the patronising one, but I can't help it. It does lighten my mood a little to see that I've hit a nerve. I didn't think I was someone who liked the concept of payback, but this conversation is starting to prove otherwise.

He grits his teeth, jaw working side to side as if he's contemplating spitting some pointed retort at me to stay out of things that don't concern me, or maybe to simply tell me to bugger off. I wonder, when the look softens for a fraction of a second, if he's debating telling me. Spilling whatever's eating at him to some relative stranger, just to ease his mind. But he obviously thinks better of all those things, because he settles for turning away and ignoring me.

I say, 'Well, this is going to be a *lovely* wedding.'

Time until 'I Do'

17 hours

Chapter Seven

Gemma

Oh, God, this is just what I need. First the cabin crew actually *did* misplace my bridesmaid's dress – which, for all I joked, was a fucking nightmare – and *now*, after waiting for them to track down where they'd put it, there's a massive queue to sort out where I go from here.

'Here', apparently, being France. Honestly, who goes through *Orly* for anything? What happened to good old Charles de Gaulle?

A gym-bro guy with glitter in his hair and no luggage except a rucksack runs past me, panting, 'Shit, shit, shit,' under his breath. He looks like a kid who got lost on a stag do and is late going home to Mummy and Daddy.

He probably *is*.

He joins the huge queue I'm heading for, tearing at his hair as he counts up how many people are in front of him.

Yeah, you and me both, buddy.

I'm on the phone to Kayleigh as I cross the terminal, though I only get her voicemail. There's a big, fake smile pasted on my face as I talk. Like it'll help me pretend I'm totally genuine – or maybe it's just force of habit for whenever I'm dealing with Kayleigh.

'Babe, you will *never* believe what's happened. It's an absolute mare of a sitch. The flight got diverted to France because of a bit of rain, can you even? Absolute *mare*. Anyway, sure they'll fix me up on a new flight *tout suite*, so it's no big. Do not even stress. Not sure if I'll make it in time for a cheeky beveragino tonight but I promise, I'll make up for it in the morning with the champers, lol!'

I will make up for it with vodka, neat.

Can the maid of honour get away with being completely rat-arsed during the ceremony? I wish.

'So, like, I'll deffo let you know as soon as I know when my next flight is, but *please*, do not stress. It'll all be totally fine. Promise. Love ya! Say hi to Marcus for me!'

I hang up, knowing full well she will be stressing out.

What a waste of a massage that will be. Boo-hoo.

I wonder if there's somewhere here *I* can get a massage? I deserve one.

I also wonder if this is either karmic retribution or the universe trying to throw me a line. First with the dress, and then the weather. . . I mean, I have practically *made this happen*. I am a witch from *Macbeth*. I am the Grim in the tea leaves of Harry Potter's cup. I am Nesta from *A Court of Thorns and Roses* with her pointy death finger.

I've brought this on myself. Spoken it into existence. Manifested not being able to make it to the wedding.

But God, if I don't show up there – at the very least, by tomorrow morning – she will never let me live it down. Oh, we'll laugh about it, and she'll say it's all good and it's not my fault, but she will hang it over my head like a guillotine for the next ten – twenty – years, easy.

It'll be the thing she brings up jokingly whenever I'm a

bit late to meet up. 'Ooh, didn't get diverted through France again, did you? Thought this was going to be a repeat of my wedding, haha!'

It'll be the thing she throws back in my face whenever she gets a little bit upset with me for something. 'And this is *just* like my wedding, when you weren't there for me . . .'

It'll be the thing she brings out as leverage to overrule me – 'Well, if you'd listened to me and flown out earlier like I'd said, you wouldn't have missed the wedding . . .' – and the thing she uses to excuse her own failures as a friend – 'I think I'm owed a missed birthday party or two when you missed my entire *wedding*, Gem, the most important day of my life!'

I think about the video on my camera roll, and the resolve that *she deserves this* hardens a little more.

I will be at that goddamn wedding if it kills me.

Joy of joys, finally, a stroke of luck!

Just as I'm about to join the back of the humungous – genuinely, *humungous* – queue, I hear a familiar voice up ahead, and my heart leaps. I know that head of scruffy curls! I know that stocky build!

Leon is at the counter arguing with a flight rep, and there's a petite brunette next to him, the patient and friendly smile on her face just a bit too strained to be believable.

I breeze past the entire queue towards them, wheelie case rattling lightly behind me.

'Leon, hon! Fancy seeing you here! *Bonjour, bonjour!*' I call over, interrupting the conversation. I throw an arm around him in a quick hug he doesn't return, and when I pull away he's still blinking, startled to see me.

'Gemma. You're here.'

'Of course I'm here, silly! Looks like we were on the same flight.'

'I thought you would've already been out there. Making the most of the place.'

Yes, well, if it didn't cost an arm and a leg to get a room for a night, and if I hadn't been screwed over getting time off work . . .

'Oh, you know how it is! I thought you were going out this morning with your parents?'

'Flight was fully booked.' He shakes his head, trying to clear it. Poor guy can't handle stress *at all*. 'This, uh . . .'

He makes some vague, half-hearted gesture to the brunette, who meets me with a ready smile, this one equally frayed around the edges as the one she was using with the staff.

'I'm Francesca,' she says, 'Marcus's—'

'Oh, you're Marcus's friend! The work wife! Darling, *lovely* to meet you!' I give her a hug, too, if only to hide the wide-eyed shock that steals over my face in that moment.

The fucking *work wife*.

I swear to God. I can't. I can't deal.

But I'm not about to lay into her here in the middle of the departures hall, not when we'll have to see each other and play nice at the wedding all day tomorrow, too. I may be a bit of a bitch sometimes, but I'm not a monster.

I still can't believe Marcus invited her. I can't believe Kayleigh *let him*. I can't believe she actually *came*. This girl throws herself at him at any opportunity, has this pathetic crush on him, makes all these sad excuses to spend time with him . . .

I bet they've fucked.

38

Although, actually, this doe-eyed girl does *not* seem like Marcus's type at all. But still. Everything I've heard about her from Marcus and Kayleigh . . . I bet she has slept with him. I mean, hello, did somebody say 'office siren'? And in that ugly man's jacket, she's giving real Manic Pixie Dream Girl vibes.

Leon makes a disgruntled noise that sounds like an actual *grunt*, and we both glance over. His jaw is clenched, and he looks about as thrilled by the term 'work wife' as Kayleigh is. Francesca, for her part, has a faint blush on her cheeks. She's annoyingly good-looking. *Adorable*, all big eyes and pouty mouth, and I bet she doesn't even have fillers to achieve that look.

Anyway. Bigger fish to fry, and all that.

I turn to the man at the counter, resting my elbow on it and giving him a smile, too. Bright and dazzling and ruthless.

'*Bonjour, monsieur. Nous sommes—*'

'I speak English, madam,' he informs me with a Brummie accent.

'Right. Well, hi,' I say. 'I'm with them. We're all trying to get to the same wedding. What's the update? Have we got a new flight yet? We really *do* need to be there tonight, you see. Terribly important. Lots to do! I'm the maid of honour,' I add, really laying the self-importance on thick.

He looks exhausted already, poor fella, and gives me a terse look.

'As I was just explaining to your friends' – even *he* says it like he knows we're hardly more than peripheral acquaintances – 'most flights are currently grounded due to the storm. It's expected to clear up in a couple of hours, but—'

'So put us on a flight in a couple of hours.'

I swear, I literally see him questioning all his life choices and losing the will to live. He manages to turn his eye-roll into a series of blinks.

'We're very busy. You understand it's the bank holiday weekend. Most flights are already fully booked. With the delays—'

'What about . . . well, I don't know, a bus, or something? There's always a bus when the train is cancelled,' Francesca says, and we *all* look at her so unimpressed that she flushes beetroot.

'As if rail replacement buses are *ever* a good option,' Leon mutters.

'Would you *like* us to put you on a bus to Spain?' the desk attendant asks, and I don't blame him for the thick sarcasm. Francesca looks like she wants the ground to swallow her up whole. 'I didn't think so. Your options are: we can find you tickets on the next available flight, which *would* have been scheduled to leave tonight, but we can't guarantee how long that delay will be while this weather continues—'

'You have *got* to be kidding me,' I say. 'We aren't waiting around all night to *maybe* get on a flight!'

'*Or*, if you prefer, we can put you up in a hotel overnight. I should be able to seat you on the ten a.m. flight—'

'No!' all three of us cry out, and all three of us lurch towards the counter, making the guy reel back in alarm. He almost falls over, and I'd laugh if the situation wasn't so absolutely bloody dire.

'That's no good,' Leon says, fighting to keep his composure. 'The ceremony is at ten thirty.'

'Then I suggest you wait here for the next available flight.'

Leon huffs and steps back, and work wife Francesca is

dithering, fidgeting, which is all super unhelpful. I brace both hands on the counter, and try not to give our new Brummie pal a death-stare when I smile at him.

'I don't think you're understanding our predicament here. We have *a wedding*. My best friend is getting married, and I need to be there. *He* needs to be there. *She*' – I jab a finger at Francesca – 'needs to be there. What do we need to do to make that happen?'

'Take it up with Zeus,' he deadpans.

Leon snorts, so I look at him. 'Is that the manager?'

'It's the Greek god of thunder. You know. Like in *Hercules*? King of the gods? You and Kayleigh are as bad as each other, I swear.'

Right, well, *thank you* for that assessment, dickwad.

The man at the desk prints us each a boarding pass. He hands them over, and I take all three.

'Please proceed through security to the terminal and monitor the board for more information. Your flight details are on the boarding passes, and there are some food vouchers for use within the airport by way of apology from the airline for the inconvenience.'

'But—' I protest.

'Wait a minute,' Leon says.

Francesca cries out, 'Hang on, we haven't—'

And the man bellows, 'NEXT!' and I guess . . . we're done.

I debate planting my feet and telling him absolutely categorically *no*, we are not done here, but I . . . kind of don't think it's worth it. Is it the *worst* thing in the world if I miss the drinks tonight? I'll have already missed dinner, even if I got on a flight leaving right now. And so what if I don't have to put up with Kayleigh's self-satisfied smile and perfect, perfect life for a couple more hours? Besides, I've got Leon to vouch for me.

And frankly, I need to reserve my energy for getting through tomorrow, not haranguing this man into bumping someone else off an earlier flight for us. Because it's an *us*, now, we're a *team*, all three of us doing our damnedest to get there to celebrate Kayleigh and Marcus.

If we're stuck together, somehow, that will soften the blow . . . won't it?

Hell, knowing Kayleigh, *nothing* can make this better. It's an unmitigated disaster. I can't wait to not live it down for the rest of my life.

But I put on a brave face, another winning smile, and turn to Leon and Francesca. 'Come on then, you two. To security we go. *Tout suite!*'

Chapter Eight

Leon

Flight AFR13 Orly to Barcelona
DELAYED – Expected 02.35

'You have got to be kidding me,' I mutter, more to myself than to either of the girls. They flank me – Gemma with her arms crossed and hip cocked out to the side like she can glare the flight information board into submission, Francesca nervously dithering with her bags and phone, biting her lip. I knead a knuckle to my forehead, closing my eyes and shifting away from the glare of the board, and the flight that's now nine hours away.

Is this an omen? Stuck halfway to Barcelona until the morning, caught in a storm. It's got to be.

But an omen against what? The wedding? Or the talk I suddenly planned to have with my sister?

I look at the board again like it holds all the answers, but it just says the same thing.

DELAYED.

It's not good news, obviously, but it could be worse. Like, not getting there in time for the ceremony at all.

I must say it out loud, because Gemma snorts. 'I told her it was a bad idea to have the ceremony at ten thirty in the morning, but she was adamant. She just *had* to have so much time scheduled for photographs . . .'

'Oh,' Francesca says, 'that explains it. I did wonder about it being quite so early.'

I'm hardly listening to either of them, though, trying to mentally calculate ahead. It's almost two hours from here to Barcelona, it'll take – what, thirty minutes? An hour? – to get through passport control, then it's at *least* an hour's drive to the venue . . .

It's cutting it close for me to find time to talk to Kay before she starts getting ready for the wedding. To sit her down and ask if she's *really* sure about this, *really* sure about him.

It's a fine line to walk – voicing concern enough to give her an out if she wants to take it, without making her feel like we'll all judge her if she chooses Marcus – but now, at least, I've got time to think about it. Really hone what I want to say. What we *all* should have said a long time ago.

It won't give *her* much time to think about it, but there's nothing I can do about that now. Nothing I can do about any of this, except wait.

Obviously, Gemma's freaking out. She's the maid of honour. She's got a *role* to play, things to do. Kay's running a tight ship with this wedding, and Gemma's been involved in *all* of it.

I'm not saying Gemma took over as if it was her own wedding. Or at least, I'm not saying that *to her face*.

So, she's probably got tasks to complete, people to oversee.

She's probably mad she's missing out and can't swoop in and take over, too, but I won't dare voice that either.

I don't know why Francesca's all worked up, though. She looks ready to cry, or hyperventilate – so much so that I have this weird urge to reassure her. I push that aside, though. She's not my friend; she's *definitely* not Kayleigh's friend.

It's just a mate's wedding, I want to tell her, *calm down already. You'll make it.*

Unless . . .

She mentioned 'a guy' to the air stewardess on the flight. She can't mean Marcus, can she? Alarm bells start ringing in my head – I remember Kayleigh calling her an interfering harpy, her voice a little too shrill to let us believe it's some silly little joke. Maybe it wouldn't be so bad if Francesca *didn't* make it? Kay would probably prefer it if Marcus's work wife wasn't, you know, there with his *actual* wife.

She doesn't look like much of a harpy. But she must be, or else why would Kay be so bothered – so *threatened* – by her?

Is Marcus actually oblivious, or just choosing to be?

Is Francesca? Doesn't she *know* what she's doing? Some 'best friend' of the groom she is, when the only time she's ever mentioned is when Marcus is cracking a joke about his work wife and Kay's eye twitches as she tries to laugh along.

I look at Francesca as if the answers will be written all over her face. Like there'll be the word 'HOMEWRECKER' in scarlet lipstick across her forehead.

Which there isn't, of course, and she glances over like she can feel my gaze on her, and jolts a little at whatever expression is on my face. I wouldn't be surprised if there's writing on *my* face that says 'I DON'T TRUST YOU', at this point.

She frowns back at me, big eyes narrowing.

'How,' Gemma demands, stealing both our attention, 'has our flight been delayed *already*, in the time it took for us to get through security? This is actual madness. This is not happening. What are we supposed to *do* here for the next nine hours!' she cries.

And she's looking at me. More specifically, between me and Francesca, as if we're all buddies now, all in this together. The only reason we've not parted ways yet is because she's still holding onto all the boarding passes and food vouchers.

The need to be in control is something she and Kayleigh share. It's not hard to see why they're such good friends. They're alike in a lot of ways.

I don't know why she's looking at me – us – like we've got the answers.

The sheaf of papers is still pinched between her thumb and forefinger, hanging at her side where her arms are folded, and I reach out to take them, divvying the pile into three and handing them out.

I say, 'I don't know about you guys, but I figure I'll set myself up with a cup of tea and find a seat somewhere. We're going to be in for a long wait, and that's if we're not delayed any more than we already are.'

'A cup of tea does sound good right about now,' Francesca murmurs.

Gemma is nodding along fiercely. 'Yes! Perfect. Definitely what the doctor ordered. Come on, let's go find some seats before the whole terminal is full. Set up camp!'

She strides off towards the escalator to our right, where there are big signs pointing to the food court, and Francesca is already following.

'It wasn't an invitation,' I say, even though neither of them hears me.

I trudge after them; it's not like I've got much choice.

Upstairs is busy. The seating area is clustered in the centre of the space, essentially on a wide balcony overlooking the main concourse. The booths are an orangey leather and there are stools upholstered in pale green velvet, and some of the tables have entire trees growing up through the middle of them. It's actually a lot less pathetic-looking than I'd expect for an airport food court.

It's still a far cry from the white-and-gold glamour of Kayleigh's wedding venue.

Most of the tables and seats are taken; everybody who's already here has clearly had the same idea as us, but Gemma makes a beeline for the centre, weaving deftly between the crowded tables and finding an empty one for us. It's small, only intended for two, but she snags an empty chair from nearby and whirls it into place for us before throwing her coat over it, marking our territory.

Francesca and I are a lot less nimble on our way to join her. I hear her muttering, 'Sorry, sorry, excuse me,' behind me, and my suitcase keeps catching on the legs of people's chairs. I make sure to keep my satchel tucked in close, where it won't catch on Francesca's jacket again.

We all arrange our suitcases on the empty side of the table, Gemma collecting them neatly together before beaming up at us both from where she's tucked into the booth.

'I'll have a flat white, oat milk – and two shots of vanilla syrup, if they have it.'

Oh, great, so I suppose one of us is buying her drink, then.

'And if they don't?' Francesca says, but Gemma only laughs. Francesca heads over to the counter in the corner where they're selling sandwiches and coffees, and I'm once again left with no choice but to follow. It's not as if I'm going to expect her to buy my drink, too.

Francesca pauses to browse the case of pastries near the tills. A middle-aged man who's just paid turns, attention fully on his phone, and walks straight into her. He must stand on her foot – hard – because she jumps away with a pained expression.

'Oi,' he barks. 'Watch where you're going.'

I scowl; what a douchebag.

But Francesca only mumbles, 'I'm so sorry, I was just—'

'Not bloody paying attention!' He *tsks*, noisily, and marches off to wait at the end of the counter for his drink – immediately burying his nose back in his phone. I almost say something myself when, instead of calling the hypocrite out, Francesca just bows her head and takes it, scurrying to the back of the queue.

I'm not sure what I thought was going to happen. I've got Kayleigh's voice in my head calling her manipulative, a harpy. Did I think she was . . . what, going to *seduce* him into apologising?

Obviously not, but . . . That meek wallflower behaviour doesn't exactly scream 'man-stealing harlot'.

Even as I join the queue right behind her, I try to hang back. I look at the sandwiches in the open-front fridge (none of which look hugely appealing) trying to look busy, but Francesca is staring hard at me. It's like a physical *thing*, laser beams driving into my skull that are impossible to ignore for too long.

48

So, eventually, I give up, and ask her, 'What?'

'I think we got off on the wrong foot.'

'*What?*'

She clasps her hands in front of her, her purse and phone held between them. The purse is battered, old, a faded navy leather. Her phone case is the clear plastic kind with pressed flowers in. Actually, her whole look is ... eclectically mismatched. I can see the enamel badges crowded on her denim jacket in more detail now – one that's a pink and white stack of books, one saying something I can't read in swirly writing, an astrological sign, a yellow tulip, a video-game character, a red and white mushroom with a cutesy face, a Taylor Swift one. I wonder if she's collected them lovingly over the years, gifts from friends, or if it's all just to *look* 'quirky', in that way female characters do sometimes in movies. Try-hard, fake, alluring for being so off-beat and 'not like other girls'.

That would check, knowing what I do about her.

'I think we got off on the wrong foot,' she repeats. 'On the plane. Or in the queue downstairs. Maybe both?' Her voice goes up more than it should with the inflection of the question – nerves, I think. She bites her lip, then stops, then tries to smile. Her head cocks slightly to the side as she does so, which some distant corner of my brain registers as cute. Or annoying. That's yet to be seen.

She goes to say something else, but I cut her off.

'You're Marcus's friend from work. Francesca.'

'Actually, we're very good friends outside of the office, we're—'

'You're the work wife.'

She blushed, earlier, when Gemma said it. I noticed. But now, she reels back a little, as if the words are a physical blow.

'We're friends,' she reiterates, but even she doesn't sound very sure about that now.

'Right. And I'm Leon. The bride's brother. There – introductions done, we're off on the right foot. Better?'

The words come out sharper, meaner, than I'm used to hearing myself talk, and she looks a little hurt by it, but that only solidifies something that's unfurled in my chest. I've never been the protective big-brother type when it comes to Kay. Even if I'm older by four years, she always acted like the elder sibling. She was loud and bright and brave, and I . . . mostly just faded into the background. Coasted along in her shadow.

But God, if Francesca isn't bringing that out in me now. I think it has more to do with my dislike of Marcus than a protectiveness over Kay, but that's something to deal with later.

Or, you know, never.

Maybe Francesca *is* just his friend. Maybe she really doesn't see anything wrong with it. Maybe she thinks she's just here to support a mate and celebrate his wedding, and doesn't know the impact she's had, how much Kay sweeps it under the rug.

She swallows, hard. I hear it. She closes her mouth where it's parted into an 'O' of shock, and lifts her chin. I hear the sharpness of her inhale. Her eyes – the ones which were so wide and shining just a second ago, like she was about to cry – turn icy. They're pale blue, I notice. Almost grey.

Even though she doesn't say anything else, I get the message loud and clear: *Fine, if that's how you want to be. Fine.*

I don't bother to apologise.

Chapter Nine

Francesca

Quite honestly, I would be perfectly happy to take my cup of tea and hole up somewhere far, far away – or as far away as I can get in a compact airport terminal for nine hours – from Kayleigh's awful brother and her intimidating best friend, and pass the time until the flight with my Kindle, daydreaming about what I'm going to say to Marcus when I see him, how he'll react, what *he'll* say . . .

He calls me his 'work wife'.

He *talks about me*.

That has to mean something, doesn't it?

But I can't just run away – not least because I have the maid of honour's coffee, and she has all my bags.

So I go back to the table she secured and pop our drinks down.

'One oat milk flat white, extra vanilla,' I confirm.

'Ooh, you are a star!' Gemma wraps both hands around the paper cup, pulling it towards her and making an appreciative noise as she inhales the sweet-scented steam. She doesn't mention paying me back for it, and I'm not sure how to ask without sounding rude, but I suppose it was only a couple of quid. It's alright.

She taps her phone screen, which has a bunch of notifications showing, but apparently not the one she wants to see. 'Don't suppose you've heard from Marcus, have you?'

'No.'

I texted him while we were in the queue for security, letting him know about the change of plans. I was meant to be joining him and the groomsmen and a couple of others for some drinks after dinner, but I definitely won't make that now. I reassured him that I'd be there soon, though, and wished him a fun night with everybody.

Gemma clicks her tongue. 'Damn. And Kayleigh's phone is off. They'll be doing cocktail hour before dinner, at this point . . . Oh, well. They'll find out soon enough, won't they! Nothing to do about it now.'

I give a little laugh, but it comes out nervous and awkward. Gemma is polite enough to pretend she doesn't notice and just keeps smiling at me.

I'm not sure what to make of her. She's constantly plastered all over Kayleigh's social media – they've been friends since they were preteens, all through school, even getting jobs at the same company and living together. They're *inseparable*. And they're always out at bars or cool gigs or hosting glam little dinner parties, living their best lives.

Gemma is as striking in real life as she is online. Coppery-auburn hair in a choppy, chin-length cut and in artful waves – I honestly can't tell if they're natural or if they took her two hours with a Dyson Airwrap; glasses with thin, octagonal frames that she make look chic and fashionable, and a glowing complexion. I don't think she's even wearing any makeup right now. She's not *pretty*, exactly, but she oozes confidence and charisma in a way I only wish I could. This is a woman who knows exactly who she is, and wants to make sure everybody else knows it, too.

But her smile looks sharp. Dangerous, somehow, and maybe a little bit fake. I don't think those eyes miss a thing, for all the blank, casual expression on her face.

It's like, for a second, she can see right through me. Like she *knows* why I'm really here, what I'm planning to do.

It's like she *knows* that when I say no, I haven't heard from Marcus, what I mean is that he left my message on read. With a thumbs-up reaction.

But he probably just saw it quickly and didn't have time to reply properly. He's always doing that. He'll text when he gets a chance, he always does.

I dither next to the table, taking my time putting away my purse, pretending to rummage through my bag for something, wondering if I can make an escape now. Could I invent some work I have to do? What if they catch me in a lie, though? This isn't a very big airport, they're bound to see me, and see I'm obviously reading a book instead of working, and they'll know I lied to them . . .

Leon has joined us by now, slumping into the extra seat that Gemma has pulled over to our small table. 'No word from Kay,' he says.

'We were *lits* just saying!' Gemma flaps a hand at me. 'Honestly, you'd think the pair of them would wait to completely ignore the rest of the world until the honeymoon, wouldn't you! Cheeky buggers. Oh, Fran, hon, sit down already. You're making the place look untidy! Not like we've got anywhere else to be, is it?'

She laughs, and even that's somehow both pretty *and* manufactured. Like, it's almost *too* nice to be real.

53

I shake off the thought. Just because Kayleigh can be a bit up herself . . .

I glance at Leon. *Obviously a family trait.*

Still. I shouldn't hold that against Gemma, and we *are* all stuck here for the next nine hours – and for the entire long weekend beyond that, at the same resort.

If the wedding even goes ahead . . .

And what if it *does* go ahead? What then?

'You alright?' Gemma says. 'You look all out of sorts, Fran.'

'F-fine. Yeah.' I sit down, shoving my bag between my knees and onto the floor. My stomach is in knots.

I hadn't really thought that far ahead . . . My plan sort of began and ended at talking to Marcus and confessing my feelings to him – and then he would say he felt the same, and . . .

Right now, faced with the maid of honour and the bride's brother, those daydreams feel naïve and juvenile. I can practically hear the gentle admonishments my friends and family would make if they knew the whole truth, all the 'I told you so' looks I'd get even as they comforted me in my heartbreak.

How my older sister would give me a cuddle and rub my back and say, 'Well, it's his loss! But, really, if he was *engaged* . . . don't you think you should've gotten over this crush a while ago?'

How the girls from uni would jump on a group call immediately, and we'd all order ourselves Deliveroo and gossip as per our usual routine. They'd cuss him out for hurting me just like they did after he started seeing Kayleigh, I'd cry, and then they'd say, 'Yeah but Fran, hon, he *had* a chance with you, and he didn't take it. And even if he had, you lose them how you get them, so you're sparing yourself some heartache down the line . . .'

As if they know *anything* about us.

I swallow the lump in my throat, but it doesn't go away, so I take a few tiny sips of my too-hot tea to try to clear it, though that only succeeds in scalding the tip of my tongue.

Marcus and I – we have something *special*. That night we spent together, it meant something. It wasn't only a one-night stand, some random hook-up, or a drunken fumble with a mate that you both laugh about the next day.

You don't touch somebody you don't care about like that.

You don't lie there whispering about your deepest fears and biggest dreams with them until dawn begins to sneak in around the corner of the blinds.

And you don't flirt with them for years around the office, have everyone talk about you like you're such a pair, always find excuses to drop by each other's desks or mundane little things to message about during the workday, and then text all the time when you're apart, even long after you've gotten a girlfriend, if they don't mean something to you.

Gemma and Leon are busy talking about some of his family, and I sink deeper into the memories. Marcus popping up on our work's internal IM system to suggest getting lunch together. The arm he'd sling over the back of my chair when we were both at after-work drinks, the random texts we'd shoot back and forth, *always* initiated by him because he'd seen or thought of something that reminded him of me.

I felt that spark the very first time I saw him. All that build-up, culminating in the perfect night together . . .

He only chose Kayleigh because he thought *I* didn't choose *him*.

Those feelings, that flirtation, it's never really gone away. No matter how careful I've been to make sure I respect the fact he's with someone else now, to keep things just friendly and not overstep the mark.

But that connection we have . . .

The way he acts around me . . .

I just *know* if I tell him I feel the same way, that I'm in love with him, too, he won't go ahead with marrying Kayleigh. And I have to tell him. He has to know.

I *have* to be brave enough. Don't I owe that to both of us? Shouldn't he know, before he commits to somebody else for the rest of his life?

I've been staring off into the distance, and a noise at the next table draws me back. Gemma is still chattering away, swiping across something on her phone as she does so – Instagram, it looks like – but Leon only seems to be paying her the bare minimum attention.

He's too busy frowning at me.

He's actually quite attractive, if only he didn't look like such a miserable, bad-tempered grouch. He holds my gaze even after I catch him looking, and the deep breath he takes as he straightens up in his chair feels pointed, somehow, like he's trying to tell me something.

I don't know him well enough to understand what point he's making, but I do know it makes my own temper spike again – hot and sharp and raw, the taste of it acidic and unfamiliar in my mouth. Why does he have to be so hateful? Is this why he's not on Kayleigh's socials; she decided to cut his horrid attitude out of her life and not make time for him?

He's made it perfectly clear he doesn't like me. He sounded *very* disdainful when he said I was 'the work wife', which I think I'd be a lot more offended about if I didn't secretly thrill at the implications of that. That he thinks I'm a *threat*. Whatever Marcus says about me . . . Leon must have caught on to the fact that I matter to him.

Maybe there are cracks in Marcus and Kayleigh's relationship that run deeper than he's let on. Leon must know that, too, but has chosen to resent *me* for it, blame *me*, instead of simply accepting that they aren't right for each other.

That's got to be it.

Yes, I think, I'm *definitely* doing the right thing by confessing my feelings to Marcus before the wedding.

But even as I cling to that thought, my shoulders hunch, and I have to look away from the weight of Leon's stare, suddenly too much to bear.

Time until 'I Do'

16 hours

Chapter Ten

Gemma

By some miracle, we've whiled away a whopping thirty-eight minutes with our drinks, and it really *is* a miracle, because Francesca is dull as ditchwater, barely even *listening* never mind saying anything, and Leon is doing his best impression of a Neanderthal, doing little more than grunting when spoken to.

I know it's his sister's wedding and he's missing out on a family reunion tonight, but he really needs to chill out. *I'm* the one who'll get it in the neck from Kayleigh when she finds something that isn't going perfectly and wants me to come in and argue with somebody to fix it. *I'm* the one who's supposed to be doing a last-minute check of the seating chart and making sure all the guests have arrived okay and that the flowers are correct and the caterers have everything in hand, and . . .

Speak of the devil.

My phone starts buzzing across the tabletop. 'BITCH', it says, with a sparkle emoji.

'Ohmigod, it's her. I'll be back!' I leap up with my phone in hand, hurrying away from the food court to try to find somewhere quieter. The concourse is packed now, and there's

61

a huge queue at the little coffee shop at the top of the escalators, so I head downstairs as I answer the call.

'Hang on, it's crazy loud here! One sec, babe.'

As I do a quick scan of the area – it's a circular space lined by shops, the only exception passport control and the gates, but I find an empty hallway behind me, and dart down it. I think it leads to the loos.

Kayleigh is already talking anyway, somehow managing to hit that weird combination of hissing *and* shrill she's always been so good at.

'I cannot believe this, Gem! Delayed? *All night?* Are you kidding me? What am I going to do? You were supposed to be here! This is *exactly* why I thought you should've come out the other day, or at *least* got the morning flight out –'

Easy for her to say, when half the reason I couldn't get the time off is because I've been picking up *her* work while she's out of the office, and I can't even complain about *that* because it turns out she's the one who got the fucking promotion.

It's now officially *my job* to pick up the slack for her.

She's still going, so I wait for her to pause for breath, only half listening as she panics about all the potential things that could go wrong between now and tomorrow morning, repeating how I should've taken the morning flight, then throwing in a few crocodile tears while saying she's so upset I'm not going to make it to the 'rehearsal dinner'.

I don't even know where she's gotten that from. There's no *rehearsal* of anything. It's just that everybody who's flying in would have been there anyway. A few people who've booked hotels in Barcelona city are taxiing in for the evening to see friends and family, make the most of it. All Kayleigh did was arrange cocktail hour for anybody who wanted to join.

I say Kayleigh; I mean, she told *me* to organise it with the hotel.

Maybe if I hadn't been lumped with so much of her wedding planning, I might not have looked so burnt out at work, and they would've given me the promotion. There's a joke in there somewhere, I'm sure. I'm the punchline.

Then she says, 'Honestly, I shouldn't have even *bothered* with that massage this afternoon. What a waste of time.'

Boo-fucking-hoo.

But I make a sympathetic noise. 'I know, right? I'm legit *so* sorry, babe. If I could've been out of work sooner for the early flight, you know I would've . . .'

I don't even bother trying to defend myself on that front. She *knows*. She doesn't care about the truth; she just wants to play the victim.

Not wanting to get thrown under the bus totally alone, I add, 'Leon's stuck here, too, you know. We both feel *awful*. I wish there was more we could do . . .'

'Can't you get a train? Or rent a car? How long can it take to drive here, anyway?'

In all honesty, maybe we *could've* gotten a train – I think we were too thrown by Francesca suggesting a *bus* to really consider it. Besides, Kayleigh's whole rant has been so emotionally draining I think I'd actually rather wait it out here at this tiny airport terminal.

I can't blame any of her attitude on the stress of planning a wedding. This is just – Kayleigh.

She's my best friend; aren't I supposed to forgive her stuff like this? Love her in spite of it?

'Oh, hon, you know we would, but we've already gone through security and everything. I don't think we could leave even if we wanted to,' I say, which is sort of true. It's just that I don't plan to ask and find out. 'Listen, Joss and Andi and Laura know all about the dress and bouquets and everything, so if anything goes wrong, they can help sort it. And your mum's there! She'll have a handle on things till I get there.'

'Yeah, I guess.'

Joss is going to just *love* stepping up so she can undermine me. She's been Kayleigh's friend the longest, and I don't think she's ever forgiven me for the fact Kayleigh picked *me* as her bestie.

'Just enjoy the night, yeah? And then when you wake up tomorrow, I'll be there waiting with a mimosa in hand ready to help get you ready for your big day. Promise!'

Kayleigh sighs, but it's not her argumentative one this time. Phew. At least that's one storm that's blown over – for now. She says, 'Have fun stuck in an airport all night. Sounds miserable as hell.'

'It is.'

'Lucky you, having to hang out with Leon all that time. Is he there now?'

'Nah, I left him upstairs. Oh, and you know who else is here? *Fran.*' My mouth is moving before I can think about it; my tone is catty enough to match Kayleigh's. I feel like a puppet given a script, but I can't stop it.

'Fran?' she says. 'Who the hell is—'

'You know, *Francesca*. Marcus's Francesca. *The work wife.*'

Kayleigh's gasp is loud and so melodramatic it does a full one-eighty back to deadly serious. 'No! Oh my God.

64

What do you think of her? Isn't she such an annoying little cow?'

I snort. 'She's too boring to be annoying.'

'Please. She's such a prim and prissy piece of work; it's *so* embarrassing the way she's always throwing herself at Marcus. You know he only invited her because he feels sorry for her?'

'Oh, totally.'

Secretly, I've got other theories. I think he *loves* the attention. I think Marcus enjoys the whole 'cute girl fawning all over him' thing a lot more than he makes out. I think Kayleigh knows that, too, but because we're besties, we both pretend like we're not thinking it.

And . . . I don't think Fran's actually *that bad*. Boring, yeah, but . . . I don't know, Kayleigh always made her sound so self-righteous and insufferable. Prim and prissy, like she said. I haven't seen that yet. She's just . . .

Nice. Boring, but . . . nice.

I actually feel kind of bad, bitching about her with Kayleigh now, but . . . old habits die hard, I guess. And the nagging feeling of guilt, that itch of discomfort, the lingering little voice I shut down a long time ago saying that I'm being needlessly malicious – that's an old familiar feeling, whenever I'm talking to Kayleigh. I've long since learned to accept that.

So I ignore the nauseating twist in my stomach and laugh at the high-pitched, breathy impression she does of Fran, even though it sounds nothing like her, and I say, 'Oh my God, *accurate.*'

'Let me know what she says. A running commentary any time she talks about Marcus, okay?'

'Oh, you've got it. Absolutely.'

And I know I mean it, too. I know I'll text her everything Fran says, exaggerate a little, throw in a bunch of mean-spirited emojis, and laugh to myself about it, and pretend it's totally harmless fun.

There it is again, though. That little twist. Another knot forming in my stomach.

Then Kayleigh says, 'By the way, you heard, right? About the job?'

Shit. I'd really been hoping to avoid talking about this. Bury it, until next week. Pretend for a couple of days that it wasn't true.

She just has to drive the knife in, though, doesn't she?

'I did.' I swallow, and force myself to exclaim, 'Congratulations! I'm so excited for you!'

Lie, lie, lie. Can't she hear it?

'Ohmigosh, I'm *so* relieved, you have *no* idea how hard it was to not tell you! But it wasn't my place, you know? They wanted to make sure everything was all done properly, tell you themselves. Follow due process and all.'

Lie, lie, lie. I can hear it.

'Totally.' The word scratches out; my throat is bone-dry.

'It's so exciting, though! Guess the best gal won in the end, huh?' She laughs to take the sting off, an old trick, but I only feel a total sense of numbness.

My voice doesn't even sound like mine when I say, 'For sure. Hey, you owe me one for setting the whole thing up in the first place for you, huh?'

Kayleigh's laugh this time is curt. Patronising. She doesn't say anything else.

'Well, anyway, I'd better get back – my coffee'll be getting cold, and you would not *believe* the line to get a fresh one. Total hell. Get the girls to send me some pics from tonight, yeah?' I say. 'Can't wait to see! Can't believe I'm missing it.'

'Me either. Miss you, babe.'

'Miss you too!' I chirp, but when I finally hang up, my breath comes out in a long rush, and I sink down the wall I'm leaning against until I'm crouched on the balls of my feet, and I press the heels of my wrists to my forehead.

I wasn't very pretty or book-smart or sporty at school, but I could be popular. Kayleigh took me under her wing, and the rest was history. I knew how to work people, and I used that to my advantage. Then at work, it was so cut-throat that being *nice* and *kind* and *compassionate* would've only held me back. I know who I am; and worse, Kayleigh knows who I am. Who she expects me to be.

Sometimes, when I have a little distance from her, like right now, it wears on me.

It makes me think . . . that I don't always, necessarily, *like* who I am.

That's the sort of thinking that gets you down if you give into it, though, the kind of thing that sends you spiralling into an existential crisis. So you can't think about it too much. Just like how you can't let yourself think too long and hard about your dad walking out, or your mum never caring, or your girlfriend breaking up with you when you thought she was going to propose . . . Or your best friend beating you out for a promotion, getting the guy, buying the home, and stealing your dream wedding.

It'll bury you, if you're not careful.

It'd ruin a better person. So, sometimes, I'm glad I'm not like that.

67

I can't afford to let it fester. It's the sort of thing you harness, channel, let drive you to something bigger and better, use it to get what you want instead of wallowing. It's the only way to cope.

Which is why I know that in all likelihood I'll gossip ruthlessly via text with Kayleigh about anything Fran says and does, and why I have that video on my phone. There, ready, waiting.

Chapter Eleven

Leon

Gemma can't be gone for more than five, maybe ten minutes at most.

It's an eternity.

Without her chattering away about the wedding and the venue and the guests, the silence swallows us, made all the more obvious by the clamour of voices and hiss of drinks machines and rattle of suitcase wheels and shouts of 'Order number eighteen! Eighteen?' from the food vendors.

Francesca sits quiet. She alternates between fidgeting with her empty cup or the pins on her oversized jacket and checking her phone and looking around, people-watching. She looks my way several times, like she wants to say something, but never does. It's probably for the best.

I don't have much to say to her.

The only common ground we have is Marcus, and I'm *really* not interested in talking about him right now. Especially not with someone who, I'd be willing to bet, thinks the sun shines out of his arse.

I don't even know why she's coming to the wedding. Marcus invited a few of his mates from work to the wedding, so maybe he genuinely felt like he *had* to include her, but . . .

The whole thing just feels *off*.

I get my notebook out, pretend to focus on it, but the words swim on the page. It's three sides of scrawl about what a prat Marcus is, how Kay deserves better, a very much *non*-exhaustive list of occasions he's been rude to the family or affects Kay's behaviour and she seems not so much like her usual bubbly self . . .

Kay's always been well liked. People flock to her – and to Gemma, too. They both have that kind of charisma that draws people in. But while Gemma can be a bit blunt and snarky, Kay's got that softer, sweeter edge. She's always been like it; and then Marcus came on the scene and suddenly it was all about him, and their life in London, and her social circle, and her Instagram, and getting the *right* throw pillows and the *right* gin glasses; and things like that were more important than making time to come home to see her family.

And when she did, she'd be the Kay we all knew and loved, but there would be these flickers of someone else. Some stranger who turned her nose up at Mum's coat or ignored Dad when he tried to talk to her about a new album he'd been listening to, who sat down to a lamb roast and waxed lyrical instead about the fancy lamb shank at a posh restaurant they'd been to recently, and didn't clear her plate when she used to ask for a slice of bread to mop up every last drop of gravy.

She calls, sure. She checks in. Even remembers, some-times, to ask how Dad's doing. She makes vague plans to visit, promises she'll be home soon, swaps links to clothes and beauty products with our little sister Myleene . . . But she never bothered to visit Nana, all that time she was ill. Her plans would always fall through at the last minute, laden with apologies and excuses, and it'd *sound* like Kay, except we all knew it didn't, not really.

Being with Marcus . . . It's not good for her. It's turned her into someone else. Someone none of us recognise.

Nana's voice rings loud and clear in my memory. It's so vivid, I can almost feel her frail hand gripping mine, hard enough to hurt.

'It's up to you to look after them, you realise that, don't you? I won't be around forever. Your mother's an avoider and Kay is too flighty, and Myleene's too young. And your poor dad . . . You're going to have to step up, Leon. You're going to have to take care of this family.'

Nana wouldn't have let it get this far. She would've stepped in, done something, tried to piece this family back together before it fractured for good.

I thumb through the pages. Can I really say all this to Kayleigh?

And the fact this doesn't even skim the surface . . .

'Is that your speech?' Francesca asks, her tone pleasant and friendly in a way that she has no right to be. She's smiling, doing that thing where her head is tipped slightly to one side. I get the sense she's trying to offer an olive branch.

I close the notebook before she can see, keep my palm on top of it. 'No.'

'Oh. I just thought . . . I mean, Marcus mentioned you'd be giving a speech instead of Kayleigh's dad, because he didn't want to—'

'He gets stage fright. And he's not well. It's not that he doesn't want to.'

'Oh! Well, that's . . .' She fumbles, falters, tries again. I grit my teeth, wishing she'd shut up. We *really* don't have to pretend to be polite, here. We just have to . . . coexist. In silence, preferably. 'That's very generous of you to step in.'

'Kay asked me to.'

Her smile strains around the edges, muscles quivering in her cheeks with the effort to keep it in place. 'So have you got your speech sorted? If that's not it, I mean. How are you feeling about it?'

'Fine.' I still have to write the damn thing, hopefully won't even need it at all, but . . . 'It's fine.'

She nods, looking a bit put out, but unfortunately for me, not entirely deterred. Then she points at my bag and says, 'You must travel a lot.'

'Huh? Oh . . .' I see what she's noticed: all the patches sewn into the bag, covering the front, the strap. It's not so different to the pins all over her denim jacket, except – 'It's my dad's. They're his. He used to travel a lot. It's . . . This is his bag.'

She smiles, a little brighter this time. Her head ticks sideways towards her shoulder. God, I wish I didn't find that so endearing. 'Do you have the travel bug too?'

'Um . . . I don't really get to go anywhere these days. This is probably the first time I've been abroad since . . .' Since the early days of Dad's diagnosis. Since my parents' holiday budget had got redirected into adapting the house for him, or the occasional burst of private medical care. I clear my throat. 'Not for a long while.'

72

'A bit of a homebody?' she guesses, and it's grating, how *interested* she sounds, how *genuine* it feels.

'Not really. Well, sort of.' I've got nothing against travel, but it's hard to commit to going away when I'm constantly worried that I might be needed at home – that something will happen, and I won't be there to help, to make it easier for the rest of them. Francesca, watching me with a patient smile and wide eyes, looks so engaged with the conversation that I almost want to blurt it all out. I swallow the urge and settle for saying, 'I've got too much keeping me here.'

'Oh! Oh, do you have a partner? Children?'

'No.' I scowl; I don't have a girlfriend for the same reason I don't travel, when it comes down to it.

I must be curt enough that she finally gives up on her attempts to make small talk, and we lapse into a silence I'm grateful for. My skin is prickling, the discomfort of that subject like a physical itch.

I glance at Francesca, who is people-watching once more. She doesn't even seem *that bad*, which somehow makes it worse. Unless the cutesy innocent nice-girl thing is all an act? It's got to be. Kayleigh's never had *anything* good to say about her; I should be on my guard, watch for her to slip up. That's what a good brother would do, right? Help find some ammunition to evict the work wife from Marcus's life permanently.

Or, maybe, find evidence that there really *is* something going on between the two of them, and use it as ammunition to stop the wedding going ahead altogether . . .

Gemma's still gone when Francesca's phone buzzes. It's lying flat on the table, and we're so crammed in that when

I glance over automatically, I can clearly see it's a text from Marcus. A *long* one, by the looks of it.

She snatches it up, but not like she's trying to hide it.

Like she's just excited to hear from him.

And – I see it. I *see* that giddy look on her face, the brightness that sparks in her eyes as she devours his text, a faint dusting of pink colouring her cheeks.

That's *not* the reaction of someone who's 'just a friend'.

I can't resist a dig. Testing the waters, a little. 'Boyfriend?'

Now, she flushes, all the way down her neck. She pulls the phone a bit tighter to her, eyes widening. She knows she's been caught out.

'N-no. No, nothing like that. It's . . . it's just Marcus. Replying about how we're all delayed.'

I nod, and it's like another tally on the board against him.

'He's just worried,' she goes on, the words running together a bit too quickly. 'Because of the weather. If we'll all make it. Because we're missing out on everything tonight.'

'Sure.'

'It's not . . .' Francesca swallows, trailing off, and I can't help but smirk at her expense. *Not what?* I want to press. Not what it looks like? Not like she isn't harbouring a crush on a guy who's *about to be married*, inserting herself into a relationship that doesn't concern her? She squirms in her seat. She's *got* to know how guilty she looks.

What is she even doing, coming to this wedding?

Is she really going to stand around flirting with the groom, cosying up to him any time she can get close enough? Is she going to be one of those women who wear a white dress to someone else's wedding and end up on Reddit? Is she only doing this to humiliate Kay? Francesca can't be oblivious, even if Marcus is.

Are they in on it together? Is it an affair?

If Marcus was going to dump Kay for his 'work wife', I wish he'd done it months ago, before we got to this point. I wouldn't be sorry to see him go. Maybe then, we'd get Kay back.

Something burns, boils, in my chest. Angry and corrosive.

I really *hate* Marcus. Not just for what he's doing to Kay, but for what he's doing to our whole family. And whatever part Francesca is playing in it – I hate her for it, too.

She tries again. 'We're . . . just . . .'

'*Best* friends,' I say. 'Right. I remember.'

This time, when the silence settles, it's charged, tense. Both of us are on high alert, neither of us saying a word.

Gemma sweeps back over to the table, jostling her way through the gap behind me to get back into the booth and throwing herself down there with a melodramatic sigh. She dumps her phone on the table, not noticing the tension crackling between me and Francesca.

'Phew! Well, that didn't go as badly as I thought it would.'

I swivel towards her, and that anger is still there, poison in my veins. 'Is my sister saved as "bitch" in your phone?'

Gemma blinks, owlish behind her glasses.

'With a *sparkle emoji.*'

I grunt, not sure that's really an answer, and then she mutters under her breath, 'Besides, it's not like it isn't *true.*'

Francesca lets out a laugh, though she claps a hand over her mouth and coughs to try to hide it, and Gemma glances her way with an appraising look, cool and curious. The slight smile that curves her mouth is something I can only describe as sly.

That hatred burns a little hotter in my chest.

Chapter Twelve

Francesca

Leon pushes away from the table abruptly, his chair knocking into someone behind him. He mutters that he needs some air and trudges away, his thick legs and broad shoulders making him clumsy as he manoeuvres between people. I feel my whole face burning, my palms turning clammy, a wave of panic rising – is he going to call Kayleigh? Tell her about me, about . . .? It was only a text, but he clearly doesn't think very much of me or how Marcus calls me his 'work wife' . . .

Maybe it would be a *good* thing if he told Kayleigh something was going on between me and Marcus? She might call off the wedding. But then what if Marcus thought I'd lied, and never heard me out, and we lost our chance all over again?

For all my excited, romantic notions leading up to this weekend, I'm starting to think it won't be as painless as it looks in the movies after all.

Gemma pushes her bag into Leon's empty chair to keep it reserved, though she's pulling a face as she watches him go.

'What crawled up his arse and died?'

Me, I think. But I say, 'He's not always like this?'

Gemma scoffs. 'Are you kidding me? That guy wouldn't say boo to a goose.'

'I'm not sure *anybody* would choose to say boo to a goose. Aren't they quite aggressive?'

Gemma ponders it for a moment, then bats it away with a sharp flick of her hand. 'Whatever. He's a softie, is my point. I don't know *what* this whole . . . this Jon Snow act is about.' She glances at me, then adds quickly, 'All broody bastard. It was a joke.'

'I got that.'

'Like *he's* got anything to stress about.' Gemma snorts. She reaches for her cup, then clicks her tongue when she remembers it's empty. 'Like Kayleigh's going to be blaming *him* if anything goes tits up because he wasn't there. He'll miss out on a pint with some of the cousins, oh *no*. Meanwhile, I've got an entire to-do list of things the bride is expecting me to see to because she just *looooves* the drama and acts like everything is going to go wrong . . .'

She trails off with a testy sigh, glowering into the distance.

'That sounds tough. But I guess it's very stressful, planning a wedding. Anybody would get a bit worked up about it,' I say carefully, although I'm thinking that sounds an awful lot like the person Marcus talks about. I shouldn't badmouth the bride to her best friend; but Gemma is entitled to vent, isn't she?

She seems to realise she might have spoken a bit out of turn, giving me the impression that she wasn't saying it to me, so much as getting it off her chest. Gemma plonks an elbow on the table, resting her cheek on her fist to pin me with a look.

But then she says the *last* thing I'm expecting, and tells me, 'Fran, I'm gonna level with you – this has *nothing to do with the wedding*. This isn't a bridezilla situation. She's just a pill. Do people say that anymore? Either way, she is.'

I'm not sure I've ever heard anybody called a 'pill', but it doesn't sound very nice.

'But you know,' she adds then, 'Marcus is too, so they're great together.'

'Marcus isn't . . . He's . . . I mean . . .'

One of her eyebrows quirks up slightly behind her glasses frames, and her gaze sharpens.

'I don't really know Kayleigh that well,' I say, 'we've only met a few times. I just mean that he's . . . I'm surprised you think that of Marcus, is all I'm trying to say.'

She gives a crisp laugh. 'Well, you know him. You know what he's like. Hardly a saint, is he? Mr Goody Two-Shoes, like Leon over there.' She jerks her head in the direction he left, grin widening as she rolls her eyes with affection.

But I can't join in, can't say anything. That's not the Marcus I know, not at all.

Does Kayleigh bring out a worse side of him?

Or is it . . . is it me, bringing out something better in him?

My heart gives a little flutter inside my chest, like a hummingbird. *See?* It seems to say. *You are meant to be. Whatever the two of you have, it is special, because he doesn't have it with her.*

Gemma is waiting for me to say something, but I'm not sure that defending Marcus is the right move. It'll sound like I'm agreeing that Kayleigh is awful, and I don't want to do that.

Offence might be the best defence here, so I settle for

saying to Gemma, 'Maybe it upset Leon because you called his sister a bitch.'

She shows all her teeth now. 'I didn't hear you disagreeing.'

'You caught me off guard, is all.'

'Please. We *both* know she's a bitch. If he wants to stick his head in the sand . . .' She holds her palms up in surrender. 'Anyway, it's obviously not *me* he's angry at. Cut the tension between you two with a *knife*, my God. It's like you were two seconds away from either mauling each other with your bare hands or fucking.'

I choke on my inhale, my cheeks heating. 'That is *not*—'

Gemma laughs. This one sounds less pretty than before, more brash – more sincere. 'I'm just kidding. That poor boy . . . Oh, he's a missionary man. Right? You see it.'

'Um . . .'

I have no idea how we got here, but I do know I'd like to steer the conversation anywhere else.

Gemma must sense that and take pity because she leans in a bit closer, eyes sparkling with childlike mischief, and she folds her hands under her chin. 'So? What *did* you say to piss him off? What's he got against you so bad? I've never seen him this riled up.'

'I . . . didn't, really.' It's not exactly reassuring to hear that this *isn't* normal for him, though, and therefore must be to do with me. 'I just – I got a text from Marcus. He was weird about it.'

'Why?' Then she gasps, and jokes, 'Was it a dick pic? I'm not being funny, but I'd be pretty mad if I saw my brother-in-law's dick, too. And they never look very good in photos, do they? Like, I've never *looked* at a dick pic and thought, *Wow, that's attractive, consider me turned on.* Have you?'

'Uh . . . n-no.'

'Women just photograph so much *better*. And I'm not saying I don't love a good penis, but they're ugly things, sometimes, aren't they?'

An awkward smile cracks my mouth. 'Kind of, yeah. But, um, that wasn't . . . I mean, it wasn't anything like that. From Marcus. He was just saying it was a shame I was stuck here. Well, that I wouldn't make it for drinks with everyone after dinner tonight. Not that it's a shame I'm stuck here with *you* guys, of course, but . . .'

'Let's see.'

'Um.' I seem to be only capable of stuttering and stammering in the face of Gemma's unabashed confidence. I feel like a bumbling idiot, while she's a queen of self-assuredness. She's even holding her palm out, ready and waiting for my phone.

It's so invasive that I'm too shocked to be outraged. Does *she* suspect something of me, like Leon? She will, if I refuse to show her the text.

Left with no other choice, I unlock my phone, which is still open to our texts, and hand it over.

Gemma takes it delicately, finger poised above the screen as she reads.

There's nothing incriminating.

It really is just a text.

Hey babe, just catching up properly on this now! That SUCKS, I'm so sorry you got caught in the weather. Grr! Fingers crossed you make it sooner than later — won't be the same without you. I was counting on you being here to kick Tony's arse at pool with me, lol! We'll have an extra shot for you. Keep me posted about the flight, yeah? Safe travels and can't wait to see you tomorrow! xx

Gemma reads it at least twice, then scrolls further up the chat. I swallow down the noise of indignation and protest that rises in my throat, and fight to keep my hands from snatching my phone back.

I know what she'll see. Me letting him know about something that happened at work that he would've found funny (he did laugh-react); me wishing him a nice few days in Spain ahead of the wedding and him sending back a selfie giving a thumbs-up at the camera from next to the pool, beneath a big straw parasol.

There's nothing to *see*.

Not unless you go looking. Not unless you're reading between the lines, and thinking about how he's sent me a shirtless selfie he didn't really *need* to send but obviously *wanted* me to see, or thinking about the two kisses on the end of his text, or the in-jokes and tongue-out winky-face emojis sprinkled throughout, or . . .

On the surface, it really is just a friendly chat. Something that, if Kayleigh saw, he'd be able to say, *No, don't be silly, there's nothing going on, that's just how I talk* . . .

But Gemma's not an idiot, and I know she must be seeing all the things I see.

The same things I can't tell my friends about, because they know Marcus is engaged and *I* pretend it's all just friendly chat to them . . . And the same things I screenshot and send to my sister to eagerly dissect, knowing there's a flirty edge to them.

Gemma hands the phone back to me.

'Leon should get his head out of his arse,' she says. 'And seriously, who types "grr" in a text like that? What an ick.'

I laugh. I think I laugh, anyway. There's a ringing sound in my ears and the relief that she *didn't* find anything is positively crushing, smothers all the air out of my lungs. I say something like, 'Tell me about it,' and count my lucky stars. I think I need a second or two to recover, actually, so I stand up and pick up her empty cup, along with my own.

'I think I'm going to get another drink. Do you want one?'

'Yes please! Same again.' She beams at me, and pushes her glasses up her nose with the tip of her middle finger. 'And then you can tell me all about why my best friend's fiancé is busy flirting with you when he's about to get married.'

My stomach plummets through the floor.

And Leon's voice behind me says, '*What?*'

Chapter Thirteen

Gemma

Ooh, the drama.

It is *delicious*.

I live for it, really, I do.

Francesca stands there, speechless and ashen, mouth gaping open, looking for all the world as if her soul just left her body. Off to one side, Leon, eyes wide and mouth tight; but it's not the white-hot fury I would've expected – it's more like . . . vindication.

And me, leaning forward with my elbows propped up on the table, and I just *know* there's a glint of excitement in my eyes, my smile something toothy and vicious – which, really, is not so much to do with Francesca at all.

What a tableau we must make. A veritable Renaissance painting. All three of us caught up in this storm (the figurative *and* literal kind) while the dull hubbub of the airport continues around us. People balancing trays of food, families wrangling tired or unruly children, solo travellers bent over devices trying to block it all out and get some work done – all of them oblivious to the absolute hellscape that's about to unfold here.

And oh, it is *excellent*.

Kudos to Marcus, of course, for the plausible deniability. His texts walk a very careful line of 'just being friendly!', but I *know*. Any self-respecting girl dating in the social networking era would know. I mean, we used to log off and back onto MSN to get our crush to notice us when we were kids.

We know.

Marcus's texts aren't the kind of stuff you'd get a guy sending you on a dating app. They're somehow worse. Charming, casual in the way only an established relationship of any kind can be, and *juuust* long enough that he's obviously invested even though, from the quick scroll I just had, he only reacts a very little to anything Fran says and never asks her questions. He's doing the bare minimum to prove he's interested in what she has to say, knowing she'll respond to whatever self-centred crap he spouts.

He hasn't got to waste time fluffing her ego with compliments, trying to win her over. He's joked to us all often enough about how she obviously has a crush on him, how pathetic and sweet that is, how *sorry* he feels for her.

It's the kind of way Kayleigh talks to me. It's so easy to recognise.

Whatever Marcus really thinks about his work wife's crush on him, he's absolutely guilty of pandering to it.

Which, knowing Marcus, he wouldn't do unless there was a benefit to him. He doesn't do *anything* without putting himself first. He's a lot like Kayleigh that way.

Does Kayleigh know he's indulging Fran with all these texts? Does she even know they *text*? Pretty regularly, too. There's at least one message from him every day for the last week or so, and that was only as far back as my scroll took me. I can only imagine what's further back in the chat history. Surely she would've mentioned it to me before if she knew.

But I'm not thinking, *I should tell her; my best friend is about to marry this man and look at this scumbag, red-flag behaviour; she needs to know, I have to tell her.*

I'm thinking, *This is fucking great.*

It's all I can do not to burst out laughing. This isn't even *surprising*, coming from Marcus, and Kayleigh would go absolutely ballistic if I did tell her, which is a real double standard coming from her, and how much fun would it be to watch her perfect life implode then?

She certainly enjoyed it plenty when it was my life imploding.

I wouldn't even need the video, then. I could be the architect of her destruction without even really getting my hands dirty.

I *am* her best friend, though, so I know my barely contained glee comes off as righteous indignation and a 'Ha, gotcha!' to Francesca and Leon, which is all that matters.

Leon turns more fully to Fran, now, and she shrinks in on herself, both our empty cups huddled into her body.

'*What?*' he repeats tightly, then throws a glower my way. I barely blink in reaction. 'What the hell are you talking about? Did you know about this?'

'I just found out. I got a look at their messages. Looks like darling Marcus is playing away from home.'

There's a flash of emotion in Leon's eyes that takes me a moment to process, it's so out of place.

It's the kind of look *I'm* trying so hard to hide.

He asks, head snapping between the two of us now, 'Why?

86

What's he said? Is this that text he just sent you? Is that what this is about? Let me see.'

Fran is shaking, now, poor thing, but manages to sound fabulously indignant when she says, 'Marcus and I are *friends*. There's nothing to see, alright? I don't expect to go digging through *your* phone looking for rubbish I can blow out of proportion. But *fine*, if you want to look, *fine*. Go on! I've got nothing to hide!'

She wrestles her phone into one free hand to unlock it, the text thread still up on the screen, and slams it down on the table before storming off.

I hope she remembers the oat milk.

Leon has picked up the phone before he even sits down, so focused on the messages that he half falls back into his seat, almost misses the chair completely. I watch his frown deepen as he concentrates, reading slowly, scrolling back up – and then down again, rereading, like he's missed something.

He lowers the phone to look at me, and exactly like I thought he would, he says, 'Am I missing something here? I thought you said he was cheating.'

'I didn't say *that*.' I huff, and take Fran's phone to put it on the table. I love her phone case, all pressed flowers in pink and yellow. So cute. Basic, but cute. I point at the screen. 'Read between the lines, Leon. *Look*. Like how he only texts in these chunky paragraphs – probably because it's when Kayleigh's not in the room, or asleep or something, rather than texting back and forth throughout the day? And he doesn't even reply to half the stuff she says, but he'll heart-react so it *feels* like he's paying attention, so poor Fran is probably out here telling herself, *Look how much he cares about me!* Bless her.'

Leon nods, once, slowly, absolutely not getting it.

'Like, did he need to send her a shirtless selfie? Or this gym-mirror selfie, post-workout? Like hell he did. And look, that message he just sent her – wish you were here, won't be the same without you, need you here with me, and all that crap. It *sounds* friendly, but if you've got a raging crush on someone and they send you messages like that—'

'It's not going to *feel* friendly,' he concludes, finally catching on. He leans back in his seat and rubs his hand across his mouth, frowning at the screen.

It's startling, how much he and Kayleigh don't look alike. She's all dainty, sharp edges and refined features and graceful stature, whereas Leon is . . . *clunky*. Squarish face and squat nose and unruly hair, thick limbs and clumsy, calloused hands. He does a lot of weightlifting – he makes a lot of really boring, dry posts about his progress on his Insta Stories – but it's a far cry from any sort of gym-bro energy.

Sometimes, I think if I really wanted to get under Kayleigh's skin and piss her off, I'd fuck her brother.

But that feels weirdly Freudian and I'm sure a therapist would have something to say about that, so.

'So . . .' Leon clears his throat, shuffles in his chair. 'Are they having an affair?'

'I don't think so. An *emotional* affair, maybe . . .'

'I knew something was dodgy, whenever Kay mentioned the work wife. I mean, who says things like that anymore? It's . . .'

'It's *very* pick-me girl,' I say sagely, nodding, though I'd be willing to bet Leon doesn't know what that is. Honestly, he thinks *I'm* an idiot for not knowing who Zeus is off the top of my head, but he wouldn't understand the nuances of pop culture if they bit him on the arse.

'I knew it was bothering her. She always acted like it was some big joke, though.'

'Well, yeah. What else are you going to do in that situation? It's not like she doesn't have a harmless little flirt with guys if we're out at a bar, or everyone's round to dinner.'

Leon recoils a little. 'She what?'

I roll my eyes. As if we've got time for his rose-tinted glasses when it comes to his sisters. (I mean, you just *know* he'd go to his grave denying that little Myleene's ever touched weed, but she was high as a kite the last two times I saw her.)

'Anyway,' I carry on, 'obviously Kayleigh whinges about the work wife thing behind Marcus's back. He always treats it like a joke. The way he talks about Francesca, mocking her and saying how sad the whole thing is, you'd *never* guess—' I snort, cutting myself off before I can say –

'Hardly surprising, though, coming from *him*.'

It takes me a beat to realise that *wasn't* me saying it, and that yes, it did, in fact, come from Leon. I've never heard him say a bad word about *anybody*.

This is a delightful turn of events.

Truly, spectacular.

'Mmhmm,' I say, which is non-committal enough to brush off if I'm ever challenged on it, but just sympathetic *enough* that Leon carries on.

'Selfish prick. I should've – *fuck*, we should've known he'd do something like this. I knew he was bad news. Right from the start, Mum said—'

He cuts himself off, though, so abruptly I just know

whatever he was about to say would've been juicy and damning. He shuffles in his seat again, shoulders bunching, and clears his throat awkwardly.

'Didn't your nana not like him?' I prompt, fighting to keep my voice neutral. If Leon doesn't like Marcus much, if his mum doesn't either . . . I know Kayleigh huffs and puffs and rolls her eyes a lot about going home, but she's been griping about visits back home for *years*, way before Marcus was on the scene. It was like she'd . . . outgrown them. Was sick of the drive back and forth, the poky little terraced house they'd pile into for a family dinner and feeling obliged to stay in the childhood bedroom she shared with Myleene, them not understanding why she wanted to live in London or cared about things like dry-cleaning her silk blouses and drinking bubble tea.

She had her own life now, and they didn't fit. And I guess with Marcus on the scene, she decided they were even less of a priority. Which makes even *more* sense if they never actually liked him . . .

Oh, the drama she's been keeping from me.

So as much as I want to grab Leon by the shoulders and yell, 'Spill the tea!' I stay put in my chair, hands folded in front of me, giving him a sympathetic look, and I mention his nana instead.

The same grandmother that Kayleigh cut off and called a bitch after the last time she saw her, then cried crocodile tears over at the funeral.

Leon is so visibly affected by the mere mention of his nana, though, my heart does genuinely bleed a little for him. It's always so easy to gobble up Kayleigh's melodrama and take it at face value, I forget sometimes that it's all a story she's rewritten to put herself at the centre of. But Leon's face crumples, and he swallows hard, even looking a little misty-eyed, and I remember that his nana looked after me in the school holidays when my parents couldn't, and she showed me how to bake the best chocolate-chip cookies I've ever had in my *life*.

I bake them sometimes still, when I need a little pick-me-up, and something cosy to turn off my mind.

I feel such a wave of compassion – of sympathy for his loss, a shared moment of grief that his nana has gone, a shame for trying to throw it in his face even in some small way – that I reach out to put a hand on his arm. Leon's mouth twitches in a wobbly attempt at a smile.

But whatever he's about to say about his nana or Kayleigh or Marcus is stolen by Francesca plonking down three steaming paper cups on the table, looking ready to face the wolves.

Chapter Fourteen

Leon

I'm not sure that I'm quite ready to tackle Francesca's whole 'emotional affair' mess with my soon-to-be brother-in-law, but I can't deny I'm relieved that she's back; it gets Gemma off my back for now. She can be like a dog with a bone, so I'm sure she won't forget that thread of conversation any time soon, but at least I have some breathing space.

Admitting the truth – that collectively, we don't like Marcus, or the person Kayleigh is with him – is harder than I thought. *A lot* harder.

I'm not sure how I'm going to manage to say any of it to Kay herself, when it's tough enough trying to vocalise it to someone who already sees that Marcus isn't some saint.

As for Francesca – I don't even know where to start. I can't help but acknowledge that it's Marcus who sends the borderline-flirtatious selfies, Marcus adding kisses to the end of his texts, Marcus keeping the conversation going when he could easily just let it die off.

Francesca's not the only guilty party, but there's got to be a good reason Kayleigh called her a *harpy*, right?

Luckily, I get a few moments to stew over all that as she plonks some takeaway coffee cups down on the table and then doles them out to us. She glances at me as she pushes one in front of me, along with a couple of sugar packets.

'Milk and two sugars, right?'

'Uh, y-yeah.'

She must've heard me ordering earlier. I'm surprised she noticed the sugar packets I dumped in. I have been trying to cut them down, but . . . if ever there's an excuse to indulge a bit, isn't it for a wedding?

Even one you wished wasn't happening?

Maybe *especially* then.

'Oat milk, two vanilla shots,' she adds, to Gemma, who grins and says, 'Thanks, hon,' as if they're best mates, and she didn't just out Francesca for flirting with an almost-married man.

I'm surprised Francesca even bothered to get us drinks. I thought she was just . . . storming off.

I must get a look on my face, because she says sharply, 'It's not poisoned.'

'Didn't think it was.' Although . . .

No, that seems like more of a Gemma scheme, if anybody was going to do it.

As I dump the sugar packets into my tea, Francesca sits down and looks between me and Gemma, then at the phone. Her spine is ramrod-straight even as she picks at her nail varnish, making her look like she's been called into the headmaster's office, not sure if she's allowed her phone back after getting caught using it in class or something.

Gemma takes a noisy sip of her drink and smacks her lips.

'So, *have* you shagged?'

Francesca makes a sort of choking noise, face flushing, and stammers until Gemma cuts in, 'That doesn't sound a lot like a *no*.'

'We haven't – I mean . . . It's not like *nothing* happened,' she says, 'but it was before he even met Kayleigh. Everyone at the office always expected us to get together, but then obviously she came on the scene, and it's not like Marcus and I could just *stop* . . .' A guilty glance at the phone, then a panicked, plaintive look at each of us. Her eyes are huge, and framed by thick, long lashes. 'Nothing's happened since then. I knew he was with somebody, and—'

'Didn't stop you texting him, though,' Gemma points out.

'We'd just, you know, message at work sometimes, meet up for lunch or go to the pub with everyone after work . . . *He* asked for *my* number, for the record.' Francesca's chest puffs out, her eyes shining with emotion now. 'To make sure I got home safe, after a night out got a bit rowdy.'

I don't know why she seems proud of that. Why she says it like it's some badge of honour, some accomplishment to brag about. Gemma pulls a face, though, obviously hearing something I don't, like she did with the texts.

If Francesca didn't look so worked up, I'd think Gemma was just pulling my leg.

But Marcus's 'friend' barrels on, the words pouring out of her now, and I don't think we could shut her up if we tried.

'I haven't been *pursuing* him, if that's what you're thinking. I'd never go after someone in a relationship like that. We were friends before, and now we're friends again, but – but we were *more* than that, once, and we missed our chance, we both moved on with our lives . . . But that's only because he thought *I* rejected *him*. This whole thing was just – it was one stupid moment, one wild miscommunication that spiralled out of control, and now . . .'

94

Gemma's mouth is slack, hanging wide open; she's so stunned I don't think she even blinks.

I'm not sure I understand what I'm hearing. Or – not sure I believe it, rather.

Francesca's on a roll, though, and says, 'We have a real *connection*, and you can't just ignore that, it doesn't just go away, even if we've *both* tried, and now – now he's marrying someone else, and he doesn't even know I feel the same way about him as he does about me, and he *has* to know, it's my last chance to tell him, and he—'

'Whoa, whoa, hold up.' Gemma recovers first, places both palms flat on the table, peering over the top of her glasses. 'You think he's in love with you?'

Francesca blushes a deeper shade of red, which gives her away. *Yes*.

'Ohmigod,' Gemma breathes. 'Oh – my – *God*.'

I remember all the things I've heard second-hand about Francesca. That she practically stalks Marcus around the office and always shows up uninvited to after-work drinks, laughing at his jokes and vying for his attention. That she's *too* friendly with him when he's invited her to get-togethers with other colleagues and Kayleigh's there, says things like how they're so in sync with each other, really *get* each other, makes sure she sits next to him.

Maybe all those things are true.

Marcus has always maintained that it's sad and pathetic but it's nothing, he's above it, it's a joke. He's not interested, doesn't give her the time of day outside of sharing mutual friends at work and being nice to her around the office.

But those texts.

He wouldn't bother replying if he didn't care. He wouldn't

95

be so chatty and send selfies and tell her all about his day if he wasn't interested on some level.

So maybe all those things I've heard about Francesca are true.

But – maybe all the things she's telling us now are, too.

And she sits there, back straight, shoulders squared, all steady and set, because she really believes . . . he's in love with her. Like she's in love with him. Like she thinks she's the main character in a romcom or something.

It's so completely ridiculous that I snort, and say, 'So, what, you're going to race to the wedding and yell 'I object!' and tell him he can't marry my sister because he should marry *you* instead, and the two of you will ride off into the sunset, happily ever after?'

'I – n-no, that's not . . . Well, I—'

'Ohmigod,' Gemma gasps. 'It is, isn't it? That's totally what you're planning to do. You're going to *tell him*. You're going to try to break up the wedding.'

Francesca blushes to the roots of her brown hair and I wait for Gemma to erupt – even before she's had a chance to digest this news, I can already see her leaping to her feet and screaming at Francesca – *How dare you/that's my best friend/what world are you living in* – and probably ending up getting security called to calm her down for causing such a scene . . .

But instead, she throws back her head, opens her mouth wide, and lets out a cackle like she's auditioning for *Hocus Pocus*. She laughs so hard there are tears streaming down her cheeks, and she bends forward, clutching her sides and wheezing.

I look at Francesca, who looks at me, equally confused.

And I know I should say something. No matter what Gemma's reaction is, I should be outraged, too, should be jumping to berate Francesca and tell her to back off, this is my sister's fiancé she's talking about, my sister's wedding she's planning to ruin.

Would that . . . be so bad, though?

I mean, if there was any kind of sure-fire way to make Kayleigh see what a narcissistic, callous prat she's engaged to, it's by having him jilt her at the altar for the girl he's always telling her 'not to worry about'.

Which would be horrible, and heartbreaking, and devastating, yes, but . . . *necessary*?

We'd all be there to help her pick up the pieces, of course, and reassure her that it's for the best. Him running off with someone else would be a good excuse for us all to hate him until Kayleigh's over him enough to stomach hearing all the other ways he wasn't right for her.

Francesca sucks in a breath, as if to brace herself for whatever rage I'm going to launch at her in my sister's defence. Next to me, Gemma is still gasping for breath, laughing too hard to say more than a broken syllable or two at a time.

And I sit back in my chair, arms crossed, and say, 'To hell with it. Rather you than Kayleigh. You're welcome to the bastard.'

Gemma starts howling with laughter all over again.

Chapter Fifteen

Francesca

I – don't believe this. I must be hallucinating. Or dreaming?

Is this some nasty plan cooked up between the two of them while I was gone, some way to humiliate me?

No, I don't think it is; Gemma looked too aghast when I admitted to everything, and is absolutely beside herself now. I don't think anybody could fake that sort of laughter. People are looking over, staring, the uninhibited sound carrying above all the general commotion.

As for Leon, the hostility he displayed earlier has vanished and he leans back in his chair, crossing his arms. 'To hell with it,' he says. 'Rather you than Kayleigh. You're welcome to the bastard.'

I *have* to be dreaming.

This *has* to be a trick.

I overheard what they said about Marcus mocking me . . . That can't be true. If anything, *they're* the ones mocking me.

But Leon's blank expression, the way he slouches in his seat as if to say he really couldn't care less, the bite in his voice that's not directed at me, but at Marcus – it rubs me the wrong way. Maybe it's because I was so ready for a fight, or maybe because he kept getting my hackles up earlier, but I scowl at him again now.

'Don't talk about him like that. This isn't his fault. It's – it's nobody's fault, it's just . . . What we have, it's real, it's special, and I just don't think it's right that he should get married to somebody else when I *know* he has feelings for me, and I feel the same way about him. It's not just us I'm thinking about, it's Kayleigh, too. Isn't it punishing her, if we let her marry someone who isn't in it one hundred per cent? It's not as if Marcus has been cheating, like we've been carrying out some sordid affair behind her back—'

'It's an emotional affair,' Leon tells me bluntly.

It's—

Wait, *is* that what it is? Is that what we've been doing? All the things we don't quite say in our texts, all the sidelong looks and secret smiles, the hugs that we let go of the split-second before they become more than a quick greeting or goodbye?

Oh, God. It is, isn't it?

I've been having an affair with an almost-married man.

I kept telling myself we were treading that line, but . . . Just because we haven't kissed in that time, does that make this any less wrong? Isn't that exactly why I can't tell my friends or my family the entire truth about him, why I feel such guilt whenever they ask me about him? Didn't I know, deep down, how wrong we were to carry on like this?

This is what I've been avoiding admitting to myself every time I back myself into a corner with too many little white lies. When Marcus and I spent the night together, *obviously* I told the gang from uni everything. They sent me Ben & Jerry's over Deliveroo when I cried down the phone to them after rejecting him in the office a few days later. When he started dating Kayleigh officially, I couldn't tell them that there was *still* something going on between us, however innocent. Because of *this*, because part of me *knew* they'd tell me I was the other woman. And my family think he's just a friend at work I have a bit of a crush on, someone whose friendship I don't want to risk losing so that's why I haven't made a move . . .

And all that time, with each little white lie twisting the truth of our relationship, I'd tell myself, *This is part of how it's supposed to be*. The whole 'forbidden romance' thing, the 'true love conquers all' fairy tale everybody wants to believe in. It wasn't a *red flag*, more like . . . another hurdle in our journey to be together.

I feel ill, suddenly. It's a mockery of the butterfly sensation I get in my stomach any time I imagine the look on Marcus's face when I finally tell him I love him, too.

Is Kayleigh even really that cold and nasty, or is that just the idea I've built up of her in my head, so I can lie to myself that this is all okay? In her shoes, wouldn't I have been a bit frosty towards someone my partner was so invested in?

Then Leon says, 'You weren't *really* planning to try to break up the wedding, were you?'

'I . . . I don't know.' I *do* know. But I swallow, hating myself, hating the mirror that's being held up to me right now. If we hadn't been diverted for the bad weather, this wouldn't be happening; I'd still be in wilful, blissful ignorance. 'I guess I just thought I'd . . . try to catch him for a quiet moment tonight, and I'd tell him how I felt. And then . . . Then . . .'

'Then he'd run off with you, instead of marrying my sister.' Leon nods, though, not really expecting a response. He takes a swig of his sugary tea. 'Well, good luck to you. Like I said – you're welcome to him. She's better off without him.'

'W-what?'

'She's better off without him,' he reiterates. 'And none of us will be too sorry to see him go. Nobody in our family was exactly thrilled they got engaged in the first place, so good riddance to the both of you.'

I gawp, but Gemma has got a hold of herself just enough now to claw at Leon with one hand. 'Wait-wait-wait.' She takes another second to gather herself, and says, 'Are you serious? Like, genuinely, *nobody* likes him? Are you kidding me right now?'

'Why?' I blurt. 'Why don't any of you like him?'

Objectively, it's wonderful news that Kayleigh's family don't approve of Marcus, and as much as they might hate him for leaving her for another woman – for *me*, I'm the other woman, oh, God, how is the reality of this only just sinking in now? – they already disliked him, so that'll soften the blow. Maybe he'll even be *relieved* not to marry into such a hostile family.

Because really, if they're anything like I've found Kayleigh and Leon to be, he can't be excited about becoming part of such a family? He probably feels obligated, knows he's too far in to back out now. And at least with Kayleigh, he has a relationship he's sure of, while he doesn't believe *we* could be anything more than friends.

That doesn't stop me wanting to jump to his defence, though.

Leon scoffs, and there is a bitterness in the twist of his

mouth as it draws into a smirk that sets my temper on edge again.

'Where do I even start?' he says, and then reaches into the front of his bag and throws something onto the table.

It's a notebook. The green leather-bound one I saw him writing in on the plane and then studying earlier, when I asked if he was working on his speech.

It lands, open, and though Gemma and I both lean in and angle our heads to try to decrypt his scrawling writing, he's already talking again.

'He's pretentious, self-centred, rude, arrogant . . . He always thinks he's the smartest person in the room, thinks his money makes him better than everybody else, acts like everybody is beneath him and he's doing you a favour just by being there at all. And he's hardly *ever there*, for the record. I can count on one hand the number of times I've met the guy in the time they've been together. We used to see Kayleigh regularly, or she'd at least FaceTime to check in – but now he's on the scene, we hardly even get that much from her. And when they *do* visit, it's like they can't wait to get away again – like *he* can't wait to get away.'

'Well, I'm not surprised, if you're all so horrible to him,' I mutter, and Leon cuts me a look, his eyes narrowing. The hostility returns full-force in that moment; I can practically feel it prickling across my skin, and this time I stare him down.

He snarls, 'We have been *nothing* but nice to him—'

'Oh, clearly. Just like you've been nothing but nice to *me*—'

'That's different.'

'I'm sure.' My voice is dripping with contempt; I've

never heard myself like this before. It must get under his skin because Leon shifts in his seat, and all I can think is, *Good*.

'Even when he showed up unannounced the first Christmas they were together and we'd never met him before, we did our best to make him feel welcome, went out of our way to help him feel at home—' He breaks off to narrow his eyes at me as if daring me to challenge him, when I obviously can't; I wasn't there, I don't know. 'But we all can tell, it's not good enough, nothing is ever up to his standards. Or Kayleigh's, now, which is all to do with *his* influence.'

Gemma snorts. 'Damn, say it with your whole chest, Leon.'

He doesn't even seem to notice her comment, barrelling on regardless.

'He's constantly talking over people, interrupting, doesn't even do you the courtesy of listening politely and making small talk or pretending to be the slightest bit interested in what's going on with his fiancée's family. Always criticising, offering 'advice' nobody's asked for, while never lifting a finger to do anything himself, of course. When he *does* deign to come and see us, I've never heard him so much as offer to help carry plates from the dinner table. And Kayleigh's followed his lead, of course, started acting like she's above helping out in her own home. Our dad's sick, he uses a cane these days, but they'll let him wait on them hand and foot before they even think about pitching in to help.'

I don't point out that it's not her home, it's her parents' – because I have to agree with Leon's disdainful tone, that it's the very least she could be doing. She's not *really* a guest when she grew up there. And if her dad really is unwell like that . . . Gosh, I can't even imagine. I can't fathom acting that way if it were my parents.

Instead, I say, 'What makes you think it's not him taking the lead from Kayleigh?'

'Excuse me?'

'Well, if you think he's such a terrible influence on her – what if you're wrong, and she's the bad influence on him, and that's why you think all those things of him? Alright, so he's a little bit opinionated—'

'He's an argumentative prat.'

'Pot, kettle,' I point out, and Leon makes an angry noise in the back of his throat that has Gemma smothering a giggle into her hand. She has to turn away a bit, flapping a hand in front of her face to try to breathe before she sets herself off into another fit of laughter.

Leon says, 'Always playing devil's advocate—'

'He enjoys a healthy debate!'

'You can do that without belittling everybody around you – something he's never bothered to learn how to do and clearly doesn't care about, either. You know he had my mum in tears after he left once, lecturing us on veganism and how we were all contributing to the ruin of the environment for the next generation – even saying *maybe that was why my dad got sick*. And then he's there not two days later, out with some people, hunting. For *sport*. And posting photos of the pheasant they ate, after.'

'He – well, that . . .' That can't be the whole story. Can it? Maybe Leon and Kayleigh's mum said something aggravating, or got the wrong end of the stick. Although Marcus *does* love playing devil's advocate to stir up a chat, can come

104

off a bit . . . a bit *brusque* sometimes. Even I can admit that sounds like him.

A leaden weight settles in the pit of my stomach and there's a tremble in my hands as I reach for my drink.

'He's not a bad person,' I say, and my voice is a bit wobbly, too. I try again. 'I'm not saying he's perfect, nobody is, but you don't know him like I do. He's sweet, and caring, and funny—'

Both Gemma and Leon scoff at that.

I only dig my heels in harder. They don't know. They *don't*.

'He can light up the whole room when he walks in—'

'He's an attention seeker,' Leon insists. 'He *demands* that attention, doesn't earn it or deserve it.'

'And he can make you feel so special, like the most important person—'

'Yeah, because here's this raging narcissist giving you the time of day.'

Gemma, again, makes a noise of agreement at that, nodding along.

I say, 'Maybe he's got a bit of a – a polished, hard exterior, but he's not like that deep down, not really. He's such a softie, has such a big heart—'

'One,' Leon snaps. 'Give me one example. Go on.'

He sits up straighter, and Gemma has an elbow on the table, cheek on her fist again, watching our exchange like a tennis match – though it's abundantly clear she's rooting for Leon, is on his side. I'm not sure if that's because they both hate me as the other woman, or because she really doesn't think much of Marcus either.

Isn't that a sign, that he and Kayleigh aren't right for each

105

other? If her own brother and her best friend don't like him? Are quite literally fighting to *prove* how dislikeable he is?

Leon taps the open notebook.

'I've got pages of instances he's offended or upset our family here, and that barely scratches the surface. So go on. Give me *one* example of a time he was such a glowing example of a good human being.'

I open my mouth and falter, mind racing, reeling.

It's only because there are so many, though. It's like when someone asks you to name a book you like, and you suddenly forget the title of any book in existence.

How am I supposed to choose just one?

And how am I supposed to find the *right* one – one that proves he isn't worthy of their hate, but isn't so convincing that it makes Leon think Marcus *should* marry Kayleigh. It's mean and scheming and feels wrong, but I know that it is, ultimately, helpful if he doesn't want the wedding to go ahead either.

It's someone on my side, if not in my corner.

Where to even start?

'He always tells me to text him that I'm home safe, after a work night out,' I say, but that's – no, that's not enough, is it? That's too ordinary. 'He always picks up the tab if we go for lunch or anything, and he always holds the door, which is . . .' *Chivalrous*, I want to say, but it's still not big enough.

I reel off more, knowing one will strike gold. He compliments my outfits or hair sometimes, noticing if it's something new. He makes sure I'm included in casual after-work outings, always sends me things he's seen online or out and about that remind him of me, he's stood up for me in tough

106

meetings a couple of times with senior managers, he always brings me cake when—

Oh, no, that's something I do for him. One of our little rituals. I bring him a slice of cake whenever there's a birthday cake in the office. It's a nice excuse to see him and talk for a few minutes, and he always looks so happy to see me.

Gemma's face creases, lines carving across her forehead and her mouth downturned as she grimaces.

Of course I'm not helping his case, I think; this isn't doing anything except showcasing all the ways he gives me attention he probably shouldn't be, drives home the emotional affair we've been conducting, and that's not going to paint him in a good light at all.

But Gemma reaches over, places her hand on mine, and squeezes tight.

'Oh, sweetie, no. Oh, no,' she says, and she sounds as concerned as she looks. Pained, almost. 'He's breadcrumbing you.'

'What?'

'I don't think I want to google that,' Leon mutters.

Gemma *tsks*, and the table jostles a little as she kicks him lightly. 'It's not a sex thing, you pervert. It's a boy thing. A dating thing. When people do the absolute bare minimum and sprinkle in *just* enough effort and flirting to make you think they're interested, when all they're doing is stringing you along. Because the attention makes them feel good, or they enjoy having this weird power over your emotions, or they're just dickheads. Whatever. Girl, you *cannot* be this blind. Are you seriously going to break up a wedding because a guy is breadcrumbing you?'

'He's – he's not doing that.'

She's making assumptions. She doesn't know. It's just all so much more than I can put into words, that's all.

She gives me a sad, sorry look. 'Even if he's not – but he is, believe me, I read those texts . . . Whatever weird little pseudo-romance the two of you have going on, I'm *telling you*, he's not in love with you.'

'You don't know what you're talking about. You have no idea—'

Leon, to my surprise, is the one who interrupts.

And it's in my favour, for once.

He tells Gemma, 'Lay off her. If she thinks he'll pick her over Kayleigh – let her go ahead. And if he doesn't, well, fine. But at least Kay will still know what kind of man he is, and this can all be over.'

Gemma keeps her gaze on me for a moment, and bites the inside of her cheek, mulling over something. Whatever it is, she makes her mind up swiftly, and gives my hand another squeeze before drawing back to appraise Leon, eyes full of suspicion.

And – something clicks.

Something out of place and weird and so completely minuscule and forgettable is suddenly thrown into sharp relief, and I gasp.

'You,' I say to Leon. 'You wanted to talk to Kayleigh. You had something important to chat to her about before the wedding. *You were going to break up the wedding, too.*'

Chapter Sixteen

Gemma

Stop. I cannot deal. This is all too much.

I definitely have unfinished business with darling Fran – I mean, God, the level of bullshit Marcus has been pulling to string her along all this time, to the point where she's so convinced he's in love with her that he'd ditch his own wedding to run off with her instead . . . She needs a reality check, yeah, but I think she also just needs someone to look her in the eye and tell her that she categorically deserves better.

Which, you know. Maybe she doesn't? Admittedly, I don't know her all that well, beyond the last couple of hours in this godforsaken airport halfway to Barcelona, and she *has* been going after a man who's engaged.

But this is Marcus we're talking about, and I reckon this girl is every last bit as doe-eyed and naïve as she looks, and fell for it hook, line and sinker.

Either way, she needs someone to pull her out of that delusion.

But *now*, it turns out, she's not the only one with a secret agenda.

Leon?

Quiet, unassuming Leon, the king of avoiding confrontation?

As if.

Obviously, also, there's me and *my* agenda, but they don't need to know about that. Shit, if they want to take care of this, more power to them. I'll stand by and watch as Kayleigh has to pick up the pieces.

Francesca is gawping at Leon, looking just a bit self-righteous (deservedly so, in my humble opinion, after he kind of laid into her), and when I swivel to him, he's grouchy and defensive. Shuffling around in his seat and scowling at the table, staying completely mute.

The pair of them are as bad as each other. Doesn't anybody learn to regulate their emotions and think about what they're showing to the world? Aren't they the tiniest bit concerned about at least *trying* not to look so guilty?

'You were, weren't you?' Fran presses – and would you look at that, she *does* have a backbone after all! Somewhere in there. There is hope for her yet. 'You wanted to talk to her so you could – could tell her all this rubbish,' she says, waving a hand at his notebook full of Marcus slander, 'and stop the wedding!'

I don't want to be left out, so I say, '*That's* why you were so wound up about not making it there until the morning, isn't it? Because you were worried you'd miss your chance to catch Kayleigh before the ceremony.'

Leon gives me a disgruntled look. 'Hardly sounds like *you're* his biggest fan, either. You can't talk.'

'*I* wasn't about to stand up and yell "I object!" and run in wielding my Burn Book.' I pick up the notebook and

110

wave it around theatrically, if only for a moment to relish the ridiculousness and excellence of that mental image. '*You're* planning to tell her that her whole family hates the man she's marrying. Respectfully, Leon, what the fuck?'

'Me? What about *her*?'

I am dealing with toddlers. God, give me strength.

Fran looks down, fidgeting with one of the enamel pins on her jacket.

'*She*,' I say, 'is doing this because she thinks she's the main character in a cheesy romance movie. Which I'm normally all for, but that's beside the point. She's doing it for *love*. You're doing it to be spiteful.'

But when he shakes his head, his expression clears, his resolve hardening. I see it settling into his features like stone. Clean-cut and sure.

'You're wrong. I'm doing this because it's what we should've done a long time ago. There's never a good time to say, "We don't like your boyfriend", especially when he's always *there* and you're engaged in the blink of an eye. We all kept our mouths shut because we love Kay and want her to be happy, but this relationship *can't* be making her happy. It's changed her. She's not the same person. And if it comes from me . . .'

He takes a deep, shuddering breath, and it's oddly vulnerable for someone who looks so set on their course. My heart bleeds for him a little.

'If it comes from me, then the worst that happens is she cuts me out of her life. But she'll still have Mum and Dad, and Myleene. It's not like she makes time to talk to me much these days, so I'm sure it won't be difficult for her to stop altogether. And they can blame me, too, say they didn't know and it was all my idea, so they don't have to lose Kay. But at least someone tried.'

'Oh,' Fran gasps, and she gets as far as reaching for Leon's elbow to lay a hand on his arm in comfort before she thinks better of it. Her fingers barely graze his sleeve before she retracts her hand, but her eyes are misty.

She's not the only one. The emotion is shining in Leon's eyes, too, and while I wouldn't be surprised to see him cry, I *am* surprised it's over this.

I'm surprised that it got this far. That I never stopped and considered how it must feel on the other side of their relationship with Kayleigh, beyond the whinging and fed-up comments I constantly hear from her whenever the topic comes up. I guess . . .

I guess I sort of assumed the familial distancing was mutual.

Like it is for me, with my family.

And I knew they had this idea of who Kayleigh is – ever since we were in school, she'd always act differently around her parents, which I assumed was so normal I never thought twice about it till now – but I never thought they'd be *clinging* to it. Reaching for her, even as she slaps their hands away.

My heart really *does* bleed for him now. For all of them. Kayleigh's family are good people. Average, normal, ordinary, *good* people. It's so sad to think they all feel that they're losing her, that they have to fight for her.

What's that like? I want to ask. Maybe Kayleigh, maybe Leon. *What's it like having a family who want to fight to be in your life?*

How can you throw that away, like it means so little?

There's a pang in my chest so sharp, so tight, it *hurts*. I rub absently at the top of my sternum like I can massage it away, but it doesn't budge.

Quietly, Fran says, 'I'm sorry, Leon. That's . . . That must be really hard on all of you. That must've been a really hard thing to decide to do. It's . . . I think it's very brave of you.'

He laughs, but it's a hollow, barking sound. 'It was an impulsive, stupid thing, but . . . It's the only thing I *can* do. She wants me to stand up there and give a speech saying how happy we are about the wedding, how thrilled we are to have Marcus join the family, and . . . Surely there's part of her that *knows?* I mean, Dad – my dad doesn't do crowds, he'd probably pass out if he tried to give a speech. But he didn't even want to *try* – not after she told him he couldn't walk her down the aisle. His eldest daughter's getting married, and he doesn't even want to *try* to stand up there and say so much as, "Congratulations, both." Do you have any idea how sad that is to see?'

I don't.

I can't imagine. I really can't.

He looks at Fran for a long moment, and her pretty features bow with sorrow for him. Leon doesn't bother to glance my way. He knows as well as I do that I won't understand.

We were never a close-knit family, anyway, even before we fell apart.

'It's a more honourable bloody reason to call off a wedding than an affair,' he mutters then, and I give him another kick under the table. This one might be a little harder than the last. I'm not sorry about it.

I mean, poor Fran. However dodgy her motives are, she's not mean-spirited about it. I mean, she actually *said* – honestly *believed* – it was for Kayleigh's sake, too, because it'd be sad to be married to a man who had feelings for someone else. I'm not saying it's honourable, but he doesn't need to be a prat about it.

I open my mouth to say something – about his plan, this little speech he's going to give, if he'll give his parents a heads-up.

But instead what comes out is a soft, 'What makes you think that's going to change anything?'

'Huh?'

'Marcus. If she doesn't marry him. If the wedding doesn't go ahead.' I lift my gaze to his. Leon's eyes are the same colour as his sister's. They're warmer, though. More . . . human. 'What makes you think she's going to be the person you all want her to be? What happens if she's not? If it's not him? What if she's still that bitch, and the only difference is that you're all finally starting to realise it?'

Leon regards me for a long moment, letting my words sink in, turning them over in his mind to make sense of them. My heart is racing under his steady scrutiny, and there's an acrid taste in my mouth. Did I just say that? Am I really doing this? No, of course I'm not, I'm Kayleigh's best friend, why would I be sat here saying any of these things, even suggesting it?

But *I am*.

The complete and absolute conviction Leon has that the reason his sister is acting out is because of *Marcus*, and not because she's just that person at her core . . . The fact he's willing to lose any chance of a relationship with his sister to fight for her, the fact he's planning to break up the wedding at the last second to 'save' her . . .

She doesn't need saving.

She doesn't deserve anybody fighting for her.

She's a liar, a master manipulator, every bit the self-serving and self-centred, stuck-up, nasty piece of work her whole family think Marcus is.

If Fran can sit there and say that Kayleigh deserves to know if her fiancé has feelings for someone else, aren't I entitled to say Kayleigh's family deserve to know if they're chasing a ghost?

And Leon – poor, lovely Leon who's just trying to do the right thing for his family – is staring at me as if he can't fathom a world in which his sister *is* that bitch.

'What makes you think,' I say, and I can barely hear my own voice over the roaring in my ears, 'that if he's not on the scene, she'll come home to visit more, and be nicer to everyone, and stop acting entitled and too good for you all? Do you think she'll stop getting rid of the birthday presents you all give her, stop whinging about having to come visit when she'd literally rather be doing anything else, stop *lying* and making up excuses so she doesn't have to waste her time on you all, unless it suits her? She's been taking you all for granted since long before Marcus was around. You just didn't want to see it.'

'That's not—'

But the floodgates have opened, and I can't stop.

Half a lifetime of resentment, of feeling less-than, of getting knocked down every time I think I can stand on my own two feet, of that horrible, bitter, black hole in my chest . . . That fucking phone call before the flight out, letting me know she'd stolen the promotion *I* worked for, the one that wouldn't even exist if not for me, just one more thing she's taken from me and expected me to turn the other cheek over . . . It all comes pouring out, to the last people on earth I should be telling.

I don't know who I'd be without Kayleigh. I don't know how *not* to be her best friend.

But I hate her. I hate her.

And I can't – stop – *talking*.

Chapter Seventeen

Leon

'No,' Gemma snaps at me with a sudden vehemence, her eyes blazing, jaw set. 'It's true. Just because you're all in denial, doesn't mean it's not true. I'm telling you, the Kayleigh you all think you know and love – she's not real. She's good at *seeming* good, and she's good at presenting a bit of a front when it suits her. Like how it suited her to be this precious, darling, golden child who had parents that doted on her and thought the world of her. It was never *her* fault if she got in a bit of trouble at school, then, was it? It was never *her* fault if a party got a bit out of hand and she was home late. She'd have been helping tidy up, or looking after somebody – right? I can tell you for a fact that's a lie. She's a *liar*, and she always has been.'

I scoff. 'Please, every kid tells a couple of little white lies to avoid getting into trouble with their parents. That doesn't mean anything.'

But the words sound hollow, and it's like they're coming from somebody else.

My brain feels fuzzy, foggy, and Gemma's words are a harsh static tearing through it. I hear what she's saying, but none of the words connect, I can't process them enough to make sense of it.

The only coherent thought I have is, *Why is she saying this? Why does she look so upset?*

I could count on one hand the number of times I've ever known Gemma to be upset. And most of those were when we were at school, when she was just a kid. She's always so in control.

She's Kayleigh's best friend. They've been thick as thieves since they first met at twelve years old, and that's never changed. They've lived together, worked together. Their lives are so entwined that you couldn't separate them if you tried. Isn't Gemma supposed to go to bat for her, defend her, stand up for her?

Why is she tearing Kay apart now?

Gemma is barrelling on, though. Her voice shakes, but the look in her eyes is unyielding. I can't look away.

'You think Marcus is a piece of work? You think *he's* the bad influence on her? Let me tell you something – I have *never* known Kayleigh be more herself than when she's with him. Marcus is the first guy she's dated that I've thought, *Yup, that's the real Kayleigh.* She doesn't have to try to be someone else – someone better – when she's with him.'

'N-no, that's not . . . She isn't . . .'

'You don't *know* her, Leon. *I do.* And I'm telling you, your sister is a stone-cold bitch. Which is great, sure, I love it about her—'

'Doesn't sound like it,' I mutter, because there's venom in the way she spits the words.

'But that's who she is. With her perfect life and perfect home and perfect job and perfect man and *perfect fucking wedding*—'

'Careful,' I warn. 'You're starting to sound jealous, Gem.'

The noise that rips out of her throat is a breathy laugh so incredulous and bitter, it only proves my point.

'Yeah. *Yeah*, I'm jealous. She gets *everything*, all the time, and she doesn't care who she hurts in the process. If this wedding turned into a raging shitshow because Marcus jilts her at the altar and it comes out her family all disapprove of the whole thing, I would stand by with the popcorn, because it's the *least* she deserves. You know I'm the one who pitched for the promotion, but she caught wind and swanned in like she was entitled to it, and then *she* got it instead – and badmouthed me to our boss in the process. And now she gets to piss off to Barcelona for three weeks while I'm stuck picking up the slack for her, so she can enjoy herself and not stress about work. *I* found that flat for us to rent, but then she's calling up the landlord and persuading him to sell so she can buy it – with *Marcus*, leaving me stuck in this shitty house-share with a girl who always steals the orange juice and someone who never pulls their weight with chores, and now it's *my* fault she moved out and the three of us have to pitch in to cover her rent while we're looking for someone else.'

'That's not what happened.'

It's not. This is a warped version of everything Kayleigh's told us.

A role opened up at work, so she interviewed and Gemma did too, but at the end of the day, she got it. She was just the right person for the position, but she was sure something else would come along for Gemma eventually. And the flat was kismet, a lucky find at the right time, everything just working out suddenly and perfectly, falling into place so she and Marcus could take the next step.

Isn't that how it happened?

'You wanna bet?' Gemma snaps. 'You want to know who she really is, Leon? Huh? Do you?'

She rises halfway out of her seat. Her hands are bunched into white-knuckled fists on the table and she leans towards me – over me, looming and snarling, teeth bared and lips peeled back – and she's trembling.

I'm not sure I do want to know.

Not if it's coming from someone who looks as hateful and angry as Gemma does right now, I think, but that's not quite true.

Not if the answer is someone who does this to her best friend.

But I don't say anything; I just sit there, staring, waiting. Dreading.

'When your nana took Kayleigh aside and said she wasn't very keen on Marcus, and thought that her big, glamorous new life in London wasn't doing her any good, told Kayleigh that she needed to sort out her priorities because she was pushing all her family away and hurting them and they'd raised her better than that – Kayleigh laughed in her face. She told her she was an interfering busybody who couldn't tell her what to do and just because Kayleigh had it all when the rest of you don't, she didn't have to sacrifice it to make the rest of you feel more comfortable about your own sad little lives. She was *awful* to your nana. And when she died, Kayleigh said, 'Good riddance to the old bat.' *She said that.* Then she went and cried at the funeral and hugged you all and said how much she regretted that she hadn't made time to visit. You know why she didn't visit? Because she – quote – wasn't going to waste her time being lectured to by some jealous old cow. Your nana held up a mirror, and

Kayleigh didn't like that, so she smashed it to pieces, and didn't lose sleep over it.'

I can't say a word. I'm completely numb.

Because – it *feels* true. I can't even try to deny that.

Kay kept promising to visit, kept sending her best over the phone with one of us, kept making excuses. She cried on the phone to Dad one time about how it was just too hard, the idea of seeing Nana in that home, so frail and unwell, but it's not like she ever acknowledged how hard it was for all the rest of us. Myleene cried after every time she went to visit Nana, but she still went every couple of days. Fuck, Myleene would *plan* to go in to visit whenever Kay was supposed to – because we all knew Kayleigh would never actually show up. Our little sister would sack off plans with her friends and hockey sessions and have to do her homework late at night just so she could be there when Kayleigh let everyone else down.

She didn't visit *once*.

We all blamed it on Marcus, on this new life she had with *him*, on her busy job. We believed whatever excuses she gave because the alternative was . . .

This. Exactly what Gemma is saying. Which is so cruel and unthinkable, none of us would have ever dared contemplate it.

I knew Nana had spoken to Kay about Marcus. I knew Kay didn't exactly *listen*. But to hear she said those things – that she'd cut Nana out of her life without a second thought . . . That's not the Kayleigh we all know.

Gemma must see that something she's said has struck home, because she pauses to catch her breath. She wipes her cheeks briskly, getting rid of the few tears that have fallen there. I stammer something, a few half-formed words in half-hearted protests – she's got it wrong, that's not what happened, Kay would never, that isn't her.

'No,' says a quiet voice on my other side, making me jump. 'That sounds exactly like her.'

Christ, I'd all but forgotten Francesca was even there, never mind listening to this character assassination. Instinct tells me that of course she'd say that, she's trying to steal Marcus and is no peach herself, but when I look at Francesca, her expression is weirdly apologetic. She looks *sad*, like all of this is hard to hear.

She looks like I feel.

Which makes no sense, but she carries on in a gentle voice, 'I thought maybe it was all in my head. Or – I suppose, maybe, part of me realised that my friendship with Marcus was obviously a bit more than that, and she saw it and was jealous and quite right to be standoffish and annoyed. But she's never struck me as a . . . very *warm* person. She's certainly never talked much about her family to make me think you were all particularly close. Marcus says she's quite . . . exacting,' she says, in that way that's obviously more diplomatic than whatever he actually said. 'And she can be a bit difficult and abrasive.'

Gemma has sunk back into her seat now, and grabs her coffee. 'What else has he said about her?'

Francesca shrugs. 'It's just been a few remarks here and there. I've probably read too much into them.'

'Like *what*?' I demand.

'Stuff like . . .' Her eyes track to one side as she thinks. 'If he's working late, he'll joke about how he's got a girlfriend with expensive taste he's got to look after, or if we all go for

122

a drink after work sometimes he says he *should* get on home, but needs a break from her. It's . . .'

Francesca frowns, squirming in her chair, then says quickly, 'Actually, it's all very nasty and misogynistic, and they all join in about it, but I've always told myself it's just that he's settled for her and it'd be different if he was with someone he really cared about.'

'A fixer-upper,' Gemma says, nodding, then spits, 'Pig.'

I grunt in agreement, not quite trusting myself to form a coherent word. Francesca's comments about Marcus are hardly a revelation. The problem wasn't that he acted like Kay needed to be some stay-at-home wife with no life of her own, it was that she was suddenly doing things like hiring cleaners that she did nothing but complain about for 'not doing their job well enough', then scrunching up her nose when we'd ask why she and Marcus didn't just tackle the housework themselves if it was causing such an issue.

That Kayleigh sounds more like the one Gemma's been talking about.

The one that, apparently, Francesca has witnessed too.

I press my fingertips to my eyes, rubbing them hard. There's a headache throbbing at the front of my skull and suddenly the clamour of the airport comes pouring in. Scraping trays and squeaky wheels and chaotic footfalls, dinging phones and beeping tills and voices placing orders and chattering blithely and complaining about delays.

How can the rest of the world be carrying on like normal, when everything has changed?

I drag my head back up, and my eyes go straight out to the concourse and high ceiling and billboards beyond the edge of the balcony where the food court is. A mirrored tower rotates slowly there. And somewhere past all of that, outside, there's a storm raging on, keeping us all stuck here.

Fifteen hours until the ceremony suddenly doesn't feel long enough.

Chapter Eighteen

Francesca

Leon falls quiet, and Gemma's tirade is over – for now. She looks like she has a lot more to say, but she also looks exhausted. Ashen and limp, worn out by her own explosion.

I can't blame her; I feel pretty wrung out, too.

This confrontation has been so emotionally draining, such a rollercoaster of revelations, I think we need this beat of quiet to take a breather and digest it all.

The airport around us is noisy, chock-full of people waiting miserably and impatiently for flights. There's a clatter a short way off, and I glance over to notice a tall, broad young man tripping over a barstool, spilling half of his beer as he does so. He must be on a lads' holiday or something. There's a streak of silver glitter in his gelled hair. Elsewhere, there's a group of people in gimmicky T-shirts, obviously on some sort of stag or hen do, laughing too loudly; at the table across from us a ginger man and woman sit close, ignoring each other in favour of their phones. They look so alike, right down to their mannerisms as they swipe and type, they *have* to be related.

Gemma has slumped in the booth, legs and arms splayed out, frowning at a spot on the table, eyes tracking slightly back and forth as she thinks over something. Between us, Leon sits rigid and awkward in his seat, mouth slack, apparently contending with the fact that his sister isn't the person he thought she was – and that maybe Marcus isn't the villain he believed him to be, too.

My body tingles with that pins-and-needles numbness. It makes me feel both detached and grounded, all at once; not quite myself, but too sharp to ignore.

And my mind is spinning so fast I'm not even sure *what* I'm thinking.

This is the first time I've properly been able to *tell* anybody what's going on with me and Marcus, all the complicated dynamics and nuances at play. The gang from uni would probably have staged an intervention long ago if they thought I was seriously pursuing a man who was engaged, and I suddenly suspect they might accuse him of 'breadcrumbing' and whatever else, like Gemma did. And my family . . . Gosh, I don't think they would ever look at me the same way if they knew the truth.

There's just . . . there's a lot of layers. There's so much to it they could never really understand.

At the very least, it's a relief to finally get it off my chest.

It's certainly a bit reassuring to learn that Kayleigh really *isn't* such a good person. I know it doesn't excuse my own behaviour with Marcus, but at least it confirms my belief that he can't truly be happy with her and I'm doing the right thing.

But then . . .

Am I really? What if *they're* right? What if *I'm* no better than Leon seeing Kayleigh through rose-tinted glasses, refusing to see all those bad traits? What if it's not because he's unhappy with Kayleigh, and Marcus really is that person, too?

And worse – what if he's been showing me who he really is all along, stringing me along with the bare minimum like Gemma said? Have I been misreading everything this entire time, seeing only what I want to?

But that kiss. That night we spent together.

That wasn't a lie. That was real, and it mattered; it isn't some collection of tactfully distant text messages that could be misconstrued.

Maybe it sounded to Gemma like what Marcus and I have isn't anything worth fighting for, but I know how he makes me feel. I know how *different* it is to all the other guys I've dated. I know those butterflies that erupt in my stomach whenever his name pops up on my phone, the giddiness when he smiles at me when he sees me, the way my skin tingles when he touches me or hugs me.

That's what matters.

And it's worth risking it all for.

It has to be.

I don't stop to ponder what kind of man Marcus must be if he chose Kayleigh, knowing that she's the kind of person capable of all those heartless, selfish things Gemma told us about. Stealing promotions and screwing her over with accommodation and cutting her own grandmother off.

I have to have faith. I have to see this through.

I have to *know*.

I've already spent the last few years wondering what if; don't I owe this to *myself*, at the very least?

'Are you . . .?' The words leave my mouth before I can check them. They're raspy, and I wet my lips, trying again when both Gemma and Leon glance over. I ask Leon, 'Are you still going to talk to Kayleigh before the wedding?'

He opens his mouth, but has no answer.

I feel so awful for him. He's stuck in such an impossible situation, jeopardising his own relationship with Kayleigh for his family's sake and to try and salvage it for all of them, and worse, now he's faced with the idea that it might not be worth it at all.

I know we got off on the wrong foot, but I think I misjudged him badly.

Nobody who would do something like that can be so terrible at their core, not really. And the pressure he must've been under in the build-up to such a conversation, it's no wonder he was a bit short-tempered with me. Or with anybody, really.

Gemma lets out a dry bark of laughter. 'You've *got* to be kidding me. You're still going to try to break them up, aren't you? You still think Marcus is going to pick *you*.'

I bristle. So maybe I don't have designer coats and cashmere jumpers, and my idea of a weekend splurge is to order some takeaway and open a bottle of wine, maybe visit my family for a board-game night or have a group video chat with the gang from uni, and maybe I don't get my nails done unless it's a special occasion, and I'm a bit on the short side – so what? I don't own my flat and I can't drive and no matter how many TikToks I watch I'll never figure out what my colour palette is to make the most of my wardrobe, but *so what*?

I know how he held me when he kissed me. I know how he smiles at me, how he hugs me, how I'm on his mind so often he texts me about all these little nothings, just to share them with me.

My lips purse tight and my shoulders bunch. 'So what if I am?'

And when neither of them says anything, I add, 'You've both made it quite clear that you don't like Marcus – or even Kayleigh, really, if I had to hazard a guess – and I don't imagine either of you would be too sorry to see the wedding called off. What does it matter to you if I *am* still going to talk to him?'

Gemma's face is lined with disdain, and I realise how much she must have been masking her emotions earlier. She drags a hand through her hair, shaking it out, and regards me shamelessly.

She says, 'I didn't say I was going to stop you.'

Gemma looks at Leon, then, and I automatically follow suit.

He looks a bit startled, but shrugs. 'Yeah, go . . . go for it. Not like it'll make things worse, is it? Shit. *Shit*, what am I going to do? My parents are going to be wrecked.'

I reach to give his arm a little squeeze, but stop myself like I did earlier. We aren't friends; he still probably doesn't like me, let alone want my comfort or reassurance.

He buries his face in his hands. 'How much longer have we got?'

Gemma checks her phone. 'Well, I hate to break it to you, but the flight's delayed *again*, so now we're not taking off until nearly four o'clock. Which gives us, oh . . . nine hours, thirteen minutes. I think we're actually worse off than the last time we checked.'

Leon groans in distress, but I almost get the impression he hopes it would be longer.

Gemma must think the same, because she jokes, 'Do you

129

need more time to get your head around all this? I can probably make that happen. I already almost lost my bridesmaid's dress – which is another reason your sister is totally heinous, for the record, it's *hideous* – and accidentally sort of manifested not making it to the wedding at all. I'll just point my finger and make it happen, say the word.'

She points, wielding her index finger like a weapon, and pulling a theatrical grimace.

I laugh. 'How very Nesta Archeron of you.'

Gemma blinks, dropping the finger and expression both, but before I can explain it's a reference to a book, she grins. 'I knew I was going to like you, Fran. Dubious taste in men, fabulous taste in book boyfriends. Right!' She slaps the table and pushes herself to her feet. 'I don't know about you two, but I don't think I can stand to stay here much longer wallowing in . . . whatever this whole mess is. If I'm going to be stuck at an airport, I might as well try eighteen different perfumes in duty free. I'm going shopping. Are you coming?'

Leon grumbles incoherently, but manages to shake his head behind his hands. I nod, although I'm still trying to contend with the whiplash of Gemma saying 'someone like *you*' and then declaring she likes me because I made a reference to a romantasy novel.

She's right, though. I'd rather mooch around some shops for a while instead of sitting here in our strange, sad, angry little trio, hashing over a wedding none of us are very happy about.

'Are you sure?' I ask Leon gently.

'Yeah. Yeah, you guys go ahead. I'll . . . hold the fort here, or whatever. I just need to think about this a little, that's all.'

130

'Take your time,' I say, but I wonder if part of him would rather avoid me for the next several hours until the wedding. Maybe he's hoping that because I'll talk to Marcus, he can blame everything on the two of us, and it'll soften the blow of such a confrontation with Kayleigh for him. I wouldn't blame him.

Gemma grabs her handbag and I pick up my tote, slinging it over my shoulder. She gives Leon's shoulders a fond squeeze as she scoots past him.

'Here if you need more Kayleigh slander to uproot your worldview, buddy.'

'Is that meant to be reassuring?' he mutters. 'Because it really isn't.'

Gemma laughs, though, like it's all a great joke, and I murmur a goodbye to Leon as I follow her out of the food court, the two of us stepping onto the escalator down. Below us, the airport opens up. It's not a very big terminal and the shops are all in a round. The few rows of seats are packed to bursting with impatient, tired travellers waiting out the storm. People are even camped out on the floor, clustered around plug points to charge their phones.

The change in scenery offers some breathing space, and helps my head feel a little bit clearer.

At the bottom of the stairs, Gemma steps off first then waits for me, and winds her arm through mine, linking us at the elbows like schoolgirls.

'Come on, Fran,' she says brightly, and seems perfectly sincere. 'Let's go shopping!'

Time until 'I Do'

15 hours

Chapter Nineteen

Gemma

We were all in such a daze earlier from our unscheduled layover that we rushed through duty free, and I hardly got a look at anything. It's the best part of the airport experience, if you ask me. All these lovely products and perfumes waiting to be admired and sampled, a white-lit haven of decadence and extravagance just begging you to slow down and browse and *indulge*. It's a really lovely juxtaposition when you're racing to grab a coffee before they close the gate for your flight.

Although now I think about it, that rush to the plane is probably *because* I linger too long in duty free.

We pass straight through the overpriced chocolates and the little foodie section, past the bizarrely placed vintage cherry-red Mini beneath a display of red, white and blue umbrellas hanging open from the ceiling and with a cursive neon '*Ohlala*' on the roof, and past the booze which is, for some mind-boggling reason, always near the sunglasses.

I point that out aloud, and Fran says, 'I think it goes well together. Buy a litre of vodka dirt-cheap, and a pair of sunglasses to hide your hangover the next day.'

I laugh. She's not nearly as boring as I thought she was

going to be. Then again, *nobody* who's scheming to steal someone else's man while looking as innocent as she does can ever be *truly* dull, I suppose.

Once we're back at the beginning, near signs informing us in very loud, large letters, NO ENTRY PAST THIS POINT as it'll lead back to the security check, I pause and turn, and taking a deep, centring breath.

The brands spread out before us, and there's something delightfully French and sophisticated about the whole thing that I'm only just getting to appreciate. I mean, there are *chandeliers* hanging from the ceiling! How very Versailles. There's the usual Kiehl's, Clinique, Dior, Jo Malone – but there's also a neat little Cartier stand, a collection of Diptyque candles I cannot *wait* to get my nose into, a whole section dedicated to travel minis that are a cut above *anything* Boots would be selling in their holiday section, and even—

'Is that . . .' Fran pauses, squinting, as if she can't quite believe it either. 'A Victoria's Secret? In an *airport*?'

'When in France,' I say, and add it to my mental list of things to peruse, then set off. Fran follows. She's got a real puppy-dog energy about her, trailing around with those big eyes, a bit skittish and a bit over-eager. I don't hate it. I'm sure I remember hearing at some point that she's a couple of years older than me and Kayleigh, but I bet this is what it's like having a little sister.

The two of us work our way methodically around the cosmetics and beauty stands, not really talking as we rub tiny blobs of face cream onto the backs of our hands or read the details on bottles of toner. There's some pop music playing through the speakers, and I hum along.

I love shopping.

Well – I love the browsing part. I love *window shopping*. The whole ritual of curating a wish list in my mind of what I'm going to spend my money on, what's worth it that I'll feel really *good* about.

It's something that *did* honestly start off as another bit of one-upmanship between me and Kayleigh: I splurged on a Kate Spade handbag for my first job, so naturally she spent her first paycheque on some Louboutin loafers. And then when she made sure to keep up on all the latest trends to be the more fashionable one, I made it my mission to have a capsule wardrobe made up of sustainable investment pieces gradually gathered over time, like it gave me some moral high ground over her.

Although admittedly, all the bikinis I got for this holiday are from Shein. I mean, Christ, I'm not *made* of money. And I *did* put myself into some credit card debt buying up a bunch of very expensive pieces from niche brands at the start. But that's by the by.

Still, whatever messy, gross feelings I have tangled up in my friendship with Kayleigh, I have learned to truly *savour* the experience of shopping.

'I think this is one of my favourite pastimes,' I tell Fran. Not that she asked, but the silence is starting to get to me a little, and my head is feeling a bit too full of my own thoughts. She's polite enough to *pretend* that she's interested, I figure. 'Shopping, searching for *the* perfect thing. It just makes my soul happy, you know? Like a good book on a rainy day. I'd say it's even up there as one of my all-time best hobbies alongside sleeping in late, and getting a really good coffee somewhere.'

I half expect her to challenge me on whether those are really 'hobbies' – or God forbid, she's going to be one of those girls who crafts book-nook dioramas and knits hats for orphaned dogs, or something, and get on her high horse about it.

It's what Kayleigh would do.

But Fran only smiles and catches my eye. 'Girl hobbies. You know, between that and the *Court of Thorns and Roses* reference, I think we're on the same side of TikTok.'

I *knew* I'd like her.

There's a little glint in her eye, too, a twist of cheekiness in that smile.

Oh my God, look at us! We're *bonding*.

'So aside from reading smutty fantasy books and throwing yourself at almost-married men, what else do you do?' I ask her. Suddenly, I'm interested – beyond the gossip I'm no longer going to tell Kayleigh all about but shamelessly enjoy myself, and beyond polite small talk. I want to know who Fran is, underneath that ugly denim jacket and neatly plaited hair.

She baulks, stammering uncertainly.

We've moved onto the Chanel lipsticks by now, and I pull her hand up to hover between us so I can swatch some. She's got a lovely olive undertone to her complexion – and with her features, I bet she can pull off a dark, bold lip colour beautifully.

'No boyfriend?' I ask her, and though she stays tense, she shakes her head. 'Oh, come on, I'm not going to lay into you. I mean, it's an incredibly shitty thing to do, have an emotional affair with a guy you *know* is marrying someone else, to the point where you've convinced yourself he'll leave the bride for you – but also, Marcus has obviously been playing you like a fiddle to encourage that delusion. So I will cut you a little slack there. And frankly, I don't care either way. You want to mess up the wedding, I'm all for it, like I said.'

'Why?' We're both staring at the lines of lipstick I've been painting on the back of her hand, and her voice sounds stronger this time when she repeats, 'Why? You're supposed to be Kayleigh's best friend. I know everybody has their flaws, and we love and accept the people who are important to us anyway, but – the way you talked about her, it's like you don't have a kind word to say.'

'Yeah, well, she doesn't have a whole lot of redeeming features.'

'What are they? I mean . . . I mean, genuinely. Why are you friends, if you don't like all these things about her? If she stole your job and flat and things.'

My jaw clenches, and my grip tightens around the lipstick in my hand. I feel Fran's eyes burning an inquisitive little hole in my skull.

It's a question I've asked myself so many times, I have the answer ready at the tip of my tongue.

'Because she stuck with me. Because we've always been friends. Because – we go together.'

And if I don't have Kayleigh – who do I have?

She'll keep the gang. She's the one good at crocodile tears and sunshine-y smiles. She'll make out like she's the wounded party and they'll all take her side, and I'll be the vicious bitch who hurt her. They're all our old school friends, and I probably wouldn't pick them these days anyway, but it still hurts to know they'd choose her in a heartbeat. Joss definitely would. She's never liked me. But then again, Joss is a whiny piece of work with zero personality, so.

Kayleigh's key redeeming feature is that she hasn't abandoned me. That she puts up with me. That she knows exactly who I am, and keeps me around anyway, which is more than I can say for pretty much everybody else in my life.

It's why she knows she can take, and take, and take, and I'll never confront her about it, because I don't have anywhere else to go.

'You know I was the one who was supposed to go out with Marcus?' I blurt, surprising both of us. Francesca's hand jolts in mine.

What's the harm in telling her anyway? She's the work wife. I'm the maid of honour. Nobody would believe her over me.

'I didn't know that. He never mentioned . . .'

'Yeah, well, I was. I found him on Hinge. I matched with him. And obviously you tell your best friend everything, you send them the screen recordings of a cute person's profile and screenshots of the messages to dissect them, right? And one morning he mentions he's going to check out this new coffee shop, and then the next thing I know, *she's* gone there, and she's flirting up a storm with him. She knew I'd already arranged a date with him for the next weekend, but of course she has to get in there first. They spend the whole day together, then grab a casual after-work drink that turns into dinner that turns into another date on the Friday that turns into him cancelling on *me*, because Kayleigh's swooped in and taken him.'

Fran's slack-jawed, and I can *feel* the sympathy pouring off her. Or maybe it's guilt, because she knows she's doing the same thing, but like, a thousand times worse.

I carry on, 'Which like, fine, whatever. It's not like we

were dating or I'd slept with him or anything, and it's not like he knew. Actually, it's one of the *few* times I thought he was a decent bloke – cancelling on me because he was really into this other girl he was seeing. But of course, *she* gets the guy. She gets the flat. She gets the job. She won't let me have anything. Even the wedding—'

I cut myself off, seething.

I shove the lipstick tester back and storm over to the Diptyque and Jo Malone section, as if angrily sniffing extortionately priced candles will calm me down. Aromatherapy at its finest, I'm sure.

'What *about* the wedding?' Fran asks me, coming up beside me. With her big watery blue-grey eyes and sad mouth and looking like she *cares*. 'You're not . . . I mean, you're not in love with Marcus, are you?'

I snort at the hilarity of the very idea. It relieves a little of the tension coiled tight inside my body. 'Absolutely not.'

'And you're . . . not in love with Kayleigh?'

'Again, no.' I raise an eyebrow at her and deadpan, 'This is not *Love Actually*, and you are not Laura Linney at Peter and Juliet's wedding. For the record.'

A little smile tugs at her mouth before vanishing in favour of that all-consuming concern I would suddenly just *love* to run a mile from. How dare she be acting *nice* to me? She's trying to steal my best friend's fiancé. She's the work wife from hell. She's not supposed to be a halfway decent human being. Especially not to me.

'So what happened with the wedding? Is it just that she's getting married at all, or . . .?'

I slam down a candle a little too hard. It makes the plastic shelf wobble.

'It was *my* wedding. I was the one who wanted to get married abroad, had browsed a few venues, narrowed down which city I wanted to get married in, had an idea of the costs and the menu and the number of guests and . . . I wasn't engaged,' I add, 'but I was . . . I thought it was going to happen. I was with someone who . . . She was . . .'

I think of the way Brittney looked at me, so fed up, like the entire conversation was an inconvenience. '*I can't keep doing this, Gem. Do you have any idea how exhausting it is to be around you? You're always trying way too hard, expecting way too much. Clingy isn't a good look on you. I thought we were just having fun.*'

'Fun' which lasted for eighteen months, and was exclusive, and a total kick in the teeth when it ended when I thought it was . . . something else. That all those deep chats about what we wanted for the future *meant something*.

I shake myself, feeling Fran's big eyes boring into me.

'It doesn't matter now, anyway. We were together for a while and I thought it was going well and then it *wasn't*, and then Kayleigh got engaged and stole my dream wedding. Made it all seem like it was everything she wanted, too, and I'm her best friend – what was I supposed to do except help her out with planning it all? It wasn't like I'd be using it anytime soon, was it?'

'She said that?' Fran gasps.

'Not in so many words. But I knew. We both knew that was what was happening.'

I pick up another candle. It's pear and freesia.

It smells a bit like Mum, and there's a lump in my throat. I take another deep breath in through my nose, let my eyes close for a moment, then put it back down.

Fran says softly, 'She doesn't sound like a very good friend, Gemma.'

'No,' I say. 'She's not.'

But she's all I've got.

Chapter Twenty

Leon

The flight gets pushed back *another* twenty minutes. Not a single flight has left in the time we've been here, which makes me feel . . .

The exact opposite of hopeful.

Maybe even a bit grateful?

I'm beginning to toss around the idea of abandoning the flight altogether. Finding an information desk and requesting to change my ticket to one back to the UK. Getting the bloody Eurostar to London, even, at this rate. I can pretend there was a problem with my ticket for the connecting flight, that I got sick, *anything* but making it to the wedding.

I was already stressed out about the idea of sitting Kay down for a serious conversation about Marcus's behaviour and his effect on her, but at least that had felt like I'd be doing the right thing, ultimately.

But after everything Gemma said . . .

What if she's right?

What if it's not worth it?

Will it break Mum and Dad's hearts even more if the wedding doesn't go ahead and Kay's true colours start showing? Will she become even worse?

There's a voice in my head saying, *You know your own sister; it's not her it's Marcus, it's London, it's the job, it's Gemma* . . . But at what point do we have to accept that those are all just excuses?

For all I can say that Gemma's just jealous and bitter and Francesca's clearly biased, it's frighteningly easy to recall a dozen tiny interactions with Kay over the last few years, even before Marcus was around, that hit wrong. Expressions she pulled, things she said, so minuscule and forgettable, but together, now, they all add up to say, *She's not the person you all think she is.*

I don't know how to fix this. I'm the oldest, I'm supposed to look out for the family, and – I've failed, so badly. Is this how Nana felt when she tried to talk to Kay, just for her granddaughter to throw it in her face and never see her again? She never told us they'd had a full-on *argument*. She saw what Kay was really like, and took that to her grave rather than upset us all any more about it.

Can I do that, too?

Is it worth it, if it spares the rest of the family some heartache?

Come on, Nana. Give me a sign, tell me what to do.

Is this storm and this layover a message to go home, to forget about the wedding and the chat with Kay and everything else? Go home, apologise for the mix-up, and keep my mouth shut.

Or is this the universe's way of telling me that I needed to realise I was on a fool's errand, forcing me to spend time with Francesca and Gemma in this airport to learn the truth, and do something about it? Tell the family she's a lost cause – or confront Kay and tell her she has to change, or else be

145

done with us to save everyone worrying about her, causing all that pain?

I wish I knew. I wish there was a right answer.

At the next table over, there's a redheaded couple. The guy jostles against my chair as he returns with some drinks, and his girlfriend mutters a thank you before sighing at him, 'I *told* you we should've pulled the honeymoon card. They always give preferential treatment when they know you're on your honeymoon.'

'Well, it's too late for that now,' he huffs, and both of them busy themselves with their phones. I swallow a laugh; they're hardly the picture of newlywed bliss. The 'honeymoon card' would be a hard sell coming from them.

I jolt out of my thoughts when my own phone starts ringing: Myleene is FaceTiming. I dig out my earphones quickly and connect them before I answer.

I barely manage to say 'Hello' before my little sister is pulling a face and informing me, 'You look like absolute shit. Have you been drinking?'

I catch sight of myself on the screen: pale and drawn and hollowed-out behind the eyes. A stark contrast to the glow of candlelit lanterns on Myleene's cheeks and highlighting her hair in gold. She's wearing sparkly eyeshadow, and is outside somewhere. There's a whitewashed wall behind her taking up half the screen, and the other half is given over to an expanse of clear, ink-blue sky speckled with stars and silhouettes of palm trees.

'No, I've not been drinking,' I tell her, *but I could really do with one right about now*. 'Just . . . worried about this layover.'

'Fair enough. Kay's *well* stressed. Especially because Gem's not here. What kind of maid of honour leaves it till

146

the last minute to fly out for the wedding? If she'd gotten the morning flight like Kay said, she'd be here by now. You know Joss has had to step up and sort out things Gemma was meant to be doing? And Andi and Laura are having to make back-up plans for tomorrow in case she doesn't make it. *Plus* there's a whole drama between the three of them about who would get to sit at the top table in Gemma's spot as maid of honour, so it doesn't look weird in all the photos and stuff. Just because, what, she wouldn't take an extra couple of hours off work? Kay's fuming. I don't blame her.'

'Mm,' I say, but remembering that throwaway comment Gemma made about having to pick up some of Kayleigh's work for her makes it hard to be sympathetic.

Myleene, of course, is totally swept up in the drama of it all – just like Mum got swept up in the wedding planning. She's just a kid, though, nineteen, and as the baby of the family, she absolutely idolises Kayleigh: her big sister with the glamorous, perfect life she can only aspire to emulate one day.

Can I destroy that? Can I be honest with them, and sow that regret and distrust in someone like Myleene, too? I don't know if she'd even believe me. I certainly don't think she'd ever get over it.

'Is Gemma stressing out?' she asks me.

'Uh . . . a normal amount, I'd say. But there's not much we can do, is there?'

Myleene raises her eyebrows at me. 'You could rent a car and drive here. That's what Dad said. And Mum said you'd never cope driving on the wrong side of the road and you'd get too wound up and end up lost, especially in the dark. But *I* said that's what a satnav is for.'

147

'Well . . . Hopefully it won't come to that.'

'Lucky you're not one of the groomsmen, or Kay would be *really* angry with you being late,' Myleene says, laughing. 'Have you got your speech, by the way? Can you send it to me? Just in case I have to do it, if you don't make it. Kay's said to tell you that you have to send me it.'

'I'll make it.' And I suppose I'd better write *something*, as a contingency. Even if it's only to send Myleene for her peace of mind. I ask, 'Are we the only ones who got delayed?'

'A few cousins did too, and Marcus's stepbrother is stuck at Bristol.' She waves a dismissive hand. 'And that skanky girl from Marcus's work, the harpy—'

'Francesca.' I swallow a lump in my throat, and the urge to defend Francesca against the insult along with it. 'Yeah, she's with us.'

Myleene's eyes light up, and she scrunches her nose in excitement. 'OMG, say more. Is she pretty? Is she really annoying and up herself like Kay says? Has she been talking about Marcus? *Is* she really sad and pathetic, like he says?'

'She's . . .'

If Myleene had asked me an hour ago, I'd not have hesitated to say yes, she's every bit as awful as we were led to believe. Try-hard and fake and pulling that naïve act that set my teeth on edge all while being selfish and vindictive and not caring if she was hurting anybody else's feelings.

Except now, I think about how sad she sounded when I explained why I wanted to talk to Kay before the wedding, how hurt she looked when we talked about what a condescending arse Marcus is and she tried and failed to defend him. That strikes me as someone who cares very much about what other people feel. It's also easy to see why someone like that wouldn't even realise if Marcus was taking advantage of her friendship and her crush on him.

I think about Francesca's expressive eyes and heart-shaped face, how soft her hair looks and the mismatched, colourful pins on her jacket she kept fidgeting with, and that blaze of fire in her eyes when she tried to put me in my place for being rude. I probably owe her an apology for that; we *did* get off on the wrong foot.

'She's very pretty,' I tell Myleene, 'and she seems like a . . . nice person, for the most part.'

Aside from planning to break up a wedding, of course.

'Oh. That's a bit disappointing,' Myleene says. 'The way Kay's talked about her, and all that stuff Marcus says, I assumed she'd be . . .'

'Yeah. Me, too.'

'Well,' Myleene jokes, laughing, 'just watch *you* don't fall prey to her man-eating ways!'

'Ha. Right. No danger of that.'

I think about the way her head ticked to the side when she smiled. Definitely cute, I decide.

Feeling a bit more like myself, I tell Myleene to show me the view – she's out on a terrace while the partying carries on inside. Even though we can't quite see them in the dark, she points out the lush gardens and the pavilion in the middle where the wedding will take place. All the while, she's chattering a mile a minute about how Mum and Dad went to a salsa dancing class with some other relatives earlier and how cringe it is because they're all giving it a go again now dinner's over and they can 'tear up the dance floor', and how she'll be sure to video so I can see, too. She mentions that Marcus is busy getting drunk with his mates and pulls a very unimpressed face about it, and how he and Kay had a 'little spat' earlier because she thought he was flirting with the waitress, but then Kay told *everyone* how fit her masseur was, and it's a lot of pent-up wedding nerves and drama.

'Sounds like I'm really missing out.'

Myleene laughs. 'Please, you'd hate it. Consider yourself lucky you're stuck there, missing all this! Why do you think half the grown-ups took themselves off to this dance class earlier? They're not about it, either.'

'Probably for the best.'

'Yeah . . . Anyway, I should go. Promised I'd help Joss check on the flowers and stuff for the ceremony.'

'Isn't it past your bedtime?' I joke, but not really – it's getting late; does she need to be running errands like that right now?

'Bride's orders. Gotta pick up the slack for Gemma and help Kayleigh de-stress so she can get her beauty rest ahead of the big day!' Myleene salutes, stern-faced enough to make me laugh in spite of it. She might be a bit melodramatic at times, but she's nothing if not committed. She'll always step up to the plate and help out.

Not like Kay.

We say our goodbyes, and she disappears from the screen. My own reflection stares back at me.

He looks like he needs a stiff drink, and I decide I am more than happy to oblige.

Chapter Twenty-one

Francesca

There's so much I want to ask Gemma – about Kayleigh, about their friendship, about her relationship that just ended.

There's something else I want to ask her too, something far more pressing about Marcus, but it's such an ugly question that I can't stand to dwell on it, let alone ask it.

From my stints social media stalking Kayleigh – and by extension, her friends – I always thought Gemma had everything together. She wears such lovely clothes, is always posting that she's out somewhere doing something. Drinks with the other bridesmaids, her old school friends; day trips with her (ex-)girlfriend; dinner parties and movie nights with bougie snacks. I would never know she'd been passed over for a promotion, trying and failing to move, had a relationship fall apart around her – one serious enough that she was picturing their wedding.

It makes me feel so silly to realise it; because of course she's not put her entire life out there on Instagram. Don't we all just pick and choose the better moments we want to share?

It's sad, though, that she must be going through so much. It doesn't sound like she's even – or maybe, especially – been able to talk to Kayleigh, her best friend, about any of this. I get the impression she's been bottling it all up, until now – something I know about *plenty*.

I'm not sure it's my place to ask about it all, but even if I wanted to, Gemma steers the conversation away so quickly I can do nothing but go along with it.

Returning to the makeup stands, she cleans the lipstick swatches off the back of my hand with a wipe from one of the counters, and has settled on a dark, almost purplish, red that I would never normally have chosen. She finds it boxed up on the shelf and presses it into my hand.

'This is the one,' she declares.

'I don't know. I'd normally go for something . . . more subtle.'

'Let me guess – like this?'

She searches the testers, and finally comes up trumps in Clinique, with a pale, shimmery pink. It looks a lot like the NYX lip gloss I normally wear, and I feel sheepish when I nod.

Gemma shoves it back into place. 'I'm telling you, it's not doing much for you, Fran. Like, I'm sure it looks fine, but it's not going to *wow* anybody. It's probably just washing you out, if anything. That's not a lip colour that's going to make a man abandon his fiancée for you. *That*,' she says, nodding at the one in my hand, 'is.'

My fingers clutch it tighter, but it feels more like guilt than excitement that makes my stomach swoop.

Part of me suspects that she's doing this to be mean – to cut me down, to bully me into wearing something that will make me look clownish rather than sophisticated, to humiliate me in my hopes of grand romance. But she's so upfront,

152

so matter-of-fact, that I don't really believe that's what's happening. Gemma seems to be very face-value – what you see is what you get.

And, honestly, I *do* quite like the colour she's chosen. It's a far cry from anything I'd normally gravitate towards, but I've always envied women who find that perfect, bold makeup. It's amazing how something so simple can elevate your look, can make you feel like a different person.

Like . . . someone like Gemma. So at ease with who she is, so confident and unapologetic about it. I'd like to feel a bit more like that.

I say, 'Thanks. Really. I think I probably got gifted a lipstick when I was a teenager, and it was what everyone else was wearing, and I've sort of stuck with it ever since. I don't think *any* of my style has really developed in the last few years, you know. I'm so rubbish at keeping up with trends, so I just . . . stick with what I know.'

'I get that. It's comfortable, it's reliable. You don't have to take any big risks, so you never have to worry about a big failure.' She nods absently, strolling to the miniature travel-sized toiletries to rummage through, but I stand stock-still, the words hitting their mark a little too well.

How has she got me so figured out in the space of a couple of hours? In the space of one conversation, even, about something that feels so trivial?

'You're right,' I murmur. My mind is racing so fast it's practically come to a standstill, a singular blur. 'That's *exactly* what I'm like. In *everything*. I never take risks, I never try anything different or new or . . . Not in any significant way, anyway. I'm always just sort of doing what I think I'm supposed to do.'

Gemma gives me a sidelong look and a conspiratorial smirk.

'Well, I wouldn't say that. Chasing the man you're in love with to Barcelona to break up his wedding is a pretty big risk.' Then she cocks her head to one side, studying me for a moment. 'So what changed there? They do call it retail *therapy*, you know, Fran. Consider this the therapy part. Terms and conditions apply, you waive any and all right to sue over the fact I am not a licensed therapist.'

I laugh in spite of myself, then admit, 'The risk of *not* doing it and losing him forever was bigger than the risk of him rejecting me. And I thought . . .'

'You thought there was no way he *would* reject you. He was a safe bet.'

'Yes. He is.' I feel her tense, hear her click her tongue as she's about to argue, and cut her off. 'I know you think it's all in my head, but it's not. The way he makes me feel . . . I couldn't make that up if I tried. I know *he* feels it, too. And I know that I've never come close to having that sort of spark, those feelings, that closeness, with anybody else.'

'So you *do* date. You just sack it off when you decide they won't ever live up to Marcus.'

'That's not exactly . . .' Oh, God, but she's making it so easy to talk to her! And I never get to tell *anybody* this stuff. It really is a weight off to finally open up. 'It's more like they sack *me* off. No, that sounds really dirty, doesn't it? But I'm . . . I'm like the girl they date before they move on to their *real* relationship. Every time I meet a guy and think, This is it, he could be the one, so what if he's a bit of a fixer-upper? So what if I try to fit myself into a bit of a box so they like me better? It'll be worth it in the long run, this

154

is just what you do when you date – put your best foot forward, take an interest in the things they care about. And then eventually they get bored and move on.'

'All fixed-up.'

'Pretty much.' I wince; it sounds so horrible, laid out like this. I've just gotten so used to it – it's a running joke with my friends, about how much of a sucker I am for that type of guy, how eager I am for the attention – the promise and hope of romance, of love. How I'm always seeing the potential, instead of the reality. 'But Marcus was different. It wasn't just some one-night stand. He . . . stuck around.'

Gemma blinks. 'He got engaged. *To someone else.*'

'And he didn't stop caring about me, or spending time with me, or talking to me. He likes me for *me*. He stuck around,' I press, which sounds so paltry for how monumental our connection feels.

Whenever I see him, whenever we've spent time together since that night, it's always like something clicks back into place. Like finding your favourite jumper after losing it, or sitting down to a cup of tea after a long day. It feels right, and meant to be, and . . .

Comfortable.

It's *comfortable*.

Something about that realisation is jarring, the word not the reassurance it ought to be. It feels poisoned and bitter in the light of Gemma's comment about how I don't take risks and keep to what I know.

She must see something on my face, because she lays a hand on my arm and says, 'Listen, I get it, the heart wants what it wants, it's not rational, and all that crap. But your emotions are written all over your face, and you're *nice*, and he will have known exactly what he was doing. You were putty in his hands. You fawn all over him, give him all this attention and affection and whatever, even if it never got physical, and it made him feel good. And you got scraps in return, and that felt like it was enough.'

'That's not true.' But my voice wavers a little, and my lungs feel tight as the idea takes root, worms its way in and forces me to sift through memories and emotions and try to see if it might be true, after all.

I struggled to think of anything tangible that would prove Marcus was a good person earlier, when Leon was being so brutal about him, but if I'm being honest with myself – it's that so many of the gestures in our relationship of someone going out of their way for the other are all things that *I've* done for him. Like helping him sort out a last-minute birthday present for his mum, dashing out on my lunch break to pick up his dry-cleaning because he had back-to-back meetings, or bringing in leftovers of a meal I'd cooked for him to have for lunch.

And I'd do it without a second thought, because I always knew I'd be rewarded with his smile and heartfelt compliments and it'd feel so *good*, I'd feel so *worthy* and so special. He could have asked me for the moon, and I would've made it happen just to feel that way for a moment.

Always stopping by his desk with office birthday cake, just for that smile he'd give me.

How many things have I done for him like that over the last couple of years? How far out of my way have I gone to make him happy, to make his life better and easier?

What has he ever done for me in return?

And I know what I've always told myself: that it wasn't

fair to expect such things of him, because even if it was just friendly, it might make Kayleigh jealous, and I didn't do any of this because I wanted him to return the favour, this wasn't a business transaction . . .

That question I had for Gemma, the one I shoved deep down, threatens to rise to the surface, and I push it firmly away. I don't think I have the strength to contend with it right now.

Or maybe ever.

My chest hurts, and my brain feels muddled, and I'm not so sure what feels true or right anymore.

But surely I've put too much into this to turn back now?

I say as much out loud, cutting Gemma off where she's trying to tell me that Marcus is a waste of space and that I shouldn't bother giving him the time of day and how he'll never leave Kayleigh for me anyway, and she snaps her mouth shut.

'So you're really doing this?'

'Yes.'

She nods once, slowly, then several more times fast, something lighting up in her eyes. She tosses aside a tiny bottle of shampoo to grab my free hand, then drags me along behind her.

'Well, in that case, we'd better make it worth your while. If you're going to seduce him, Fran, you should at least look the part.'

We come to an abrupt stop, the Victoria's Secret logo glowing above us, illuminating us in pink. I blink to find Gemma suddenly holding up a bejewelled thong in my face, and the pair of us burst out laughing.

Time until 'I Do'

14 ½ hours

Chapter Twenty-two

Gemma

Fran's whole face lights up as she laughs, and then I'm joining her as the ridiculousness of this entire situation sinks in, until we're laughing so hard we're leaning on each other, gasping for air and bent double, people staring and frowning in our direction, and neither of us caring.

Is this actually happening?

It is, isn't it?

I'm really stuck in a French airport all night with nowhere to go but Ladurée and a sad, overpriced coffee shop, picking out lingerie for a girl I've just met to help her steal my best friend's soon-to-be husband.

There are tears pouring down my cheeks, and I can't breathe.

I'm not sure how much of it is laughter anymore, but I don't really want to know the answer to that.

Like I said, that sort of thinking is what makes you spiral if you're not careful.

It *does* feel good to finally vent a little bit about how hard it is to be Kayleigh's friend and how she treats me. *Mis*treats me. I've always accepted it as fact, but saying it out loud . . .

God, it's cathartic.

I've never told anybody that she only met Marcus because of me. He knows what happened – Kayleigh told him, and they both thought it was hilarious, but it's not the sweet meet-cute story they spin when anybody wonders how they got together. I've made a few backhanded jokes about her stealing my wedding, but nobody's ever looked at me like Fran did, feeling *sorry* about it, acknowledged that it was a really shitty thing for Kayleigh to do.

I can feel questions circling in my mind, doubts crawling out of the shadows, half-formed *what-ifs* . . . I know what my subconscious wants me to confront; these thoughts are nothing new. I've wondered plenty of times – *What if I just walked away? What if I confronted her? Why do I put up with it why don't I try to be better why—*

I know the answers to those kinds of questions, though.

It's the same kind of reason Fran is still chasing after Marcus: *because he stuck around.*

So I push those thoughts aside now, before I end up letting them drag me down.

Fran starts to sober up, taking the sparkly thong out of my hand to scrutinise. She looks me dead in the eye and says, 'Imagine the chafing,' which sends me into a fresh peal of laughter, but also chases those nasty little thoughts back into the shadows where I don't have to mull over them, and my chest feels lighter. I'm practically buoyant.

Maybe I *should* invest in therapy. This is great.

We discard the sparkly thong to pick through different garments. Lurid pink scraps of underwear, lacy push-up bras, shimmering bikinis. Fran lingers on one of those – it's turquoise, the same colour as my bridesmaid's dress.

Actually, it'd be a really lovely colour on her.

162

I say as much out loud, and she snatches her hand back. 'Oh, no, I wasn't . . . I mean, I'm not really going to *buy* any of this stuff.' Her hand curls around the Chanel lipstick I picked out for her, and she smiles down at it. 'Well, maybe this.'

'You should. You'll look gorge. And imagine – that, with *this?*' I hold the bikini up in front of her. The top part is essentially two tiny triangles with strings hanging off them, a halter-neck, and she laughs and pushes it away.

'My boobs would pop right out of that! I think that goes past "seduction" and right into "'public nudity".'

'I'm sure there are some topless beaches around,' I say, but scrutinise her a bit closer. The peasant blouse she's wearing is loose and hides her shape, and that ugly, huge denim jacket drowns her. It makes her small form look boxy and shapeless, and I remember what she said about not being sure of herself when it comes to fashion. Unless maybe she's going for more of a Billie Eilish thing . . .? In which case, she's kind of nailing it.

She moves on to a structured one-piece instead. There are little cut-outs on the side, and a diamante circle in the middle of the boobs. Even that looks too daring for Fran, though, and she quickly dismisses it. It's only when I watch her pull down the sleeves of her denim jacket to her finger-tips that I realise—

'That's a man's coat.'

She jumps, flushing red. 'Er.'

My eyes bug wide. '*That's Marcus's coat*. It is, isn't it? Ohmigod. You wear his jacket.'

'He left it at my place, that night . . .' She trails off, and her fingers touch the cuff and her lips draw into a soft smile.

Honestly, you can read her like a book. I'm not sure if it's sad and pathetic or unbearably sweet that she kept his jacket all this time and *still wears it*. It's kind of ballsy to wear it to his wedding, though, I'll give her that.

'You said he met Kayleigh just after he met you.'

'That's right.'

'So if what you have is so special, why did he bother with her when you two had a thing going?'

It's obviously the very last thing Fran wants me to ask her: she winces, looks sheepish and bites the inside of her cheek, screws up her nose and scrunches her forehead like she's half debating telling me to mind my own business.

But then she says, 'It's my fault. That's why I have to talk to him before the wedding. After we spent the night together, I saw him at the office and he came over to me saying, "Listen, about Friday night . . ." and I just *panicked*. I hadn't heard from him over the entire weekend. He looked so nervous, and I thought, *What if he's going to try to sweep it under the rug? What if he says he regretted it?* I couldn't bear that. So I just told him, "It's fine, really! We'd had a couple of drinks, it was just a bit of fun. It's no big deal." I think . . . God, it's so embarrassing to think now, but I was trying to play it cool. To *be* a cool girl about it.'

'Oh, sweetie, no.'

She nods, pulling a face at me before continuing. 'I know. And we were in the middle of the office, you know? There were people around. I didn't want to tell him in front of *everyone* that it was the most romantic night of my entire life. So I said it was fine, and he still looked nervous and he asked if I was sure. I told him I was, and he smiled a bit and gave me this weird little . . .'

She demonstrates, punching me lightly in the shoulder, hardly even touching me, her whole body swaying from her shoulders with a swagger that is actually an *uncanny* impression of Marcus.

'And he said, "So, we're all good? We're still pals? I'd hate to lose you," and I started to realise that maybe I'd gotten it wrong – that he wasn't going to reject me, but now *I'd* rejected *him*, so he had to suck it up and pretend it was all okay. He said his phone had died over the weekend and that's why he hadn't texted, and . . . Everything just spiralled so far out of control. I'd told him we were just friends, and then suddenly he was in a relationship, so it didn't feel like I had any right to take that back.'

'Until now.'

'Until now,' she agrees.

I wonder how it *actually* played out. How much is in her head that she's romanticised, and how much Marcus actually *was* invested in her until that point. I don't suppose it matters anyway. Knowing him as I do – and from what I've seen of Fran – they're hardly a match. He'd walk all over her, and she'd let him, happily.

Kind of like someone else I know, with her bestie.

I get the sudden urge to grab Fran by the shoulders, to shake her, to shout in her face, *Can't you see he's playing you? Don't you know what a fool you're making of yourself? He doesn't love you, he never will; he'll use you and take and take and take and you'll kill yourself trying to live up to some impossible expectation and count yourself lucky he even looks twice at you. Don't you know you're worth more than that? Don't you want to be worth more than that?*

But I don't say any of that, obviously.

I'm not sure if it'd be directed more at Francesca or at me, and neither of us wants to hear it right now.

So instead, I reach inside Marcus's horrible jacket she's decorated with her adorable, dorky collection of pins, and pinch her blouse so it fits tighter to her body, and then start having a proper look for something for her to wear. A cute babydoll, maybe. Definitely a hot bikini. I bet she's packed a one-piece she found in the Tesco sporty section years ago, or something.

Fran trails after me, lets me paw through pieces and suggest them for her, and it's only once I'm holding up a matching set and a really cute nightie that she blanches and recoils.

'Oh, Gemma, it's really nice of you to try to help me out, but I'm not actually buying anything, remember? I don't need . . . I mean, I'm not going to . . . Boys don't even *notice* half the time, do they? Is that really the sort of thing Marcus would like?'

With that last comment, she reaches out to touch the butter-soft silk of the nightie, and I roll my eyes.

'Fran, this isn't for Marcus. It's not about what *he* likes. It's not for any *man*. The whole point of this kind of stuff is to make *you* feel good. So *you* feel sexy and confident. Not so *he* thinks you are.'

'I guess I've . . . never really thought about it that way.'

'Sure you haven't,' I say, and when she frowns quizzically up at me I add, 'You stick to your comfort zone. Probably a raging people pleaser, too.'

She cringes, but manages a laugh in spite of herself. 'Guilty as charged.'

I toss the clothes onto the top of a display of pyjama sets

to grab Fran lightly by the shoulders. And I do give her a little shake, but just a gentle one.

'Girl, I don't know what your deal is, but you've *got* to start putting yourself at the centre of your story. Stop being some sidekick in the background of someone else's. For God's sake, you're on your way to Barcelona to break up the wedding of the man you love! If you're going to act like the main character of a romance movie, you should start believing it about yourself.'

Fran's eyebrows bunch and her lips purse, but not like she's going to argue.

Like she's heard me, is internalising it, letting it take root.

'I do always try to fade into the background and just . . . go with the flow,' she murmurs, then gives me an accusatory squint which she softens with another laugh. 'You're very good at reading people, Gemma, d'you know that?'

'Yes, I do.'

I'm just not very good at listening to my own advice is all.

Trying to lighten the mood a little – and because I'm kind of curious – I ask her, 'Was Marcus really that good in bed you spent the best part of *two years* pining after him? I mean, Kayleigh obviously thinks he's great, but personally, I have my doubts. Doesn't strike me as a guy who makes sure *you* finish too, you know what I mean?'

Fran sputters, blushing again, and I wonder if it's because we're talking about Marcus or talking about sex in general. Is this a confidence thing, or, like, a Catholic guilt thing? Although saying that, I'm pretty sure I remember hearing that she grew up with Buddhist parents . . .

She mumbles something, so quiet I don't have a hope in

hell of hearing it even if duty free were dead silent instead of pumping Ariana Grande through the speakers. There's a redhead girl nearby looking at some bras, and some people in gimmicky stag/hen do T-shirts loitering by the sunglasses. Fran looks around, as if scared they can all hear our conversation.

'Say again?'

But all I get is another incoherent mutter.

'Fran, I swear to God, if you—'

'I said we never actually had sex!' she yells, and my tongue makes a loud *pop* against the roof of my mouth as my jaw drops. She's beet red and *everybody* is staring, but she squares her shoulders. The redhead raises her eyebrows and turns away, but I think she's probably eavesdropping like hell. At a more conversational level, Fran tells me, 'We kissed, and he stayed the night, but we didn't do anything except kiss and cuddle and talk. That's what I mean when I say it wasn't some one-night stand. It was so much *more* than that. I've never had that sort of thing with anybody before. It was so romantic and intimate in a way I've never known sex be. Does that make sense?'

It does, and my heart goes out to her – but in that same way as when Leon admitted why he'd take on the responsibility of confronting Kayleigh, to spare the rest of his family losing her. It makes sense, but it's not something I can truly relate to.

I've . . . never had that.

I think, if I had, I'd want to fight for it, too.

'You're right,' I tell her. 'You can't turn back now. You deserve to know.'

Fran regards me a moment longer before snatching up

168

the underwear we found for her, bundling it together with her new lipstick. There's a spark of determination in her pale blue eyes, and she smiles at me before nodding once. I'm already smiling back, and wondering when was the last time I felt this kind of easy friendship with Kayleigh and didn't have to fake a smile for the sake of it.

Then there's the sound of someone crashing into a stand, products falling, someone shouting out, and the rattle of several suitcase wheels.

'Sorry, sorry – shit, I'm so sorry, I'll . . .'

We both look over to see Leon, his battered satchel slung over one shoulder and dragging all our luggage behind him. As if sensing us looking, he glances our way, and grimaces.

'I might've lost our table. Also, um, the flight's been delayed. Again.'

This day just keeps getting better and better.

But when I glance at Fran, she meets my eye and laughs, and then Leon turns around and knocks some boxes of biscuits over, and things don't seem quite so bleak.

Chapter Twenty-three

Leon

Some of the duty-free staff come over to pick up the products I just knocked all over the floor, and as I'm apologising and trying to help, my satchel smacks into a plastic sign and sends that flying, too.

'Please, monsieur, we have got this,' one says with a crisp smile. *Message received loud and clear.* I wrestle with the three suitcases and get out of their way before I destroy anything else. The girls are giggling – most likely, at my expense, the pair of them standing shoulder to shoulder in a chummy way that has me doing a double take. You'd never know they were strangers until a few short hours ago.

Are they bonding over a mutual hatred of Kayleigh? Or maybe my humiliating path of destruction? I wince, feeling eyes from all around scrutinising me. One half of the unhappy honeymooners with ginger hair is not far off and mutters – loud enough that I can hear – about drunkards in the airport. I duck my head, as if she can smell the single beer on my breath from all the way over there.

Francesca's holding a few things, so as I approach, I nod at the bundle in her hands and say, in desperate hopes of a distraction, 'Looks like you two have been busy. What've you got?'

Pink colours her cheeks while Gemma says, 'Lingerie! And some lippy. Look, is this knockout or what?'

She plucks the fabric from Francesca's limp hands, and I regret every decision I have made in the last half-hour that led to this moment. I *knew* I should've just stood in one spot and waited for them to come find me.

Because now, Francesca's standing there with her eyes widening in horror and looking too awkward to say anything, and Gemma's holding up a set of pure white underwear in front of her. The bra is covered in lace. The knickers are *made* of the stuff, to the point they must be more see-through than actually covering anything up.

My whole face feels like it's burning, and my pulse is roaring in my ears, and I am trying to do anything but picture Francesca in that underwear. Hiding it underneath that loose blouse and casual jeans, white lace hugging the curve of tanned hips, my hands—

'Seriously,' Gemma is saying, and I don't know if she's doing this to taunt me or if she's completely oblivious to the path my thoughts just turned down. Please, God, let it be the latter. 'Tell me this isn't the kind of woman you'd leave your fiancée at the altar for.'

Francesca finally masters herself and pushes Gemma's hands gently away, but she looks infinitely more awkward with the underwear gone, and Gemma's words ringing in the air.

'Um.' I scrub a hand through my hair, trying to think straight. 'I'm not sure there's a very good answer to that question.'

Gemma clicks her tongue. 'Spoilsport.'

She hands the set back to Francesca, who thanks her and hugs it close.

Is this really what they've been doing? Finding the best underwear to seduce Marcus?

There's a weird buzzing in my head at the thought.

'So what's the plan – you're going to strut down the aisle wearing that and he'll suddenly decide to leave Kay for you?' The mental image is so cartoonish – if only for the idea of Francesca *strutting* – that I snort a laugh.

She is the exact opposite of every nasty remark Kayleigh ever made at her expense.

'Um, excuse you,' Gemma says, and takes a playful swipe at my arm. 'She can strut if she wants to. Although,' she adds to Francesca, 'I do think I'm, like, legally obligated as maid of honour to throw red wine on you if you wear white to the wedding.'

Francesca, at least, is laughing as well. 'Believe me, if I wore *this* to a wedding, that's the very least I'd hope you'd do. Throw a blanket over me too, while you're at it.'

'You'd have a lot more than just Marcus wanting to shoot their shot with you,' I say. But that sounds not quite right, and they're both looking at me, so I try to explain: 'I mean if that's, like, the goal. I just mean that you're, you know, objectively attractive. Not that I'm trying to objectify you or anything, and everyone knows conventional beauty standards are . . . And I'm sure even if you were in a blanket you would look . . . I just *mean*—'

'Yes, Leon, tell us.' Gemma is grinning at me. 'What *do* you mean?'

I grumble a half-hearted, 'Oh, sod off.'

But Francesca catches my eye and blushes before she looks away. Her lips curve into a smile, and her head does that thing where it ticks slightly to one side. I clear my throat. Gemma watches the whole exchange – if you can even call it that – with bright eyes. I'm sure she's seeing something I'm not, like with Marcus and Francesca's text thread. I think I have some idea what it might be, but feel so ridiculous I don't even entertain it.

She *is* objectively very pretty, that's all. And who wouldn't turn heads, walking into a wedding in their underwear?

I grit my teeth, feeling like an idiot. Far more than the clumsy oaf who knocked over half of duty free.

Speaking of clumsy oafs, though, we all turn to look at the sound of someone falling over. It's some kid, a beefy guy in his very early twenties, who just went careening right over the staff crouched on the floor picking up *my* mess. He's in a rumpled T-shirt and his hair is stuck on end with a shiny silver streak in it, like he's been to a rave. A box of perfume and a necklace and a sparkly thing with a Victoria's Secret label hanging off it all goes spilling out of his hands.

'Found the target market for that thong,' Gemma is joking to Francesca behind me. 'Twenty-one-year-old boys trying to impress the girl they're seeing.'

'That poor girl,' Francesca deadpans.

'Attention shoppers,' comes a voice above, and thank God, I'm saved by the Tannoy before they start talking about lingerie again. 'Duty free will be closing soon. Please complete your purchases and proceed to the terminal. Thank you.'

It repeats in French, but Francesca gasps out loud, alarmed.

'Girl, chill,' Gemma says, checking her phone. 'We've got time. Did you want to go back to look at the shampoo?'

'No, it's not that, I just . . . We haven't got any food! What if *everywhere* closes?'

'Damn, that's a good point,' I say. 'I missed dinner in all the chaos . . . You guys must've, too. And I don't know about you, but I don't think I'll be getting a good night's sleep on the airport floor to wait it out until morning. We should at least get some snacks, a couple of drinks.'

'Oh, and we've got those vouchers they gave us! The compensation for the delay . . .' Francesca pulls a sheet of paper out of her bag. One that each of us have – twenty-five euros to spend in the terminal. 'I didn't want to use it on the coffees in case they took it away and we lost the leftover money on it. We can use those! There was that pizza place upstairs, we could get some of that, maybe, to all share? You can't go wrong with cold pizza, can you?'

Gemma claps her hands, swivelling to box the three of us in together like we're in a scrum, and she's our coach.

'Alright, gang, here's the plan. We're T-minus . . .' A quick time-check. 'Eight hours until our flight. If we all chuck in an extra twenty-five euros or so, we should be set through till breakfast. Fran, you're on snack duty. Leon, you're on sustenance and soft drinks. I will take drinks and desserts.'

'I thought you just said I was getting the drinks?'

Gemma gives me a deadpan look over the top of her glasses, and pushes them up her nose. 'Sweetie, if you think I'm staying in this godforsaken place all night and not getting at least a bit buzzed, you're sadly mistaken. And I *know* you're on board, because I can smell that beer on your breath.

Fran, hon, are you in? No pressure. You can be our sober lookout to make sure we don't miss the flight, otherwise.'

Francesca clutches her Victoria's Secret haul even closer to her chest. 'A little liquid courage can't hurt, can it?'

Gemma beams. 'That's the spirit! *Literally*, lol. Alright, go team! Meet you out by the escalators in thirty minutes.'

With that, she strides off, and Francesca and I both watch as she heads directly for the alcohol section a few feet away, snatching up a litre bottle of Malibu and a litre of vodka without even pausing.

'Looks like we're going to be in for quite a night,' I say.

Francesca laughs. 'I'll drink to that!'

Chapter Twenty-four

Francesca

Leon and I both end up in the Relay, which seems to be the European equivalent of a WHSmith – there are stacks of books and rows of magazines, plenty of snack foods and meal deals, and all sorts of paraphernalia. Most of it is emblazoned with the French flag.

I pick up a toothbrush. The entire handle is the Eiffel Tower. 'Do people actually buy this stuff?'

'What, you mean you don't have a collection of popular tourist monuments from across the world in the form of a toothbrush? The Leaning Tower of Pisa, the Statue of Liberty, Big Ben?'

I set it back on the shelf. 'You'd have to be a very dedicated collector for that.'

Leon casts a pointed look at the pins covering my coat, and I roll my eyes.

'Yes, *alright*.'

He laughs, a low rumbling sound from behind closed lips as he carries on walking into the shop. At least he seems in a better mood compared to earlier. I'm not sure he's truly on board with the idea of Marcus leaving Kayleigh for me; he must be at least a bit relieved that he won't have to have that awful confrontation with his sister now though?

We don't have long until the shops close, and most of the shelves have been thoroughly pillaged already; it's no surprise, when there must be hundreds of stranded travellers waiting around. A couple of flights have been called as far as the gate since Gemma and I set off to roam around duty free, but they've yet to board and actually depart. It doesn't bode very well for us, but the man at the front desk *did* say it would be a few hours before the storm cleared.

I'm sure it'll be fine.

I have to believe it will be. I have to channel the same confidence that drove me to buy some underwear I'd never normally even consider, and that bold lipstick. *That's* the sort of girl who gets her flight in the nick of time to stop the man she loves from marrying the wrong person.

While Leon heads over to the fridges to see what they have left, I gather some Milka biscuits, a tube of Pringles, and a handful of oat bars; we might be glad of them come six a.m. when we're all exhausted and waiting at passport control in Barcelona, wishing we had time for breakfast before the wedding.

I'm in the queue at the till behind several frazzled and tired-looking people who are stocking up on some last-minute supplies like we are. It's mostly men. Dads, it looks like. There's five of them all in a row, shoulders slumped and phones out and arms full of packets of food and precariously balanced drinks, in skinny jeans and wearing AirPods. It's such a 'glitch in the Matrix' moment I have to bite the inside of my cheek to keep from laughing. My shoulders shake with the effort, and I wish my hands weren't so full, so I could grab a photo.

'Hey, um, I forgot to ask you . . .'

Leon comes up beside me, but trails off immediately, looking at the queue in front.

He leans sideways into me, bending to mumble near my ear, 'Do you think they all know they're being real "Dad at the airport" stereotypes right now? I kind of want to make them line up and sing that Backstreet Boys song like in *Brooklyn Nine-Nine*.'

The laughter finally bursts out of me, and I'm so busy trying to keep hold of the Pringles tube, knowing they'll smash to bits otherwise, that I drop all of the oat bars. Leon's laughing, too, and bends to pick them up for me.

There's a camaraderie in the moment that I'm grateful for. I'm not very sure it'll last, not very sure who the real Leon is – the surly one who was so snappy with me or the one Gemma said was a softie – but this is a nice change.

He piles the items carefully back into my arms, and I smile up at him in thanks.

He steps back and rubs the back of his neck, reserved once more, and gestures over at the fridge section. 'I, uh, I forgot to ask if you're a vegetarian, or have any allergies, or anything. Before I go buy a bunch of chicken Caesar wraps.'

'Oh! No, no allergies or dietary restrictions here. Well, I mean, I don't like mushrooms, and I *really* don't like pistachios, but other than that . . .' I cringe, because he's staring again, looking so very serious, and I'm rambling. 'N-no. I'm alright with anything.'

'Except mushrooms and pistachios,' he says. 'Got it.'

He leaves, and I turn back to the queue, but instead of giggling at the row of dads again, all I can think about is that time we went to a new bar after work, and there were little bowls of bar snacks. It was fancy, and there were pistachios, and Marcus just could *not* stop eating them.

'Leave some for everybody else, why don't you?' I teased him. We were sat next to each other, just like always, in a semicircular booth. His arm was slung across the back of the seat and I could feel the heat of his skin radiating to the back of my neck. Even though I had my legs tucked in close to me, he was sat wide, and his knee pressed into mine. It was all I could do not to lean in closer, forcing myself to remember the boundaries *I'd* set when I'd as good as told him our night together meant nothing. He had a girlfriend, now. They were moving in together.

Marcus tossed another pistachio into his mouth and grinned at me, wide and toothy, his eyes glittering in the low lighting as he looked at me. He picked the bowl up and offered them over.

'Go on, then. Just 'cause it's you.' He winked, smiling wider, and my whole body felt like it was a split second away from either bursting into flames or melting in a puddle on the floor.

And I ate the pistachios, even though I was sure I'd told him a few weeks ago I hated them, because he was offering them to me, *to me*, but nobody else, and that felt special, and maybe it was just an acquired taste that I'd get used to anyway, and didn't I want to be sophisticated and cool like everybody else?

I *hate* pistachios.

I don't know why I did that. Why I didn't just decline the offer.

It feels so silly to think about now.

Gemma's words nag at the back of my mind, and I push them away before they start to tarnish any more memories of me and Marcus together.

That duty-free bag begins to weigh a little heavy on my arm.

Something about the time crunch starts to really trigger my adrenalin, so after making my purchases at Relay and blindly grabbing up packets of crisps and crackers at the sparse, Whole Foods-esque Monop'daily store, I dash back into duty free and go for gold. There's a sort of gourmet section in between all the confectionery and the alcohol. I grab pâté, cheese, olives, even a jar of marmalade. I'm not sure why I think we're about to sit about an airport at almost nine o'clock in the evening and make an entire charcuterie board, but I also think Gemma would absolutely do something like that, and it certainly wouldn't be the strangest thing to happen today.

In my final minutes before everywhere shuts, I manage to nab the last few pastries from one of the restaurants in the food court upstairs.

Nine o'clock arrives with no great fanfare. Shop shutters begin to draw down a little, patrons are ushered out into the terminal as much as they try to linger . . . I was almost expecting an airhorn to sound off and someone to yell, 'TIME!' and a burst of confetti at achieving my little mission – or maybe that Stephen Mulhern would pop up with a giant cheque and camera crew.

Actually, standing at the edge of the food court, holding my bags bursting with not merely snacks but rather an entire feast, I feel quite silly.

I sense someone's eyes on me, and turn to find Leon approaching. He's laden down with heavy plastic bags, three pizza boxes, and a big brown bag with more takeaway food.

'Hope you're hungry. I may have gone a bit overboard,' he tells me sheepishly.

I hoist my own bags. 'Me too. Here, let me take some of that—'

'Nah, you're alright, I've got it.'

'Are you sure? It looks heavy.'

Leon falls back half a step and his mouth cracks into a smile, a small laugh escaping him. He gives me a once-over that feels more playful, and far less critical than the one in the coffee queue earlier, and I know what he's saying: that I do not look very strong.

I'm not, I suppose, but I was just trying to be polite. I could at least manage the pizza boxes or something, give him a bit less to balance.

I roll my eyes in retort, and we both start towards the escalator down.

There's a prickle of something in my chest; not quite the flare of temper that he managed to spark before, but it feels adjacent, somehow. It makes me turn to Leon and say archly, 'I'm sure you're very capable of carrying all that. I just mean that you're, you know, objectively quite muscular. Not that I'm trying to objectify you or anything.'

His ears turn bright red, and he cringes so hard that the tendons in his neck stand out.

I grin at him to show I'm only teasing, though, and Leon relaxes before he retorts, 'And objectively, you're a bit of a smart-arse.'

'*Objectively*, it seems you're still thinking about my arse. I guess Gemma was right about the power of some lingerie.'

He makes a choking sound that sets me off giggling. I wouldn't normally be saying things like that even if I was trying to flirt with a guy, but maybe it's the fact that Leon and I aren't flirting, or maybe it is the power of lingerie, or maybe it's the sheer insanity of our entire situation and the lingering adrenalin rush, but I feel a little bit bold.

And I definitely enjoy getting the last word in, when Leon can do nothing but sigh at his own expense and shake his head in dismay.

If only I could be a bit bolder when it comes to Marcus, maybe I wouldn't be in this situation at all.

Time until 'I Do'

13 ½ hours

Chapter Twenty-five

Gemma

'Now,' I say, lowering my bags slightly, 'I may have gone a little bit overboard.'

But one glance at Leon and Francesca tells me I am not the only one. We could feast for weeks on this! Talk about a top-notch airport picnic. Well done us!

The pair of them stand looking awkward as anything, several inches apart and each turned slightly away as though they dare not so much as accidentally bump elbows. They can't still be at odds with each other, can they? I mean, she's sort of doing Leon a *massive* favour by trying to take Marcus off Kayleigh; he should be kissing the ground she walks on.

'Mademoiselle?' says a voice to my right, and I turn to see one of the Ladurée staff hurrying out of the empty shop towards me. He's terribly chic and brilliantly French, dressed entirely in black with an adorable little bow tie, slicked-back white hair, and still wearing his apron. He holds out a large bag to me.

'*Ah, magnifique, Charles*' – I'm sure to pronounce it with the 'sh' sound like the French do – '*vous êtes mon sauveur! Une etoile! Je suis plein de gratitude. Merci, mille fois!*'

I shove one of my duty-free carriers of booze at Leon,

185

who fumbles to take it while balancing his pizza boxes – and God, the smell of those pizzas? Also *magnifique*. My stomach growls, suddenly ravenous.

With my free hand, I take the Ladurée bag, and Charles and I air-kiss on each cheek. I tell him to have a nice weekend, and he wishes us all a safe flight.

When I turn back, the other two are staring at me.

Fran's eyebrows are practically at her hairline, smiling even as there's a 'what the ever-loving fuck did I just witness' look in her eyes. 'A friend of yours?'

I lift the bag. 'He is now.'

Honestly, sometimes people are just so helpful. The queue at duty free was so bad I left my stuff tucked in the front seat of that ridiculous red '*ohlala*' car on display because quite frankly, if my options were going to be to sit through the next several hours without booze or without macarons, I knew exactly where my priorities lay.

What, like I'm going to be in Paris and *not* have a Marie-Antoinette tea biscuit? Sacrilege. *Let them eat macarons!*

But I got chatting to the guy serving me in Ladurée and I asked about any end-of-day stock and if they could hold some for me if I gave him cash now, so I could go back and pay for my stuff in duty free, and . . . here we are. Besties with Charles in his bow tie and apron.

Which I explain to the others, shrugging because it was no big deal.

Fran, bless her heart, stares at me like I am the most *magnifique* creature she's ever seen, and Leon just shakes his head, smiling, not in the least bit surprised I managed this.

I add, 'Listen, Kayleigh didn't wangle a ten-thirty ceremony when "*señora*, it is not the done thing, we have a system" and get those last-minute alterations on the dress by sheer dumb luck. I'm *very* good at making things happen. Just apparently not an earlier flight. That is the one thing slightly beyond my abilities, it seems.'

'Well,' Fran says brightly, 'at least there's pizza.'

I grin at her. 'Truly, a girl after my own heart. Now come on, you two, let's set up camp and dig in!'

We end up finding a spot halfway down the long corridor towards the toilets. It's a wide space with bright lights, and there's a glass-panelled wall that we can see the passport control stands through, and – weirdly enough – little office spaces. Two people leave one, wearing full suits, and one has a little Greek flag pin on their lapel.

Leon's eyes follow them curiously. 'I can't decide if I'd be offended or not, if I had to take business meetings next to the toilets.'

'There's probably some secret corridor to bypass the usual security with us peasants for foreign dignitaries,' I say, only half joking.

We claim a corner space, tucked out of the noise of the concourse but still a good distance from the loos. I throw my jacket down to sit on, and start upturning bags to see our spoils. Leon, bless him, has even remembered to pick up a few empty cups from upstairs for us to use, and some disposable cutlery.

'A star,' I tell him. 'Thank you!'

I separate everything into piles, squealing when I realise Fran's got us basically an entire charcuterie board. A couple of ripped-open carrier bags serve as our makeshift picnic blanket, and with everything on display ready to eat, I break into the booze.

'Um,' Fran whispers, her eyes blown wide and darting around, 'are you allowed to drink that here? I thought there were rules against it . . .'

'None anybody told me about. Besides, wouldn't they have sealed the bag up if they didn't want me to drink? And it's not like it's illegal to drink in an airport; I think they just stop you flying if you're so sloshed you can hardly stand,' I add, when she worries her lower lip between her teeth, starting to look supremely uncomfortable. 'We've literally got seven hours and sixteen minutes until our flight leaves. That's *ages* to sober up.'

She looks unconvinced, but when I throw some Malibu and Coke into a cup and offer it out, she's quick enough to gulp it down.

I laugh. Poor Fran, she really is in a way.

'Talk about a hot mess,' I joke. 'Right, Leon?'

He flushes a bit, uncomfortable, and I add that to my growing tally of 'Leon being weird around Francesca'. I've yet to determine if he'd rather be far, far away from her because she's a homewrecker setting out to steal his sister's man or if the 'hot' part of my comment hit a little too close to home for him.

Or, the most likely: Leon is a dork who keeps to himself and isn't good around new people, much less women. He's been single for *ages*, and never has had much luck on the dating scene.

'What're you drinking?' I ask him, to spare his awkwardness, and showcase my little bar. 'We've also got some Smirnoff, a bit of Johnnie Walker, some of whatever this is . . .' I squint at the label. 'Blackcurrant and apple gin. And then the limon-cello. But that's more of a dessert drink, really.'

'So much for only spending fifty euros apiece.' He rolls his eyes, but points at the gin. I pour him a double measure (triple, maybe? Who's counting?) and hand over the cup. He dilutes it with some Sprite.

'They're only *little* bottles,' I say. Some of them are, anyway. Well, the gin is, and the limoncello's not *huge*. Whatever we don't drink, I'll throw in a bag to take to the wedding, add them to the tab behind the bar.

That's what I'm telling myself, anyway. And not that I'll keep them all to myself and be delightfully buzzed and therefore numb to all of Kayleigh's emotional vampire-ness through the weekend, whether the wedding goes ahead or not.

I pour myself some vodka, and only water it down a little with the Coke.

Leon notices, because he raises an eyebrow at me.

'What? I've earned this. It's been a long day.'

Fran gives a sympathetic hum, and Leon tilts his head to concede the point, but for me, this has been way more than just the upheaval of a delayed flight and the turmoil of Fran wanting to break up the wedding and Leon and his family hating the groom. Sure, *they've* had a rough day too, but they don't know the half of it. It's not a patch on the bullshit I've been dealing with.

So it all comes spilling out. I tear open a packet of crackers and some brie, shovelling olives into my mouth as I talk, telling them everything. *How's that for a rough day?* I want to bite.

I'm doing it to one-up them, obviously, to make myself

189

feel better. Like I'd do with Kayleigh, or Joss and Andi and Laura. *You think you've got it bad? Just wait, just see.*

Except it feels like they're actually *actively* listening, not just waiting their turn so they can say, *Yeah, that sucks, but I . . .* And it doesn't feel so much like a competition. It's more like . . . like I'm getting something off my chest, trying to ease the burden a bit by sharing it.

How novel.

Is this how other people feel when they talk to their friends? That must be nice.

I tell them about how our team were overworked and our direct manager stretched too thin so we constantly had to redo work and re-prioritise, and things fell through the cracks until they became urgent and we'd have to break our necks to get them done in time. So I'd looked into the budgets, crafted a role that would be an intermediary step – manage our team, but feed into our boss, and we'd ultimately be more productive and efficient at our jobs and even able to take on more, because there wouldn't be this huge gap in communication.

I tell them how tricky that was to present – impossible to get time with the right people who could sign it off, a fine line to walk between shaming our current manager for being shit at her job and showing support for how hard she was working. And I showed them all the ways *I* was perfect for that role.

But of course, it was Kayleigh who ingratiated herself with our manager, Kayleigh who went out of her way to 'be seen', even if it meant shirking work she knew the rest of us – me, always me – would pick up because it needed to be done. It was Kayleigh who went behind my back to interview for the role when they hadn't even advertised it, Kayleigh who made it sound like I was overworked and struggling and couldn't handle the pressure of a promotion.

It was Kayleigh who got the fucking job.

Just like she gets everything else.

By the time I'm done, I'm breathing hard and I've demolished most of the olives. Whoops.

I down my drink, and pour myself another.

Fran reaches over to squeeze my knee. 'That's *horrible*. Oh, Gemma, I'm so sorry. I can't imagine doing all that work, just to have it thrown back in your face like that.'

And Leon says, 'Are you going to quit?'

I choke on my vodka-Coke, which is once again more vodka than it is Coke. I can't tell if it's already hitting me and that's why my head feels so fuzzy, or if that's down to this blinding, all-consuming anger that's hit me once again.

'*Quit?*' I echo. 'Are you kidding me? What, and walk away, just let her *win*? After everything I've done there, all the grafting, the overtime . . . Just throw it all away and *quit?*'

He looks at me steadily, with a quietness and calmness that Kayleigh has never possessed. If Kayleigh is a raging waterfall with a bubbling spring at the bottom, her brother is a vast, deep lake that you could throw a stone into and it would hardly cause a ripple.

I wish I'd been his friend instead.

The thought flits away as quickly as it arrived, but something leaden settles in my stomach.

'I didn't realise it was a competition,' he says. 'Talking about letting Kay "win" like that. Isn't it just a job?'

'Well, sure, but . . .'

But I've put blood, sweat and tears into that job. I actually *like* what I do. I like the fast pace and the high intensity, even if having to redo work or down tools to focus on something else that we could've had sorted weeks ago had been pissing me off. And if I leave – if Kayleigh gets that promotion, and I leave, it's . . .

'It'll be like throwing all my toys out of the pram, just because someone said I wasn't good enough. And—' I snort. 'It wouldn't be the first time I'd heard that. *I'm* not the one who walks away.'

Wow.

I guess the booze is getting to me after all.

Fran's hand is still on my knee, and she gives it another squeeze as she says, 'Is this about your ex?'

And at the same time, Leon reaches to top his drink up with some more Sprite and says, 'Is this about your dad?'

And I burst into tears.

Chapter Twenty-six

Leon

While I could count easily the number of times I've seen Gemma upset over something, I have never seen her cry. Kay cries all the time over the smallest things, but Gemma . . .

There are fat, round tears clinging to her eyelashes and splashing onto her cheeks. Francesca gives a little gasp and starts rummaging through her bag to offer some Kleenex, and Gemma just stares ahead, breathless and tearful, looking sort of catatonic.

I almost ask Francesca if she thinks she's in shock. Actually, *I* might be in shock.

Then Gemma takes the tissue offered to her, sniffling, and she props her glasses up on top of her head to wipe her eyes. She drags in a noisy, shaking breath. 'Sorry, you two, sorry, I just . . . Wow, don't drink on an empty stomach, right?'

She laughs. It's hollow.

Francesca's face creases, and she gives me a pained, helpless sort of look. I wish I had the answers.

I don't know what happened with Gemma's ex. I'm starting to understand a bit about her friendship with Kayleigh – if you can call it that; it sounds more like enmity whenever she opens her mouth to mention her.

I do know about Gemma's dad, though. That he walked out on them when she was twelve, and he and her mum weren't married so he just stopped paying the rent and they got kicked out and ended up moving. I know he has a second family, that Gemma has half-siblings and a stepmother she met once and never again. I know that he was meant to visit and see her in school holidays, but he wouldn't show up, and she'd have to call Kayleigh and come spend the day with us lot while Nana looked after us.

I know he's a deadbeat, and Gemma doesn't talk about him, and her relationship with her mum broke down some-time when she was in sixth form. I used to come home from uni and she and Kay would be hanging out, and Mum said to me once, 'I worry about that girl, you know.'

At the time, I thought she meant that Gemma was trouble. She got detention sometimes, and she'd be the one who'd drunk a bit too much at a party that Kayleigh would have to look after (or so the stories would go), and she didn't apply herself a whole lot in school. She skated by until sixth form, when reality hit and she realised she'd have to really focus if she wanted to get into uni like Kay and their other friends.

Thinking about it now, I wonder if it was less about keeping up, and more about getting out, and if Mum worried about her for other kinds of reasons.

I never asked Gemma about it. I never thought to. She was Kay's best friend and I always assumed if there was a *real* problem, Kay would've told me what was going on.

Seeing her so upset now, though, watching her gulp down breaths and fight to stop the tears pouring down her cheeks even as they keep coming, I wish I had. I wish I'd been there, like I try to be for Kay and Myleene.

Francesca offers Gemma an open bottle of water, and she takes a swig, glancing to the brunette with a wobbly smile of thanks. I'm not sure if I should do something. Francesca's got the practicalities handled, and it'd be weird to hug her. I'm not much of a hugger, normally.

Finally, Gemma gathers herself enough to say, 'Anyway, if I leave, it's just going to prove I'm not good enough.'

Francesca and I exchange glances.

Right. Guess we're not talking about the dad *or* the ex, then.

'According to who?' I ask her. 'Kayleigh?'

She rolls her eyes, which seems like a 'yes'.

'But you'd rather work *for* her?'

Gemma flinches, cringing, and I get the impression that thought has only just occurred to her. She buries her face in her hands, groaning, 'Oh, God, I am, aren't I? As if I'm ever going to get promoted when *she'll* be the one in charge of my career. And everyone's going to know that I pitched the promotion and she got it instead and they're all going to laugh at me behind my back, and . . . How am I supposed to show my face there? How can I *not?* That's a thousand times more embarrassing. And she's going to lord it over me forever. Between that and me barely making the wedding in time . . . Ugh. God, I actually hate her.' She laughs, though, like it's a joke.

Does she mean that in the same way as she has Kayleigh's number saved as 'bitch' (with a sparkle emoji), like it's a sort of long-suffering affection?

Looking at her tear-stained face, I don't think so.

I'm about to ask why she bothers being Kay's friend if that's the case, but Francesca catches my eye and gives a small shake of her head. They must've talked about this earlier already.

Francesca rubs Gemma's back, offering her the water again.

She says, 'Maybe you're thinking about this the wrong way. Maybe it isn't that you'd prove you *aren't* good enough for them – but proving you're *too* good for them. If they've overlooked you like you said, if you've been cheated out of a job that ought to have been yours, wouldn't it be less like throwing your toys out of the pram and more like giving them the middle finger and a big 'F you!' when you find something better, at a place that *does* value you?'

Gemma snorts, the sound thick with snot. She cuts Francesca a flat look, arching an eyebrow. 'What, like you and Marcus? Give me a break, hon.'

Francesca recoils a bit. 'That's not—'

'It *is*. If anybody should understand why I don't want to leave, it's you. You're clinging to this idea of being with Marcus because it's too mortifying to admit defeat, right? And there's still a chance to win, as long as you've got skin in the game. You can still make a comeback.'

'I . . .' But Francesca trails off, not having much of a retort to that. She blinks a couple of times, turning her face away, and I wonder if Gemma's words cut a little too deep. I'm at a loss, though, not sure how to navigate any of this. I don't know how to comfort Gemma if she's taking the stance that she doesn't *want* help, like she's accepted her fate, and just like I couldn't bring myself to write that speech for the wedding reception, I can't bring myself to tell Francesca that it's okay, I'm sure Marcus will choose her.

It'd be great for us if he did, but . . .

Is she even really his type? She's so . . . *soft*. Gentle, and warm. Wouldn't he walk all over her? Take over with his arrogance and ego, while she disappeared into the background? Hardly much of a *partner*.

I'll give Kay that – she and Marcus always seem on an even keel. Equals. There's a sense of mutual respect, even if they snipe at each other sometimes.

(Is that the sort of thing you can put in a wedding speech? It's not very romantic, but it is honest, at least.)

But Francesca, who *literally* let herself get trodden on by that guy in the coffee queue earlier . . .

No. It's not my place.

She's already chosen Marcus anyway, right?

I open up one of the pizza boxes, and offer it to the girls.

They both dive in, and the tension breaks. I feel it snap, loosening the air around us, the tightness bleeding out of my shoulders. I watch Gemma sit a bit straighter where she's leaning against the wall, crossing her legs more comfortably beneath her, and Francesca gives a little wriggle, relaxing too.

We pour some more drinks, and barely come up for air as we scarf down the food, all three of us ravenous. The long day, the amped-up emotions ahead of the wedding, the late hour and the stress culminate in us absolutely tearing through our picnic like a pack of vultures.

We eat ourselves into food comas, until I can barely see straight and Gemma is groaning and unbuttoning her trousers to rub her stomach, and Francesca is struggling to find a comfortable position. She ends up going for a wander to walk off the food.

When she's gone, Gemma swirls her drink around the

little paper cup. This one is more Coke than vodka, I noticed. She seems to be making a concerted effort not to look at me, which gets my attention as much as if she was staring daggers through my skull.

So I ask her, 'What's up?'

'Just . . . That stuff about my dad . . .'

'Oh. I won't say anything to Francesca; it's okay. I'm sorry I brought it up.'

'No, it's . . . I mean, you were right. If I quit – if I walk away, I'm no better than him.'

'It's a job, Gem. Not a child.'

She grimaces; I could've worded that more tactfully. But before I can apologise, she's already saying, 'I don't just mean the job.'

It takes me a beat to realise. 'Kayleigh.'

'Yeah. I can't just turn my back the second things get hard. And she . . . You guys did so much for me when we were kids. *She* did so much for me. I wouldn't have made it to where I am without her.'

I nod, even though I know I'm only just beginning to understand. The way she talks about Kay – the things she says Kay's done, not just in general but *to Gemma* . . . At the very least, it's unhealthy. If she were saying those things about a partner, I'd be telling her those were classic signs of an abusive relationship, or at least a toxic one. She can't be happy. She certainly doesn't *look* happy.

A couple of people in white T-shirts scrawled with silly nicknames and things like 'Mate of Honour' trip past us, leaning on each other and laughing on their way to the toilets. I wonder if the wedding they're building up to is as hellish as this one.

Gemma scoffs a little, rolling her eyes like she's thinking the same thing.

My heart is sitting heavy in my chest, and I feel restless and unwell in a way that has nothing to do with overeating.

For all I'd convinced myself on the flight out that I was on a mission to put a stop to the wedding and get Kayleigh back for the family's sake, I'm not so sure that's a good idea, if this is who she's become. Who she's always been, maybe. It's feeling more nauseating by the minute, actually.

It'd break Mum's heart to feel like Kay ditched us for her new life with Marcus, but wouldn't it be worse to know Kay cut us out because she simply doesn't *want* us in her life? Not that we've been replaced, just – abandoned.

I glance again at Gemma.

'I'm not saying you don't owe her for being your friend and being there for you. But you don't have to sacrifice your whole life just to try and make up for that. And if you walked away from . . . from the job, from whatever, it doesn't mean you're no better than your dad.'

The smile she gives me is wan.

'Easier said than done.'

Chapter Twenty-seven

Francesca

'I know it's mad, mate, but you didn't *see* her. Nah, nah, I know what Jammy says, but she was *all* over me. Trust me, this is going to work. She's not like them other girls . . . What have I got to lose? She was *well* into me . . .'

The speaker bumps into me, half turning to apologise before he carries on, wandering agitatedly around the terminal as he gestures with one hand and clutches his phone to his ear with the other. It's the young man with glitter in his hair, from earlier, who dropped all that stuff in duty free. He sounds so wistful, talking about the girl he must be on his way to see.

I almost want to wish him luck.

Aren't I here doing the same thing, after all?

And isn't it so exciting, so romantic, so intoxicating?

A few hours ago, I could hardly contain myself. But now, all I can think about is how disparaging Leon and Gemma have been about Marcus; how all those fond memories I have of the two of us now seem trivial – and tainted.

He's breadcrumbing you.

Stringing me along, using me, won't pick me, would never pick me. What they said about him mocking me – calling me sad, pathetic . . . I didn't want to believe it, brushed it off, but now it gnaws at me.

I suddenly feel like a prize idiot for spending all that money on a lipstick and underwear. As if that's going to change anything . . .

But he did pick me, once, didn't he? We spent that night together. The way he kissed me . . . I felt *cherished*. And then I threw it all away because I panicked . . .

But there's Gemma's voice, again, mentioning that coffee shop he told her he was checking out, how Kayleigh went and met him there. I huddle smaller inside his jacket, the one he left behind that morning.

I don't want to ask her about it, want to hope that I'm wrong, but the mental image plays out anyway, memory warping into . . . something else.

I remember the sun pouring in from behind the curtains, how late we'd slept in, and the weight of the bed shifting as Marcus dragged himself out from under the covers. He smiled when he saw me stir, and leant down to press a kiss to my mouth. It was feather-light, and left my lips tingling. I'd have drawn him in for a deeper kiss, but was suddenly terrified of what horrific morning-breath I must have; we'd had a couple of drinks last night at the party, and I'd never brushed my teeth before we fell into bed. I hadn't even taken off my makeup! The state I must be in . . .

I was only too happy to burrow deeper under the covers, pulling the duvet up to try to hide as much of my face as I could – and hopefully smother my morning-breath.

Marcus said, 'I'm going to step out for a coffee. Maybe grab some breakfast.'

I nodded from inside my little duvet-cocoon, heart racing. 'Okay. Sounds good.'

It was like a movie, like the sort of thing that happened to other people but never to you, never in real life. A handsome boy, the one you'd flirted with back and forth for so long at work, staying the night and waking you up with a kiss and going out to get breakfast. I had some bagels and cereal in the kitchen, and I'd gotten a Nespresso machine for my birthday off my parents, but I didn't tell him any of that.

It was so much more romantic this way. So easy to picture him coming back, letting himself in as if he felt right at home here with me. How we would sit in the rumpled bedsheets (and I would have had a chance to freshen up and make myself look presentable) and carry on talking like we'd talked all night, sipping our drinks and eating flaky pastries, and then he would lean in for another kiss – to kiss some chocolate off the edge of my mouth, maybe – and we would fall back into bed again but this time it would go further, and we'd spend the entire weekend wrapped up in each other . . .

Except I kept sitting there, in the bed, half-wondering if I should make it so we didn't get greasy crumbs of pastry inside the sheets, or if that was going to suggest I didn't want us to go back to bed and send the wrong message.

I kept sitting there, my hair pulled up into a messy bun, saved with a little dry shampoo, my mouth minty-fresh.

And *I kept sitting there*.

It was two hours before I had to accept that Marcus wasn't coming back.

He'd never said he was getting *us* a coffee, my friends reasoned when I told them about it. He'd never said he was going to grab breakfast to *bring it back here*, to share.

Maybe I should have asked him to? Maybe it wasn't clear enough that I wanted him to come back, so he thought I'd rebuffed him and he was supposed to stay away.

He left his jacket, though. It was tossed over the back of my sofa. Was that a sign he would come back, or had he simply forgotten?

I texted him to ask what he was up to the rest of his day; where he'd ended up getting a coffee. I was angling to suggest we could do something together, that maybe I could join him for whatever plans he had that afternoon.

But he never responded.

I texted him later that evening – something blithe and casual, not mentioning our night together or the jacket, but again, silence.

It ate at me. *God*, how it ate at me.

But Monday, he apologised that his phone had died, and later, I learned that he'd met Kayleigh, and I hated that he didn't see my messages sooner; that I'd accidentally turned him away by something I'd not said, a cue I'd missed in the course of our brief morning conversation. So of course he was hurt and was flattered by this new interest.

He was already putting 'us' in the past because *I'd* messed up . . .

Now, though, my memory twists from him leaving my flat with a dead phone so he never saw my messages, to him wandering down the street on the lookout for a coffee shop and absently swiping on his phone, checking messages and notifications and . . .

And dating apps.

And messaging Gemma.

And then Kayleigh showing up.

And Marcus, ignoring my messages.

I'm walking in circles around the terminal and my step falters, my eyes blurry with tears. I don't dare ask Gemma for more details; I can't bear to hear that it's true – but it's so hard to shake the feeling that it is. That it was never *me* who rejected *him*.

It hurts. It's a physical pain, knifing through my heart and shredding it, and it takes all my willpower to swallow down a sob and blink back a fresh wave of tears.

What if it's really all been in my head this entire time? I *know* how it felt when he kissed me, I *know* how he smiles at me and hugs me, but . . . What if they're right? What if this is all a game to him?

Is that really the man I know? The man I *love*?

Before I know what I'm doing, my phone is in my hands, and I'm texting him.

We don't FaceTime, don't phone, because of Kayleigh. The guilt that comes with that thought threatens to rip my heart right out of my chest.

> Wish I was there with you. I miss you.

It's mere moments before the read receipt appears, and my heart somersaults. Both my hands grip the phone tight, and I wait with bated breath as three little dots appear to show he's typing a reply . . .

> Miss u too
> Not the same without you here babe xxx

And I know I shouldn't say it, but my fingers are already

204

moving across the screen, and the message is sent before I can second-guess it.

> Do you ever think about that night after Billy and Ophie's housewarming party?

Ofc xxx
Was a great party
And a great after-party ;)

My stomach is full of butterflies, I'm seeing stars, my heart is skipping a beat. I am every cliché all at once – because of a *winky face*. There's no room for me to feel foolish about that, though, because everything is taken over by the simple fact that he still thinks about it.

He thinks about our night together, that kiss, about *us*, who we could have been if . . .

If he hadn't left to chase other girls.

If *I* had just invited him to stay for breakfast, if *I* hadn't brushed it under the rug.

The phone buzzes and another text pings through, turning my eyes wide.

Shame there can't be a round two tonight lol
You're missing one hell of a party xxx

> Round two?

Since it's my last official night as a single man and all
Shouldn't I be making the most of it? ;)
You could've helped me with that
Made it one to remember

The words swim on the screen, the letters suddenly turning to hieroglyphics I can't untangle. Muscle memory guides my fingers as I force myself to type out a reply – to enjoy the rest of his night, that I'll see him tomorrow – but my stomach turns, and I have to press a hand to my mouth.

Not to contain an excited squeal because he's being so *outright* in flirting with me this time, not to suppress a giddy cry because I'm on his mind and see, he *would* choose me.

Because right now, in the light of everything Gemma and Leon have said, it just feels . . .

Cheap. Dirty.

Like I am not 'the One', not meant to be. I am just the other woman. One he would, apparently, willingly cheat on his fiancée with. It's *not* his last night as a single man, because he's not single, he's so very far from it, but if I was there . . .

If I was there . . .

Would I stop it? I don't think so, somehow. If we'd been enjoying ourselves, and I'd peeled away from the rest of the wedding guests to hang out with Marcus and his friends like the original plan was, and if he'd said something like that . . .

Would I have hesitated to invite him up to my room? To drag his mouth down to mine and let his hands wander?

Would I have felt cheap then, or like this was inevitable and he was finally choosing me?

If this is what him choosing me feels like . . .

Is this what he would say to another girl, if it was me he was marrying?

I squash that down and bury my phone deep into the large pocket of my jacket. *His* jacket. It feels chafing, suffocating, now, even if I've repurposed it, decorated it with my pins and worn it to death so it smells more like me than it ever did like him.

He thinks about us. That night, that kiss. He's thinking about me now. He wishes I was there.

As I make my way back to the others, I try to cling to those thoughts, and try not to think about the fact that they taste like ash in my mouth.

Time until 'I Do'

11 ½ hours

Chapter Twenty-eight

Gemma

With six hours and twenty-two minutes until our flight departs, thanks to yet *another* delay, the emotional confessions and confrontations are a thing of the not-so-distant past. Fran got back from her post-dinner wander with red-rimmed eyes and flinched when her phone buzzed, but I wasn't about to ask about that, and Leon *definitely* didn't. And I certainly didn't fancy diving into a deep therapy session about my childhood trauma, which really left us with only one solution: drowning our sorrows in drinking games.

Well. Drowning our sorrows and playing a game of 'what outrageous way can we stop this wedding going ahead that's even crazier than telling your sister you hate your new brother-in-law or trying to get the groom to jilt his bride at the altar for you'. Which is close enough, really.

It starts with me saying, 'Maybe I should object during the ceremony. Claim *I'm* in love with Marcus, too.'

And Leon snorting and adding, 'Say you're pregnant with his baby.'

'Or we could lock Kayleigh in a cupboard!'

Fran snorts. 'We could lock *Marcus* in a cupboard.'

'What, with you? Have the entire wedding party go

211

searching for you, and the pair of you tumble out, Marcus with his pants around his ankles, I bet? Ha! Love it!'

Fran grimaces, but probably because the idea of being caught having sex somewhere public is so mortifying, or whatever. She says, 'I could hide the dress.'

'*Sabotage* the dress,' Leon says. 'No, I've got it. Red wine on *Marcus's suit!* That preening bastard would stop the whole ceremony if he thought he looked less than perfect.'

I laugh. 'See, I *told* you he and Kayleigh are a good match.'

Then the stag/hen do attendees come back from their trip to the loos, having apparently got distracted gossiping, and they fall on us and our pile of booze with glazed eyes asking where we're off to, and obviously I say we're headed to Barcelona for a wedding, and they mention they're headed out there for a joint stag do for the two grooms, and . . .

Next thing I know, the three of *us* are being roped into participating in a makeshift obstacle course around the concourse. Half of the stags' group are stone-cold sober, but everyone's laughing loudly and giving it their all as we hopscotch around piles of bags and coats, leapfrog our way from one end to the other and have three-legged races with one person blindfolded.

We've made a solid dent in the booze, all loose-limbed and giggly. Even *Leon* is giggly, which is adorable to see. It's not as if he's always broody and sullen like he was around Fran earlier – if anything, he's normally unfailingly polite, even if he is a man of few words. But it's cute, seeing him really lighten up and let go a bit.

He and Fran are atrocious at the three-legged race.

He picks *both* of us up and wins the piggyback race, though, which somehow leads to a contest of 'how many people can

Leon deadlift?' and has one of the grooms leaping onto his back without hesitation.

He throws his arms in the air like Leon is the prow of the *Titanic*. 'I'm king of *Paree*!'

The other groom is blushing as he whoops, 'You're *my* short king!' Meanwhile, a few of the group start up a rousing chorus of 'Do You Hear the People Sing?' from *Les Mis*. Leon becomes an impromptu barricade when the best man climbs up onto his other shoulder, and then I nudge Fran and tell her to hop on. She blushes (which really, is telling me *all* I need to know) and stays put, so I cling to Leon's front like a koala.

Our human pyramid/barricade collapses when one of the bridesmaids takes a running leap and spills Leon off balance, and we're all a tangle of limbs on the floor, howling with laughter, with a slightly bruised Leon left standing in the middle.

There's a weird lawlessness about the airport at this time of night, with all these people stuck waiting for their flights in the middle of a storm. Bags abandoned willy-nilly, people sat right in the way of usual foot traffic, this bonkers little obstacle course, the lot. It's so surreal, it feels like the first time I had to queue up for pasta in a supermarket when the pandemic began. It won't feel real afterwards.

That's precisely the beauty of it, though: *none* of this is properly 'real', and I feel like I can really let go for once.

Some of our obstacle course is overtaken by children, but nobody seems to mind too much. A game of prosecco pong is pulled out of a rucksack by a *very* prepared bridesmaid. I see the redhead girl who eavesdropped in Victoria's Secret eyeing it with either intrigued disdain or coolly reserved interest. The ginger guy sat next to her is slumped, eyes closed, over the bag in his lap.

I nudge Fran and point at the girl. 'Shall we ask her if she wants to join in? Doesn't look like her travel buddy is a whole lot of fun.'

Leon looks over. 'Nah, leave them be. They're probably just pissed off their honeymoon got ruined.'

Francesca makes a sound that's halfway between a choke and a laugh. '*Honeymoon?* They're not a couple, you muppet! Look at them, they're *obviously* siblings. Twins, I reckon.'

'Come off it,' Leon scoffs, but it's with none of his earlier chagrin. He even bumps her shoulder, downright *playful*. That booze really has loosened him up. 'I overheard them talking, they were on about telling the staff it was their honeymoon to get on an earlier flight.'

I snort. 'Well, duh, who wouldn't try to use that line if it got them out of here quicker?' They're not exactly *sat* like a loved-up couple, and they *do* look eerily similar, down to the ski-slope noses and same shade of hair . . . But they are both wearing wedding rings, which gives me pause.

A bolt of inspiration strikes, and I give Leon a little shove. 'Go flirt with her.'

'*What?*'

'Well, she'll tell you if she's married, won't she? She'll be all, "Ew, creep, go away, my husband is *literally right here*."'

Leon blanches, but his eyes flit to Francesca before he says to me, 'Weirdly, becoming the airport creep doesn't sound too appealing. Besides, I'm . . . I'm not . . . she isn't . . . I'll . . .'

'Oh, fine, *I'll* do it.'

I stride over, dropping onto the sliver of empty bench

next to the girl. She looks more like Leon and Fran's age – closer to thirty – and eyes me with her nose wrinkled a bit as I sit down.

'Hi. I'm Gemma.'

There's a long pause before she just says, 'Hi?'

'Do you want to come and have a drink with us? Or just hang out a bit. This whole night is *such* a drag, but these games have been a good laugh.'

Her lip curls. 'Yes, so I heard. I think all of Paris heard, in fact.'

'Gotta show them what they're missing out on, right?' I laugh, but it doesn't land. 'Really, though, it's good fun. And you look a little lonely, over here all on your own . . .' I lean in a bit, bump her arm with my chest lightly, give her my best coy smile.

There's a good chance the whole effect comes off as more 'drunkard who's lost her balance'.

'Um, yeah, no thanks.'

'Oh. Okay.' I make a point of glancing around her, at the guy. 'Well, if you change your mind . . . your boyfriend's welcome, too.'

'He's not my boyfriend.'

'Oh?'

What does that mean? That he's *more* than a boyfriend, or the total opposite? She is giving me *nothing*. Ugh.

I give it one last shot. 'Well, he doesn't know what he's missing, letting a pretty girl like you spend a night in Paris basically on your own. You should be snogging under the Eiffel Tower! Or, you know, just indulging in a good old French kiss under the . . . lights of Orly Airport Terminal three.'

She rolls her eyes and says nothing.

I haul myself off the bench, defeated, and slump back to Fran and Leon. Leon is raising his eyebrows at me, as if my attempts at flirting are oh-so-amusing. I grimace and shove him in the chest.

'Shut up. I'm a bit rusty after Brittney broke up with me, okay? Cut me some slack.'

'Well? What did she say?' Fran demands.

'*Zilch*. Zip, nada. I am officially none the wiser. The mystery remains unsolved. Detective Coleen Rooney, I am not.'

Fran pouts and says, 'They're *so* siblings,' at the same time as Leon mutters, 'Married, I'm calling it now.' The pair of them glower at each other, but it's so non-serious and they're leaning in and I feel like I'm intruding and shit, is Leon somehow a *better* flirt than me? This is outrageous. What has become of me?

I clear my throat; they both stand up straighter.

The prosecco pong is already under way, the obstacle course fully forfeited to some children, and the three of us stay clustered just off to one side. The grooms are distracted by holding hands and looking longingly into each other's eyes, talking softly while their friends carry on their rowdy games. And I've had enough to drink that I blurt, 'So, Leon, what's up with your love life these days?'

He'd just taken a sip of his gin, and sputters. 'Um . . .'

'Oh, come on, I swear Kayleigh never says *anything* about it. Although that's not saying much, is it? She hardly gets invested in life updates from the family enough to *share* them. Your last proper relationship I heard anything about was that girl, Emma, when you were at uni.'

Fran, the little devil, is hanging off my every word, trying not to look too keen as she waits for Leon's response.

'Well, there's . . . there's not much to share,' he mumbles, and takes another drink. His ears are turning bright pink. He starts walking back towards our pile of stuff in the hallway to the loos, as if he can physically run away from the awkwardness of my question.

I am in hot pursuit, as is Fran.

'As if *Emma* was your last relationship! That was more than *ten years ago*.'

He comes to a halt by our bags and the remains of our picnic. A huff bursts out of him, and he rolls his shoulders and head back like he's shrugging off some unseen burden. 'It's just hard, okay? I feel like there are all these expectations and I don't meet them. Or like, if I tell a girl I'm "family-orientated" she thinks it's cute until I have to cancel a date because Dad's had a bad turn, and then suddenly I'm the problem for not prioritising my own life and my relationship instead. And that's if I even get past the first date . . .'

Poor guy sounds so dejected, I feel a moral obligation to fix it. He needs a hype woman in his corner! Maybe he needs a wing-woman? I could totally go out to bars with him or look through his Bumble chat history to tell him where he's going wrong. I'd say I could set him up with one of my friends, but I don't think he'd like any of them very much.

I don't think *I* like any of them very much.

We're a shallow, vain little group. A guy like Leon needs someone – hardy. Warm. In touch with her emotions.

'Do you tell them about his MS?' Francesca asks, and Leon pulls a face, wobbles his head in neither a shake nor a nod.

Ding, ding, ding, we have a winner. . .

217

'Depends,' he says. 'Don't think it'd make much difference anyway.'

I tell him, 'You're being way too hard on yourself! I mean, no shit would a girl not want to date you if you're coming in with this defeatist attitude and feeling all sorry for yourself! You need to change your outlook, Leon! *Manifest.*'

'With sparkle emojis,' Fran says, catching my eye with a cheeky grin.

'Yes! Exactly! Leon, honey, you're a catch. I mean, yes, you've got no coordination and are so clumsy it's like we can't take you anywhere, but you've got that whole beefy weightlifter thing going with the shoulders and the thighs. Those are some *good* thighs. And sure, you're not always forthcoming when it comes to making conversation, and you take a while to open up to people and that can seem a bit like maybe you aren't interested or—'

Leon peers down at Fran. 'Is this supposed to be making me feel better, d'you think?'

She giggles. *Look at you go, girl, giggling away. Look at you go, Leon!*

'No, it is!' I insist, and scowl. 'I'm not saying it right. I just mean, you're a decent guy, and you're not giving them a chance to see it. Like, you take care of your family! You own your own house! I never remember what your job is because it's something really boring, but, like, obviously that translates as being stable and sensible—'

'I'm a conveyancer.'

'Sure, whatever that is. And you're really sweet! You're always doing stuff for other people. You do all that volunteering at a dog shelter, right? I'd bet that your problem is that you're going in *expecting* these girls to feel let down by you, so you don't even try.'

He shrugs, grumbles something, and his shoulders bunch up, suggesting I've struck gold. I beam, proud of myself for helping him out, not sure how much of this will stick in the cold light of day when we're all sober, but right now I feel like an absolute genius. Fran is laughing, and pats his shoulder sloppily in a 'there, there' motion.

'It's okay,' she slurs at him. 'No judgement here; my dating life isn't much to write home about either. My longest relationship is with a guy who's marrying someone else.'

A laugh bursts out of Leon, deep and bright, and I snort so hard that I choke on my drink and it comes spurting out of my nose. It dribbles all over my face and down my front, and I spill some more from my cup down my legs when I lurch to cover my face. I kick over an open bottle of Coke, spilling it on some of the food and onto the floor.

I'm soggy and dirty and it's so worth it, because I can't remember the last time I laughed like that.

One time, when Kayleigh was hosting a dinner party – her favourite thing to do in that fucking flat, the one *I* found, the one *she* bought – I was helping her prep and I accidentally put goat's cheese into the stuffed pepper appetisers instead of feta, and you'd have thought I'd set the curtains on fire, the way she reacted. It wasn't *the vibe*, she insisted, and she made sure to tell everybody, 'We had a bit of a whoops with the peppers – so sorry, everyone! Might have to get you one of those posters for the kitchen so you can identify different types of cheese next time, Gemma, lol!'

Nobody cared about the fucking goat's cheese, but they never let me live it down, either.

Fran is fussing about handing me napkins and asking, 'Are you okay?'

'Um. Y-yeah.' My throat hurts a bit and there's a nasty stinging feeling right up the top of my nose, but that won't last. Leon has bent down to mop up the spillage and salvage the food. 'I'm . . . I'm just going to go get cleaned up.'

I skip delicately over our things – which, with the amount of alcohol I've had, is far more likely to look like the ungainly lumber of a T-Rex as I lurch all the way across into the opposite wall, my hands smacking into it and my body following. I'm laughing even as Leon winces audibly.

'I'm good, I'm good!' I turn around for my suitcase, and which one was it? There, on the end. Nope. Other end. The one with the garment bag looped over the handle.

I go to remove the dress and dump it onto one of their bags while I go and change, but in the space of time it takes me to pick it up, I'm already turning back to the others with a gleam in my eyes.

'D'you guys want to see something truly awful?'

220

Chapter Twenty-nine

Leon

Gemma stumbles the rest of the way down the corridor, giggling to herself. Francesca and I finish mopping up all the spilled drinks, dumping the wet napkins into our designated carrier bag of rubbish along with the drenched Doritos and wet, crumbling crackers, and then she tidies up the rest of our picnic. We didn't pack anything up properly earlier, abandoning it for some airport Olympics with strangers.

I must be staring, and she must notice, because she says, 'I'm always the mum friend. I can't help it. Well, *almost* always. At work, it's . . .' Her face scrunches up. 'It's a bit of a boys' club environment with a lot of them. I fell into the trap of trying to fit in so I didn't get left behind.'

'You mean with Marcus's lot?'

Her hands pause as she slots a tray of Milka biscuits halfway back into their box. 'Yes.'

'And here I thought it was just Gemma with the shitty job.'

Francesca finishes tidying up the food, but her shoulders are tense. I fight through the alcohol haze to focus my gaze on her. The way she tucks a stray piece of hair behind her ear, the way her lower lip catches between her teeth. Tiny, automatic gestures that I suddenly find myself wanting to savour.

'It's not the job, so much as . . . *them*,' she says. 'That group. I behave a bit different around them on nights out, but – Marcus started including me, and I didn't want him to stop if I was too much of a bore. And sometimes they can actually be really great fun! And they'll look out for me a bit, help me with stuff at work if I need it without expecting a favour back, always make sure I get home safe at the end of the night . . . They're not all bad, but . . .'

'Not all great, either.'

'Not really,' she admits. She fidgets with one of the pins on her jacket. The black denim is so faded it's greyish. Maybe it's vintage? Maybe she thrifts stuff.

'Cool jacket,' I say, but Francesca grimaces. 'Where'd you get all the badges?'

'Oh! Um, just . . . Well, here and there, you know.' Her voice carries, more chipper than when she was talking about going out with Marcus's gang at work, and her face brightens. 'Me and some of my friends from uni sort of made it a tradition to do Secret Santa and always get one of these enamel pins. I used to just hoard them all in a box, or put a couple on a tote bag or something, but it seemed so sad to leave them gathering dust somewhere. Some of them I got for birthdays or I just found from a creator on Instagram or something and couldn't resist.'

She starts telling me about them all – one referencing a book series, another referencing an avocado Vine from years ago that she and her sister always laugh about, one that she and a friend both bought on a trip to Dublin . . .

She's animated as she talks, smiling wide and chattering away like she doesn't really care what I think about them or if it sounds a bit nerdy or weird or anything.

Her head's doing that thing where it ticks to the side. Like she's going to tuck her cheek into her shoulder if she smiles too big.

It's definitely cute, I decide. Very cute.

She only stops because 'Lady Marmalade' starts blaring out of a phone somewhere down the corridor, and we both look over to see Gemma's head poking around the corner.

'Are you guys ready?' she yells.

'Ready!' Francesca bellows back. The pair of them are noisy enough to draw in a couple of our new friends from the joint stag do who've gotten bored of prosecco pong, and now pile in around us to see what's going on.

As Christina Aguilera starts singing the hook, Gemma hurls herself out into the centre of the hallway in a blur of turquoise. She grabs the skirt in each hand, swishing it as she struts and rolling her shoulders not quite in time to the music. I don't know if I'm drunk enough to see double, or if there really are that many ruffles on the dress.

Gemma's face is deadly serious, lips in a pout, and she swings one leg deliberately in front of the other in an exaggerated catwalk that makes Francesca shriek. She throws her arms in the air, crying, 'Yes, Gem! Go! Slay, queen!'

'Whooo,' I say, 'go Gemma.'

The bridesmaids and groomsmen are fully on board with the impromptu fashion show, cheering wildly and singing along to Gemma's phone loudly. They cry out, 'Pop off, bish! Yas! No crumbs! She's serving c—'

Francesca squeaks loud enough to smother that particular swear, which sounds weirdly affectionate coming from this total stranger in a top hat fascinator, but Gemma is beaming under the attention, the life and soul, looking happier than . . .

223

Well, happier than she has most of the night. *Definitely* happier than she did in any of the photos from Kayleigh's hen do.

She's about two feet away from us now, and throws her weight to her left, arms launching out to vogue like Madonna – and she collides with a man in a suit, who stumbles back while Gemma lets out a squawk at having almost punched him right on the nose. She nearly drops her phone as she pauses the music.

'*Excuse me*,' the suited man hisses, and skirts around her.

Gemma looks at us all with wide eyes, mouth hanging open, arms frozen outstretched, all trace of her very serious model walk abandoned now – and with no chance of recovery as a mum around my age comes out of the loos behind her with a toddler on her hip and a five-year-old held by the hand. She gives Gemma a bit of a weird look, and then notices her audience and the little bar set up around our feet, and rolls her eyes.

'Mummy,' the little boy says, 'is that a princess? I thought you said Cinderella *lived* in Disneyland.'

'Even Cinders needs a holiday sometimes,' Gemma calls after them, very serious once more, and the little boy tucks his head into his mum's side, shy. The mum throws Gemma a smile, though. There's a shout from within the concourse – the 'short king' groom, I recognise – and the stag do peel away to go see what's happening, now Gemma's catwalk is over. I peer after them, noticing he's stood on a chair and giving some loud, impassioned speech that makes his fiancé blub happy tears.

I think it might be Taylor Swift lyrics.

Once the corridor is clear, Gemma finally strikes us a pose. This one is more refined, just a hand on her hip. 'So? Isn't she stunning?'

'That *cannot* be your bridesmaid's dress,' Francesca says, appalled. 'Kayleigh usually has such great taste! What is this? What is . . .?' She clambers to her feet, stumbling only a little, and gestures at the layers and layers of ruffles arranged around the dress. They're on the sleeves, the skirt, the bodice. When Francesca turns Gemma around, I see the back is dipped low, and there's even a ruffle lining that, too.

'It's *designer*!' Gemma says, with a smile that's too toothy, and sort of manic around the eyes. 'It's *sooo* on trend, *sooo* chic. She can't have us wearing just *anything*. It needs to be standout. Especially for her maid of honour.'

Francesca takes another long study of the dress and cringes. 'Um. Well, it's . . . certainly not forgettable. It looks like something out of *27 Dresses*.'

'Ohmigod, yes! *Thank you!*' Gemma throws her hands in the air. 'That's exactly what I've been thinking this whole time! She's out to punish me, right? This is not something you make your best friend wear because you like them. Tell me.'

Now, Gemma pins me with a fierce look, and I clear my throat. 'I'm not much of a fashion expert, Gem . . .'

'Leon, look me in the eye and tell me your darling sister wouldn't make me wear this if she didn't want me to suffer.'

'Suffer' is a bit strong – it's just a dress, after all.

But I can only hold my hands up in surrender and shake my head with a breath of laughter, before reaching once more for my drink. It's almost empty; I pour myself another. In for a penny . . .

'You ever doubt what your sister's really like,' Gemma tells me, 'remember this dress. And just *look* at what she said about it in the group chat . . .'

She comes over, bringing her phone up from her side to swipe through it.

'It was all, "Oh, girls, I know Gemma's got something a bit extra special, but I hope you all understand . . ." As if she was doing me a favour! As if I didn't have to pay for the bloody thing myself!'

'Wait, I thought Mum and Dad were paying for the dresses?' I say, brow furrowing. I'm *sure* that was the conversation . . . I know my head's a bit fuzzy, but I distinctly remember them discussing it. Myleene was put out because she wasn't a bridesmaid, so they'd promised her to spend a bit extra on her dress to make up for it. I remember, because I rolled my eyes and thought Kay wasn't doing them any favours by sharing her taste for fashionable clothes with our youngest sister, and Kay had a wardrobe full of barely worn dresses that surely Myleene could borrow for the weekend; wasn't one of those good enough?

But I am not a fashion expert, as established, so I kept my mouth shut.

Gemma scoffs at me. 'Please, that budget got eaten up by the veil and the alterations. It didn't even touch the bridesmaids' dresses. We had to foot the bill for those ourselves.'

'Christ, how expensive *was* this veil?'

'You do *not* want to know.' She rolls her eyes, turns her attention back to her phone, and halts. Her face creases, her top lip hooking up in a 'huh?' sort of expression, which falls away as she studies her phone and scrolls slowly. I watch the blood drain from her face, see the usual swagger and confidence leach away too, until Gemma looks – scared. Young. Like the world just opened up beneath her feet and swallowed her whole. Her breathing turns shallow, and I'm afraid for a moment she's going to pass out.

226

Anyone else, I'd think she'd just had some bad news about a family member being taken ill suddenly. But Gemma doesn't have family, or none she's close enough to that it'd warrant a reaction like that.

I step towards her. 'Everything okay? What's wrong?'

'It's . . .' She blinks, staring blankly at her phone. 'It's the group chat. They've kicked me out so they can bitch about me. But this is . . . This is my work phone, the battery on mine was getting really low. I'm in the chat twice – you know, maid of honour, couldn't afford to miss any updates, all that crap . . . I never really message from this one, I don't think Kayleigh's even got this number saved . . .They just kicked my personal number out, not this one. Look.'

Her hand trembles as she holds out the phone, and Francesca takes it. I come over to her side to get a better look. A WhatsApp of 'Kayleigh's Wedding Party!' with a series of bride emojis is open to an hour or so ago – a string of messages that have been sent while we were laughing ourselves silly with piggybacks and three-legged races.

Gemma Cavendish has been removed from the group

Kayleigh Michaels:
Will set up the other group now so we've got a separate one if she does make it tomorrow! Not looking likely though lol

Joss Nichols-Brown:
Genuinely cannot BELIEVE she's missing your wedding. What the fuck kind of maid of honour does that??? It's not like she didn't have enough advance notice

Laura Fielding:

It's so messed up. But at least you've got us Kay!!!

Kayleigh Michaels:

Much better company lol

Love you gals xxxx

She's probably not even at the airport, she's probably shut up in her sad little room in that house-share waiting for a morning flight so she can swan in late and steal the limelight

Andi G:

Lmaoooo classic Gemma. She's always so desperate for attention

Joss Nichols-Brown:

Omg right???? SO clingy

Kayleigh Michaels:

Tell me about it! She's always been like this lol. Can't let me have ANYTHING

Laura Fielding:

You know she tried to tell me the destination wedding was HER thing? Like, what, nobody else has destination weddings? You don't own the idea Gemma, calm down

Joss Nichols-Brown:

No way!!!! Omg what a try hard

Just as well Brit dumped her instead of proposing, she'd have been copying all your ideas for her wedding otherwise I bet

Andi G:

I still can't get over that she refused to get the time off work to come early. Like she's too good for the rest of us! Bet she's been planning to skip the wedding all week bc you got the job and she didn't Kay

Kayleigh Michaels:

Would NOT surprise me

Laura Fielding:

I still can't get over that she refused to come out to drinks last week to celebrate!

Beyond bitter

Like, your best mate just got a promotion? At least pretend to be happy for her?

Joss Nichols-Brown:

She needs to get over herself

Kayleigh Michaels:

Wedding will be MUCH better for her not being here tbh. So glad I've got you gals with me!

Although I AM sad we might not get to see her in her dress . . .

Andi G:

HAHAHA PLS I NEED TO SEE THAT

Kayleigh Michaels:

You guys don't think it was too much?

Or . . . not enough? Lol! It was kinda tame compared to some of the ones I was looking at originally . . .

Joss Nichols-Brown:

Miss high-and-mighty fashionista needed a reality check

Laura Fielding:

Acting like she's too good to keep up with trends but really it's just because she can't afford them lol

Basic white tees for a basic bitch

Kayleigh Michaels:

Oh come on, she's not all bad . . .

She's GREAT at being a total pushover lol

Anyway, got to go girlies — need that beauty rest! Thanks all for such a fab night, you're the best friends a bride-to-be could ask for! See you all bright and early tomorrow morning! xxxxx

Francesca gasps, holding a hand up to her mouth, and there are tears in her eyes. I take the phone from her, scrolling back through to reread some of the messages. Is this a hallucination? The booze messing with me?

No.

It's not.

It's the rose-tinted glasses I've been wearing shattering to pieces.

I've never heard my sister talk like this. I've never heard her be so *cruel* about people. She sounds like a bully. She sounds ugly.

'You know what?' I say, fingers clenching around Gemma's phone. 'She and Marcus might be a great match for each other after all.'

Chapter Thirty

Francesca

There's a sudden flurry of foot traffic – some flights are actually leaving, boarding gates being called, and people are fitting in a quick wee before they go. I step closer to Gemma, wrapping my arms around her and bringing her out of the way. She's shaking, her skin cold and clammy, and once again, years of being the mum friend on nights out has instinct kicking in.

'We'll be back in a few,' I tell Leon, and bundle Gemma to the loos, taking her suitcase with us. The toilets are huge – wide open and aggressively lit. They're noisy, too – exasperated parents talking loudly to their children and trying very hard to be patient, a couple of old women nattering with voices like foghorns, hand-dryers blaring like hurricanes and toilets flushing like Niagara Falls. It's a struggle to process it all with the amount I've had to drink.

Gemma's drink-stained outfit from earlier is in a pile on the end of the sinks, which are a long, flat, angled bank of porcelain; her clothes have been sat collecting water as people wash their hands.

For once, Gemma is deathly silent. She wraps her arms around herself, shoulders bowed forward, staring with tearful eyes at nothing at all. Her teeth are chattering.

I can't even imagine ... Seeing those messages, her so-called friends, her *best friend*, talking about her like that ... It's so cruel. It's downright nasty. What else must they have been saying behind her back?

Are these people really her *friends*? I can't imagine any of mine acting like this. We've been a tight-knit band since the first year of uni, the kind of friends who always show up for each other but call each other out when someone's out of line, too. That's exactly why I've been too nervous to tell them about what's been going on with me and Marcus! But even then, they'd call me out to my face, not evict me from a WhatsApp to bitch about me. None of us would talk to each other, or *about each other*, like Gemma's friends did in that group chat.

And for all Gemma made it clear to us that she resents Kayleigh, I'd put money on her bottling it all up rather than badmouthing her to everybody.

Kayleigh obviously hasn't shown her the same courtesy. And Gemma told us she'd only found out about the promotion this afternoon, so Kayleigh clearly arranged a celebratory drink with her other friends and made it sound like Gemma was in the know and just didn't want to come! Maybe she even told them not to say anything to Gemma to 'not upset her any more'.

It's so – it's so manipulative, so *mean*, so ...

Is this really the woman Marcus is choosing? She can't be who he wants to spend his life with.

A headache begins to throb at the front of my skull right between my eyes; I grit my teeth against it and focus on the matter at hand. When I bend down to open Gemma's suitcase, the room pitches sideways, but I manage not to fall over. I find a pair of tapered, soft cotton trousers, and pause over a white T-shirt folded neatly on the top of the bag.

Just *touching it*, I feel like it must cost more than my dress for this wedding, and I splurged in Selfridges on that. It doesn't feel very 'basic' to me.

I root past it and pull out the next item – a pale blue button-down shirt.

I hand the clothes to Gemma. The garment bag for her atrocious dress is hanging over a toilet door, so I prompt her in that direction.

'Do you need help unzipping the dress?' I ask, but Gemma shakes her head and walks off. I turn my attention to her clothes in the sink, wringing them out as best I can and then holding them under a hand-dryer. She can't very well put sodden clothes back in her suitcase.

When Gemma emerges several minutes later, the garment bag draped over her arm, she looks like a stranger.

Well, I suppose, she *is* still a stranger – I've only known her for a few hours. But it feels like I've lived a hundred lifetimes in the span of those heartfelt and heart-wrenching conversations and with the drinking games and gossiping and lingerie shopping.

What I mean is, she doesn't look like herself. Her hair is still wavy (it must be natural, I decide, no Airwrap necessary) and a little bit frizzy, and she's still wearing her glasses, and she obviously has one of those capsule wardrobes where everything goes with everything else because she still looks effortlessly chic in that casual outfit. But there's no gleam in her eyes, no casual confidence in her bearing, no sense of absolutely rightness and belonging radiating out of her.

Gemma splashes some cold water on her face, then runs

her fingers through her hair and uses her shirt to clean the smudges off her glasses.

'Thanks,' she mumbles, as I pack her suitcase back up. She stands looking awkward and stiff. 'Sorry, I . . .'

'It's alright.'

I get back up, bringing the suitcase with me. The room spins again, and I think it might be time to take a break from drinking, maybe have a bit of food to settle my stomach. I didn't used to be a very big drinker, but I forced myself to keep up with Marcus and the gang from work on nights out. Normally I'd remember to have a couple of soft drinks between rounds of shots, though – even if I went to buy them alone, so the others wouldn't realise I'd skipped the alcohol.

It seems so silly now.

And also like a genius move I've regretfully neglected tonight. I got a bit too trigger-happy, pouring out drinks for myself, enjoying myself too much to pay attention.

Just before I turn to leave, Gemma sucks in a sharp breath.

'I didn't . . . I mean, I don't want you guys to think . . . All that stuff I told you about Kayleigh, what I think of her . . . I don't . . . It's not like I go around telling everybody. I'm not two-faced about it. Or, I am, but – only to myself. I don't go whinging about her to other people.'

'I didn't think you did.'

Gemma's brow furrows, making her glasses shift on her face. She pushes them back into place. 'I know I'm not a good person—'

'*What?* Where did you get that from?'

Her mouth opens, but she doesn't seem to have an answer.

I wonder if this is to do with her ex – or her dad, like

Leon mentioned. Maybe it's to do with Kayleigh, or maybe it's all three and then some. And while I felt a bit distrustful of her earlier, she didn't strike me as *bad news*.

Leon did, being all surly and short with me, but he's softened up since, too.

Gemma just . . . seems to say what's on her mind. She called me out about those texts with Marcus and our emotional affair, but she wasn't *wrong* to do so. It's not like I was squarely in the right, after all.

She's certainly been friendly enough in the last few hours. She's obviously got a bit of a bond with Leon despite them not being especially close, and she's even treated me like we're old pals, with all that open affection and good-natured teasing that feels like we're in on the joke with her instead of the butt of it.

'I know it's not worth very much coming from me, because we don't really know each other,' I say, 'and I *am* in the process of trying to steal your best friend's fiancé before he can make it to the altar, so I don't think that says very much about my character, either – but I don't think you're a bad person, Gemma. I actually think you're very cool and funny and loyal and the sort of person I'd want to be friends with.'

And I mean it.

I really do.

A few hours ago, if you'd told me that I'd want to be friends with Kayleigh's maid of honour – I would've baulked at the very idea. I've never taken to Kayleigh and don't think very much of her, and while I can admit I may be a bit biased there, tonight has only shown me I was right. I wouldn't have thought very much of her friends either, merely by association.

But Gemma just has this *way* of drawing you in.

I feel like I stand a bit taller around her, which is nice. She didn't hesitate to try to bolster me up in duty free – or even try to hype Leon up about his dating life a bit, too. And I always think it's nice to have friends that lift you up and make you feel comfortable about yourself just by being around you.

Gemma's like that, I think.

I can't imagine why she wouldn't be able to see that about herself, and why she thinks she's not a good person.

She sniffles, a few tears clinging to her eyelashes. She butts her glasses out of the way to wipe the back of her hand under her eyes. 'You wouldn't say that if you knew, Fran.'

'Knew what?'

Gemma looks at me, forlorn and dejected, and I want to hug her. I want to wrap her up in a blanket and let her know it'll be alright. I feel so wretched *for* her, because it must be bad to lay someone so self-assured so low like this.

And she tells me, 'You and Leon . . . aren't the only ones with a plan to ruin the wedding. I was, too.'

Time until 'I Do'

8 ½ hours

Chapter Thirty-one

Gemma

I have visions of Francesca pointing at me and screaming '*Bitch!*' like some Salem witchfinder of yore, and running to Leon who has somehow already found the video even though it's on my other phone, not the one I left him with, and the lights dimming except for eerie spotlights on the pair of them as they shame me and tell me what a heinous, horrible human being I am and then dramatically turn their backs and then I'm ousted from the wedding by security I know Kayleigh doesn't have as everybody stands to watch my downfall . . .

Except this is real life, not a movie, so none of that happens.

What actually happens is that Francesca's face furrows in confusion and she looks at me for a long moment before saying, 'What do you mean? I thought you said . . . Earlier when I asked you—'

'Yeah, I'm not trying to call it off because I'm in love with one of them, or anything. I don't want to *call it off*. I said I was planning to *ruin it*.'

'But . . . I don't understand,' Fran says. She's still peering at me like she's searching for answers, but she also doesn't bother to ask why, because I think I've made that pretty clear by now with everything I've offloaded about my bestie. 'How? What were you going to do, Gemma?'

I open my mouth, but there's a child screaming. '*But Muuuuuum, I want to go back! Alfie got to go on Space Mountain, it's not fair!*' and an exhausted mum trying to explain, 'Yes, darling, I know, but you're not big enough yet, are you? Now just try to have a wee-wee before— *DANIEL NO NOT ON THE FLOOR!*'

I'd laugh, under other circumstances. Crack a joke to Fran about how I don't know about her, but I am happy to have a child-free future ahead of me, thank you very much, motherhood is not for me.

But now doesn't really feel like the time for jokes, and all the thought does is make me think bitterly – sadly – of my own non-existent family, and how alone I am without Kayleigh.

I don't know if Francesca can sense that, or if she's grossed out by little Daniel peeing on the bathroom floor in protest, but she clasps my hand, tugging me and my suitcase along.

'Come on. Let's find somewhere a bit quieter.'

There's a constant stream of people disrupting our quiet patch of corridor now, coming and going from the loos ahead of flights *finally* departing, and the drone of overhead announcements, the clamour of voices and luggage.

'Alright?' Leon asks, with a face on him like he regrets asking because the answer is obviously, *No I'm bloody not 'alright'*. Awkwardly, he reaches out to pat my shoulder, then seems to change his mind and sort of just leaves his big, warm hand resting there for a moment before dropping it.

Before Fran can quite say anything, someone smacks her in the side with a rucksack, sending her spilling forwards with an, 'Ooph!'

Leon catches her in a startling turn of deftness, setting her back upright and asking softly, 'You alright?'

It's the lads' holiday kid off to woo a woman with Victoria's Secret underwear. He's at least got a bag of Ladurée macarons sticking out of the top of his rucksack now too, so he's not a complete shambles when it comes to airport gifts.

'Shit, sorry, sorry! My bad, I'm so sorry!'

'It's alright,' Fran murmurs, looking like it's taking all her willpower not to apologise for, you know, *standing there* and getting in *his* way, even though it was totally his fault. Leon is still holding her arm, glowering over her shoulder hard enough to make the kid cringe and run off sharpish.

'Let's go upstairs,' I say, and my voice doesn't sound quite right. It's a bit hollow, a bit monotonous. I know it's mine, I know I'm moving my mouth, but I might as well be a puppet operated by the Ghost of Gemmas Past. Taking charge, making a plan. The other two glance at me. 'There might be a bit more room in the food court, if people are starting to board flights.'

'Good shout,' Leon says. The two of them finish packing up our picnic; Leon darts off to get rid of the bag of rubbish, and Fran won't quite look at me, which checks out.

I told her. I said she wouldn't think I was such a decent person if she knew. Look at me, being right.

My bottles of duty-free booze clank together as I bag them up. They're sticky, and it feels like I might as well be ringing the bells of fucking Notre Dame for all they clink and clatter. The shame bell, from *Game of Thrones*.

Look at this sad, pathetic loser who can't cope with her best friend's success and is drowning her sorrows at two a.m. by the airport toilets, they seem to say. *Look at this evil cow plotting to ruin the best day of her best friend's life, because she can't cope with the fact that she simply* isn't good enough. *So, so pathetic.*

Out in the main concourse, the joint stag do's obstacle course has been cleared away, and the group are scattered: some playing a quiet card game on the floor, some dozing on chairs, a few slumped talking quietly as they scroll on their phones.

The kids, meanwhile, have found alternative entertainment. There's a whole cluster of them (a cluster of kids? A rampage of children? A murder of toddlers?) sat in rows while Disney tunes play from a portable speaker. A few dads are stood up in front of them performing, and I snort, because they're all dressed the same way.

What do you call that? A *man*agerie of dads?

One of them show-kicks a bit too wildly in his portrayal of Genie as he belts out (tunelessly, but enthusiastically) 'Friend Like Me', and another dad shoves him out the way. A third is shouting, 'Shut up, Charlie, you're making their ears bleed.'

'Like you're any better,' jeers another dad.

'Say that *to my face*, you Henley-wearing tosser!'

A set of over-eager jazz-hands sock one dad square in the face, and a pair of Mickey ears go flying as it turns into a full-on brawl, which makes all the kids scream with laughter. One of the mums on the sidelines sighs and pulls out a bottle of wine from underneath a pushchair.

The three of us pause to watch the drama unfold, and exchange long looks.

All I can think is: *Glad it's not just my life imploding right now.*

'Do you think we should . . .?' Leon says, and I shake my head. He's beefier than any of those dads, but Leon's so non-confrontational, he'll probably end up with a black eye before he breaks anything up.

Fran just gives my arm a little nudge, moving us away from the scene. 'They'll sort themselves out. Come on.'

It turns out the seats in the food court are almost all taken. A couple of kids are stretched out in the booth seats, heads pillowed on a parent's lap as they snooze. There are empty tables where seats have been dragged away so groups can sit together, and there's even one guy – full business suit and all – sprawled out across three tables pulled together, his legs hanging off the end, fast asleep.

I spot a shut-up restaurant to our left. There's a sign up that reads in French: *Under renovation – opening soon!*

I go over and try the door.

It's not locked.

'Gemma, what are you doing!' Fran hisses, face suddenly pale with alarm. 'You can't go in there!'

'Why not? It's open.'

'It's – well, it isn't . . . You can't go in there!'

'Yeah, I'm with Francesca on this one,' Leon says gruffly, and I almost roll my eyes because no surprises there. 'We can't, Gem.'

'What if someone sees?'

I shrug. *So what if they do?*

What's the worst that can happen? This isn't *Bridget Jones: The Edge of Reason*; I'm not about to end up in some foreign prison swapping my bra for cigarettes just because some idiot forgot to lock the door of a *restaurant*. More likely, some French police officer sends me packing back to the UK with a stern warning and a good story.

Not that it looks like I'll have anybody to tell that story to, at this rate, I think, remembering that WhatsApp chat I'm not supposed to be part of anymore.

But fuck it. I didn't get the promotion, I'm not getting the wedding, I didn't get the flat, I haven't got the partner, and I definitely don't have the friends. Very literally, *what have I got to lose?*

Out loud I say, 'Please, if security are worried about anyone right now, it's the dad-battle going on downstairs.'

So I push the door the rest of the way open and go on inside. My eyes take a few seconds to adjust to the shadows that cloak the room. It's a sit-down restaurant and rows of bottles glint on shelves behind a bar in the lights that twinkle in from the terminal. Chairs are stacked upside down on tables, but I find a big round booth over in the far corner and throw myself in, groaning at the plush cushioned seat I land on – it's a welcome relief after all that sitting on the floor.

Maybe I could just stay here? Hide forever in this dark corner of Orly Airport, all alone with my sad little life, and let myself disappear and decay and never have to face Kayleigh and her perfect fucking wedding?

But there's a clatter – Leon bumping into something and barely catching some chairs that he almost just sent spilling to the floor, and Fran saying, 'Oh, gosh, careful! Are you okay?' as she flashes her phone torch around so he can see better, and it is clear that I will not be left alone to wallow and despair.

But hey, a girl can dream.

I groan again as I pull myself up into more of a sitting position, and say, 'Over here,' so they can find me more easily in the dark. Fran swings her torch my way and I wince, momentarily blinded.

It's really the least I deserve, under the circumstances. I can only imagine what they'll say, what they'll do, when they learn the truth.

And like, sure, do I *have* to tell them? Of course I don't.

I could tell them both to piss off and mind their own business, laugh in Fran's face and say, 'God, learn to take a *joke*, why don't you!' I could pretend like I was just chatting shit, and brush off any pestering, and if Leon tries to tell Kayleigh that I've got a sinister plot in mind, who's she really going to believe? The brother who wants her to call off the wedding or the 'pushover' maid of honour who helped plan it all?

I don't have to tell them anything.

But it's eating at me, and I want to.

I'm so tired. I'm so fed up.

I'm so *lonely*.

And Fran – sweet, lovely, shy Fran – standing there and trying to be so nice to me and telling me she'd be my friend . . . It's laughable. She doesn't know me.

She shouldn't be giving me false hope for things like that.

She should at least know who I really am, first.

The pair of them settle into the booth with me, Fran in the middle and tucking herself in small. I reach for the bag of booze I put down on the floor, fishing out a fresh paper cup and pouring myself a little whisky. It burns on its way down, enough to make my eyes water.

245

Or maybe that's something else.

Leon puts my work phone on the table for me, and I take it – but only to shove it into the depths of my handbag. I find my own phone wedged between a book and my purse, and turn it back on. The battery's still low; I should find somewhere to charge it, soon. Maybe Fran has a portable charger? She seems like someone who would carry one of those everywhere.

When the phone loads, there's a notification on the screen waiting for me. Kayleigh has added me to a new group chat called 'THE WEDDING!'

Hey, ladies! Couldn't stick all the notifications and stuff in the other chat so deleted it and making this new one for the wedding weekend. Updates only please, no gossip or silliness! **@Gemma**, let us know when you land and are on the way to the hotel, keeping EVERYTHING crossed you make it in time! Looking forward to sharing my big day with you all tomorrow, best bridesmaids ever! Xxxxx

I snort. And I thought I could be two-faced . . .

Of course, when I look, the old group chat for all the wedding planning stuff with us and the bridesmaids has vanished without a trace. I wonder how long it'll take them to notice they left my other number in, that I might've seen.

I swipe out of WhatsApp and call up my photo album.

'What's going on, Gem?' Leon is asking. 'If this is about the group chat . . . what Kay said . . .'

'This is about *way* more than that,' I tell him. I find the video and lay my phone down for them. And I click 'play'.

Chapter Thirty-two

Leon

The camera swings around, showing a club. Dark, with flashing lights in shades of purple and pink. There's Kay's group of mates squashed into leather armchairs and sofas, arranged around a couple of low tables that are covered in drinks. There's a fishbowl with straws sticking out of it – the straws are pink, the ends shaped like penises. The girls are all in their party get-up, black dresses and high heels, with pink sashes that say things like 'BRIDESMAID' or 'HEN PARTY'. They're shrieking – a mix of laughter and excitement and some singing along to the music that's blaring. It's something slow and dramatic with crude lyrics.

The view shifts. This time, it shows a stage with two obscenely buff men – all muscle, all over, and I know it's *all over* because one of them is wearing nothing but a waistcoat with a plastic sheriff's badge and some tiny gold underwear so tight there's nothing left to the imagination, and the other is in the process of ripping off some assless chaps as he gyrates and holds a cowboy hat to cover his dick.

Next to me, Francesca gives a little squeak. Out of the corner of my eye I see her turning bright red and bring a hand up to her face. I'm not totally sure if the reaction is embarrassment at watching the footage of a strip club or . . .

Well, the alternative makes me feel weirdly insecure, despite the fact that manscaping to this extreme degree has never been me.

Gemma bites her thumbnail, watching us rather than the video.

The camera moves again, all the way around to the other side now, and there's a noisy whoop. The girls are shouting things like, 'Yaaas!' and 'Get in there, Kayleigh!' and, 'Last night of freedom, whooo!'

In the chair next to the person filming is something I would *very much like to never have to see*, and I cringe away, pulling a face at Gemma.

'Seriously?' I say, but she shakes her head.

'Just watch.'

In the video, Kay is wearing a white dress and white heels, and a white sash that reads in bright pink 'BRIDE TO BE'. There's a cheap veil and a plastic tiara in her hair, and a drink in her hand with yet another penis straw sticking out of it.

She's getting a lap dance from one of the strippers. He's all rippling, glistening muscles with a scanty little silver waistcoat for decoration and tiny, tight silver shorts that, again, leave nothing to the imagination. We can't see his face well, but he throws a silver cowboy-booted foot up onto the table next to Kay to thrust into her face and the whole entourage of the hen party screams in delight at that. He's covered in glitter and holds his cowboy hat above his head, whirling his arm around in time with his hips like he's at the rodeo.

'Oh, my,' Francesca whispers, both hands pressed over her mouth now.

Is this where I'm going wrong in my dating life? *Is this really what girls like?* I have to wonder. The veiny outline of a dick in their face and all those muscles and—

And that is absolutely beside the point.

Because in the video, Kayleigh grabs the stripper's waistcoat and uses it as leverage to haul herself up, and kisses him.

With tongue, which I also absolutely could've gone without seeing, thanks Gemma. It's one of those sloppy, drunk snogs given with absolutely no regard for how public it is. The stripper drops his hat in favour of grabbing Kay to pick her up. She grins, cupping his cheek, still holding her drink in her other hand.

There's got to be an explanation, though, right? Kay's not the kind of girl who goes around snogging strippers at her own hen party, a mere three weeks before she gets married.

Is she?

I look at the phone again, a sinking feeling in my stomach, because all evidence would suggest, yet again, that I am wrong, and do not know my sister at all. She is not the person we thought.

There's a sharp, stern male voice that's drowned out by squealing laughter. The stripper moves off-camera sharpish, and the bouncer is kicking the girls out of the club to loud, whiny protests. The camera judders, moves, swings around, keeps recording.

Gemma reaches to turn it off, but then in the video, someone says, 'Oh, boo, total spoilsport! That's not what your boring family are going to be like at the wedding is it, Kayleigh?'

Kayleigh laughs. It's too sharp to be written off as drunk rubbish. 'Bloody hope not. *God*, they're so drab. It's *embarrassing*. They wouldn't know a party if it bit them in the arse! Myleene's alright sometimes, obvs, but—'

A couple of girls groan. 'Nooo, all she does is follow us around like a puppy!'

The camera swings around again, and this time it captures Kayleigh pouting, but there's a glint in her eyes – bitter, angry, resentful. 'I really thought having the wedding abroad meant they wouldn't come. *So* annoying.' She clicks her tongue, and the others laugh.

The video cuts off and my blood runs cold.

Gemma gasps, a hand flying to the base of her throat before she leans all the way across the table to grip my hand. 'Fuck, Leon, I – I didn't even . . . I'm so sorry. I didn't think. I forgot she . . .'

Forgot she said she didn't want her family at her wedding, because as far as Gemma's concerned, that's an everyday kind of comment from Kayleigh.

I blink a few times. 'Is that why she said she didn't want Dad walking her down the aisle? Was she . . . trying to get us not to come?'

'No! No, she . . .' Gemma cringes, but admits, 'She said she didn't want everyone looking at *him*, worrying about *him*, and . . . and he walks too slow with his cane that it'd ruin the aesthetics in the wedding video.'

'She . . . doesn't want us there. It's supposed to be the happiest day of her life, and she doesn't want us there.'

Are we really that 'boring', that 'embarrassing'? Do we really not fit into Kayleigh's shiny new life so badly that she wants *nothing* to do with us?

The shamed, sorry look on Gemma's face tells me all I need to know.

Quietly, Francesca says, 'Why did you want to show us that video? Not just to prove a point about Kayleigh?'

'I . . .' Gemma pulls her gaze from mine, gives my hand another squeeze before pulling away. 'No.'

She swipes on the phone, and another video starts playing. This one has soft, romantic violin music playing and is a compilation of Kay at brunch, at home, prepping for a dinner party, shopping for her wedding dress, at the cake tasting, with her girls, with Marcus, by herself . . .

'You know how I'm doing a speech, as maid of honour?' Gemma is saying, as the other video continues. Even though I raise my head to look at her, she is staring fixedly at the phone, a frown bunching between her eyebrows. 'Kayleigh wanted me to have a video presentation to go with it. Something she could put on her Instagram afterwards. I had to capture all this footage since the engagement, pull it all together, so it can play in the background while I do my speech.

'And then I got that call before the flight earlier, about how *she* got the job over me, and I just . . . snapped, I guess. It's not fair. She's got everything, this perfect life, and – and why? She doesn't deserve any of it. And I just thought . . . wouldn't it really *suck*, if the presentation videos got mixed up? Like, we're all sat there, enjoying the five-course meal, and I get up to do my speech between courses and everyone's happy and she's glowing, and it's the most absolutely beautiful day, and then *that* video from the hen do plays instead, and everyone sees who she really is? And OMG, what a horrible mistake, how totally tragic, the tech guy must've

251

really messed up, this is a total disaster . . . But everyone's seen it. It's too late. Good luck salvaging your perfect wedding now, you know?'

I stare at Gemma, and Francesca pauses the compilation video.

'And obviously I'll be totally outraged and defend Kayleigh and act *super* upset on her behalf, so she'll never *actually* be able to blame me, and nobody would ever think I did it on *purpose* – but I'll know. And everyone else will know what she's really like. And I just . . . need that. I need, for *once*, for everyone else to see it, too.'

She sure does paint a vivid picture. I can imagine her own pretend horror at the 'mix-up', Kay bursting into floods of tears and fleeing the top table, the horrified murmur that would rush through the room.

How bad we'd feel – for poor, humiliated Kay, who made an honest mistake, who just got a bit carried away after one too many drinks on her hen do, egged on by the girls. Mum would go running after her to make sure she was okay, to comfort her. Myleene would probably say something like how Kay's just acting out because she knows, deep down, Marcus isn't the right guy for her, and she was subconsciously self-sabotaging – and we'd all agree, even though Dad sure as hell wouldn't know what that meant.

Except it's *not* just her snogging a stripper, is it? It's what she said about us.

I say, 'You'd probably be doing her a favour, in the end. If there's a sure-fire way to cut us out of Kay's perfect new life, it's showing us all that video. Mum and Dad would be gutted. It'd kill them.'

Gemma squirms in her seat. 'I'm so sorry, Leon. I

252

completely forgot she even said that stuff. I'd never have shown it to you if I'd realised. I was just so caught up on the kiss . . .'

I wave off the apology; it's not Gemma who has anything to be sorry for. Her eyes water, and her lip wobbles.

Finally, she pins Francesca with a glare and bursts out in a sharp, biting tone, 'So, see? I *am* a bad person. I'm not *loyal*. I'm not going after the man I love or trying to repair my family before it's too broken, I just want to destroy the happiest day of my best friend's life because I'm a jealous bitch. *That's* who I am. That's why I wasn't going to stop either of you from trying to fuck up the wedding, because I'd still get to watch her life fall apart but wouldn't even need to get my hands dirty. I was *using* you guys.'

Francesca turns the phone screen-down. Her hand trembles. Gemma, meanwhile, clenches both her hands into fists, her elbows balanced on the edge of the table as she leans low over it.

'Did she really snog a stripper on her hen do?' Francesca asks.

Gemma sniffs. 'Yeah. The guys – the performers – they were milling around a bit at the start of the night, and Kayleigh was flirting with them just for kicks, and this one guy *really* took a shine to her. We weren't supposed to be taking videos or anything either, but the bouncer was too pissed off about this guy coming down from the stage and Kayleigh's behaviour to notice. He tried to slide into her DMs after. The cowboy dude, I mean, not the bouncer. She'd tagged the club on her Insta story, so . . .'

'Did she reply?'

Gemma shrugs. 'She said she wasn't going to. But she *did*

just evict her maid of honour from the group chat and make a new fake one for me instead, so . . . Who knows? Maybe I didn't know her as well as I thought, either,' she adds, with a sorrowful look my way.

Francesca reaches over to give Gemma's arm a squeeze. Gemma hunkers down smaller, and Francesca glances my way, her eyes bright through the darkness, a pale shade of greyish-blue like hoarfrost. She looks at me plaintively, but I don't know how to help, what to do.

We are both speechless, because what do you say to something like that?

Some trio we make. The 'work wife' plotting to steal the groom, the brother of the bride hoping to call the whole thing off for the family's sake, and the maid of honour planning to humiliate her best friend in front of dozens of wedding guests.

'You were really going to do this?' I ask. 'Play that video?'

'Yes. No. I don't . . . Fuck, Leon, I don't *know*. I just wanted to get back at her. It's not like she wouldn't have gotten over it. It's not like Marcus wouldn't have forgiven her. They're both always flirting with other people . . .' She pauses, glancing at Francesca, then snaps her gaze away. 'And it's always a drama, but neither of them actually *cares*. They both just . . . It's an ego thing, you know? They like knowing they could have anyone they wanted, and they both like being the one who got picked, like it proves they're the best. It's this whole back and forth they always do . . .'

She sighs, lifting her hands to press her face into them. Her glasses bump up to her forehead.

'The worst part is, I'm so *jealous* of it. Watching them pick each other again and again and . . . And . . .'

254

She trails off, and is quiet for a long while before Francesca brings her own phone out. She opens the message thread between her and Marcus, leaves it on the table for us to look at. Gemma peeks between her fingers, curiosity getting the better of her.

Francesca takes a deep breath. 'I suppose they're made for each other, then. Marcus implied earlier that if I'd been there tonight, we might have . . . gotten together.'

The words feel like a punch in the chest. But while I'm thinking: *That bastard, I knew he was no good, we all said . . .* The part that *really* gets me is the idea of Francesca, wrapped up in Marcus's arms, his mouth on hers.

Which I have no right to feel *any* kind of way about. And, again, I remind myself that she chose him; this is exactly what she's been hoping for.

But she looks so disappointed about it, I can't help but ask, 'I thought that was what you wanted?'

'I want to be the woman he's *in love with*, the one he wants to spend his life with. Not a seedy hook-up before he marries someone else. Not the . . . the *fuck-buddy* at the office everyone knows about, carrying on an affair. I . . . want to be the one he picks,' she adds, glancing at Gemma before looking down at her lap.

Gemma snorts softly and shakes her head.

And Francesca sits there looking small and sorry for herself and sad and somehow, *still hopeful*, like this might still turn out to be the epic romance she's been imagining this whole time, like Marcus hasn't proved completely and absolutely what a tool he is, and something in me snaps.

'Why?' I ask her. My voice comes out sharper and louder than I meant for it to. She startles, looking up at me, and

255

even Gemma sits up a bit straighter to watch. '*Why*? He's shown you who he is, what he's like. He's shown you a thousand fucking times, I bet, and you keep refusing to see it. He's been stringing you along to feed his ego, like Gem said, and you don't even seem to *care*. You let him. If he was going to pick you, you don't think he would've had the guts to break up with Kay and tell you he wanted to be with you – when it's so bloody obvious you'd pick him? He made his choice, and it wasn't you. It's like you don't have a single ounce of self-respect or—'

'Leon,' Gemma says, and it's a warning I ignore.

How long has Kayleigh been stringing all of *us* along? How long have we chosen not to see it, turned a blind eye to the thousand tiny ways she's rebuffed and rejected us? Francesca *has* to see that's what Marcus has been doing to her all this time. How can she *still* want to choose him? This isn't family she's beholden to, this is . . . it's just some *guy*. She should take the out and run a fucking mile, and be grateful for it.

'He's a piece of shit!' I exclaim. 'Half the things you've said about him tonight, it's like you're embarrassed to own up to it, because you *know* – and you're still pursuing him. If you think Kay deserves him, what do you think it says about you?'

'*Leon.*'

'You're a joke to him! If you heard the way he talks about you – the *work wife* – you wouldn't be this delusional, acting like there's *any* world in which he actually fancies you. He talks about you like you're a *joke*. And I bet if you had made it there tonight, you would've shagged him, and then you'd watch him walk down the aisle and keep fooling yourself into thinking you still had a chance. You let him walk all over you! Where's your sense of self-worth? Why can't you *see*, he's never going to pick you?'

Francesca's breath hitches when I at last pause to catch mine, and before I can blink, she's scrambling to get over Gemma and out of the booth, and running for the door.

'Well, you fucked that up royally, didn't you?' Gemma tells me.

'I just . . . I—'

The door slams as Francesca runs out, and I'm already getting up and tripping over my satchel when Gemma says, 'Go after her, you big idiot! *Fix it.*'

Chapter Thirty-three

Francesca

The terminal looks almost empty compared to earlier, and the crush of movement that drove us upstairs has fallen into a near-silent lull. The dads have disbanded; I can see them scattered sullenly in different corners of the terminal, all a bit dishevelled and browbeaten. Nobody pays me any attention as I fling myself down the last couple of stairs and make a break for the toilets, fully intending to shut myself inside a cubicle and sob my heart out.

Because – oh, he's right, isn't he? Leon's *right*.

If Marcus was going to choose me . . .

He would've said something before now. He would've held off his relationship with Kayleigh to see if there was anything between us, or spoken to me about it. He's not afraid to put himself out there and take risks like I am.

He would've come back that morning with coffee and pastries, instead of leaving my bed to immediately message another girl and then hook up with someone else all weekend.

He's had so many opportunities to choose me, and he never has.

It's a joke. *I* must be a joke to him, just like Leon says. Mocking me behind my back, like I overheard them saying earlier – and who can blame him? Who *wouldn't* laugh at the pathetic girl at the office trailing after him all moony-eyed, giving him home-cooked leftovers for his lunch, fawning all over him on a night out, bringing him slices of birthday cake just to see him smile . . .

There are tears already pouring down my cheeks, and a hysteria building in my chest that threatens to crush my lungs.

I can't believe I've been such an idiot.

'Wait! Francesca—'

Oh, God, no, he's not . . .

He's not *following me*, is he?

I glance back, shocked, and – he is. He's come after me. Leon stumbles off the end of the escalator, and I let out a high-pitched noise of surprise, freezing. He catches my eye, looking stricken, and I can only imagine how *I* must look in that moment.

What is he doing? Why is he chasing after me? Is it just to lecture me some more about what a worthless idiot I am? To shout at me for getting involved with Marcus at all, like he obviously wanted to when this whole layover began and he realised who I was?

Well, he won't follow me into the toilets, will he?

He'll have to go away and leave me to cry in peace, then. Maybe he can rant to Gemma about how much he hates me instead.

I bolt down the corridor, past our picnic spot, down Gemma's makeshift catwalk.

This time, the ladies' bathroom is blessedly silent. The stall doors are all open and empty, there are no hand-dryers blaring, no overlapping voices . . .

Just my own racing heart and ragged breathing.

I hunch over the sink, trying to steady myself, and that headache that began to threaten when I was in here a little while ago with Gemma returns full-force. I screw my eyes shut, but the pain only intensifies as memories flood in – the guys ribbing Marcus and jeering, joking, the second I leave the table on a night out; Kayleigh's curled lip and disdainful look up and down when I would arrive for a dinner party; that little sinking feeling I'd push aside whenever Marcus didn't *really* reply to something I'd said but started talking about his own day instead . . .

But, but, but.

That kiss. Those sparks. The way he smiles at me.

Is it really all in my head?

A sob breaks out of my mouth, and I grip the porcelain ledge of the sink tighter.

I'm suddenly aware of a presence next to me, the warmth of a body near my arm.

'Here.'

I force my eyes open and find Leon holding out a wad of toilet roll to me, for me to dry my eyes. I take it, trying not to think about how wretched my face looks in the mirror. *I can't show up to the wedding like this, I need to look my best. Why would he ever fancy me and leave Kayleigh for me if I look like I've spent my whole night sleepless and crying and drunk?*

That only makes me cry harder, though. I wipe my nose and eyes, but Leon doesn't go anywhere. I'm surprised he followed me in at all; he must be *very* determined.

I sniffle. 'Go on then.'

'What?'

'Carry on telling me how little you think of me, and what

260

an idiot I am. How *delusional* I am to think Marcus might ever pick someone like *me*. What a horrible, conniving person I am to want to steal him.'

'That's not—'

I let out a laugh that sounds nothing like me. It's a bit wet, with all the tears, but it's a sharp, short bark of a sound, and I even manage to cut Leon a no-nonsense look. 'Please. You made it plenty obvious earlier that you can't stand me. You wouldn't have stuck around with me if Gemma hadn't corralled us together, and the only time you did look comfortable hanging out with me was after a few drinks, which is hardly a ringing endorsement. And you've clearly only followed me in here to carry on berating me for being so worthless and stupid, so—'

'No, I didn't.'

I scoff, wiping my nose again.

I thought we might actually be on better terms, given everything that's happened and all the confessions we've made, but I was obviously wrong about that. He's exactly the mean, sullen, standoffish person he first showed himself to be, and his friendlier attitude is just one more thing I've fooled myself into believing.

He's another guy I let myself think the best of, see the potential in, only to be proved wrong yet again, and made the fool.

'I don't think you're worthless,' Leon says, and moves closer. His fingers graze my elbow and I jerk my arm back when the gesture takes me by surprise. He hesitates, but I don't quite move away, too confused by the sincerity in his voice and the seriousness in his features. I could be mistaken for thinking he looks 'like a broody bastard' again, as Gemma

261

put it, but it's more like – resolve. Something very focused, and very intense, and which I'm suddenly finding it very hard to look away from.

This time, when he touches my arm, I let him.

'I don't think you're worthless,' he repeats. 'That's not what I meant by it. It's just . . . It's more like you're letting *him* treat you like you are. Like it doesn't matter how you feel, or what any of this is like for you. Like he matters more than you do, his feelings are worth more than yours somehow. Which they aren't. Because you don't . . . What I'm trying to say is . . .'

He's stammering again, like when Gemma asked him about my new underwear choices in the Victoria's Secret section. It's endearing, oddly vulnerable, and I wipe away a couple more tears. His grip tenses around my elbow.

'What I'm trying to say,' he says tightly, looking me in the eyes so fiercely it's like he's daring himself to do it, and all I can do is stare back, 'is that you're worth a damn sight more than someone like Marcus, and I think it's a real fucking shame you can't see that.'

'I . . .'

I have no idea what to say to that. It's not what I thought he'd followed me to say, not what I took from his tirade earlier, but – I believe him, when he says that's what he meant.

And I'm not sure what to do with it.

Another sob bursts out of me, and I'm leaning forward before I can think twice about it, burying my face in Leon's broad, solid chest. My fingers bunch in his shirt. He doesn't hold me, which makes me feel like a colossal idiot for throwing myself at the nearest source of potential comfort,

262

only moves his hand from my elbow. I expect him to prise me away and push me out at arm's length, but instead his hand anchors between my shoulder blades.

It's only a scrap of kindness, but haven't I already proved that I'm happy accepting scraps of affection and attention from Marcus all this time?

Leon's right – I have exactly zero sense of self-worth.

It's a vicious pain, right between my ribs, and I fight to get myself at least a little bit under control. I manage to swallow down a few gasping breaths, and shove myself upright, away from Leon. His hand falls back to his side, clenching and unclenching. I unfurl my own fingers from their death-grip in his shirt.

'I'm sorry it came out so . . . harsh,' he tells me. 'I just . . . I think I can see he's doing to you what Kay's been doing to *us*, and I just can't figure out why you'd *choose* that. Why you'd go after it, when you don't have to. She's my sister, I *have* to carry that pain. But he's . . . You can walk away. You *should* walk away.'

I sniffle. I guess it never felt like I had much of a choice, if only because I didn't *give myself* one. It was comfortable. I told myself I was happy. Told myself it was inevitable, it was a storybook romance, it was bad luck, it was . . . something I couldn't walk away from.

Could I? Could I be that person who wears the bold lipstick, the nice underwear for no reason, who walks away from this emotional affair that's no good for her? Someone who takes risks – takes *charge* of her own life a little bit?

I thought I was finally doing something that would stop me being a side-character in someone else's story, but he's right. I'll *always* be exactly that with Marcus. Just like with all the other guys I've dated before him. All those fixer-uppers I fell head over heels for, wilfully blind to a litany of red flags before they moved on to someone else.

Don't I want more for myself than that?

'He won't pick you over Kay,' Leon carries on now that I've fallen quiet, 'because even a self-centred prick like Marcus can see you're too good for him. You're everything he's not. You're kind, and sweet, and – and gentle, and . . . He'd never be able to live with himself if he picked you.'

'Oh,' I say, and it's all I *can* say, apparently, because even after I swallow the lump in my throat and try again, all that comes out is, 'Oh.'

'If he picked you,' Leon says, lowering his voice, the steady, serious cadence of it quieting some of the sadness that threatened to overwhelm me, 'he'd walk all over you and he'd probably cheat because that's apparently the sort of scumbag he is, and he'd hurt you, and . . . And I get it, you're in love with him, you know? That's . . . I don't know what that's like. I *wish* I had someone in my life I felt that strongly for, that I'd risk everything for just a chance to be with them. But he doesn't deserve it. He doesn't deserve *you*. I didn't mean to say that you were worthless, that wasn't . . . I *meant*, you're worth too much to throw it away on someone like him.'

A fresh wave of tears pricks at my eyes and spills over onto my cheeks, but this one doesn't hurt so badly. It aches, carves out a hollow deep inside my chest, but it isn't the sharp, all-consuming pain that makes me feel small and stupid.

It makes me . . .

Makes me *yearn*, for – for I don't know what. More? Maybe?

For someone who would fight for me like I've been trying to fight for Marcus, someone who doesn't offer me scraps while I give them my whole heart and act like it's enough. For someone to look at me and . . .

Say that I'm worth more. To *see* that I am.

I find my gaze drawn to the mirror above the sink. Leon's profile is highlighted there, a squat nose and scruffy hair and searching eyes and broad shoulders in a creased shirt. And there's me, cheeks blotchy and bright, eyes shining with tears and hair frizzing out of my braids, drowning in this godforsaken jacket.

I look at my reflection, see the heartache and hope and sorrow etched into my expression that I know oh so well, and . . . And I wish I didn't. I wish I could look in that mirror and see a different girl.

I wish *she* could see that she's worth more.

Leon begins to say something else but stops abruptly as I jerk away from him, tearing off my jacket. Some of my hair snags on one of my brooches and I yelp, fighting my way free.

'What are you doing? Fran—'

'I *hate* this jacket. I hate – I hate . . .' I hate the person who clung to it for almost two years like a talisman, a promise. I hate that it suddenly feels like some sort of a claim Marcus has on me, when the reality is he probably never even noticed that it's his, all those times he's seen me wear it.

I wrench my arms free, hurling the jacket onto the floor and breathing hard. My cheeks are wet all over again, and I'm surprised I have any tears left to cry.

'Are you—'

There's the *clack!* of heels on the floor as someone

265

approaches, and Leon turns pale, alarm flitting over his face as he looks towards the entrance, mortified at being found in the ladies' toilets.

He makes a snap decision, snatching my wrist to haul me with him, locking both of us inside a toilet stall just as someone comes into the bathroom. One of his hands presses into the door beside my head and my brain catches up all at once, realising that his body isn't just crowding mine against the door but is almost flush against me. My hips are pressed into his thigh. His cheek rests against the side of my head. When I breathe in, my chest grazes his torso.

I tilt my head back to look at him, and Leon shifts only slightly back, enough to look down at me. There's a question written on his face; his attention is still on the other person in the bathroom, listening, waiting for them to leave.

'I don't think I needed to hide, too,' I whisper. 'I'm allowed to be in here.'

He flushes, and I bite down a giggle. It turns into a sort of hiccup in my throat, which is still thick and raw from crying, but my reaction has him relax, a bit of a smile curving at his mouth. As some of the tension eases out of him, I feel his body sink a little more against mine.

It's strange, if only for how pleasant it feels.

'Shh,' he whispers back, 'before we get caught.'

I turn my face to reach his ear, so I can whisper even more quietly, 'I think hiding in a toilet stall with a girl is a *lot* more compromising than handing her tissues because she's crying by the sink.'

I misjudge it a bit, because my mouth ends up grazing the edge of his earlobe when I speak, and this time it's Leon's turn to sputter out a choked sound and my turn to shush him, which threatens to set me off into a whole new fit of giggles. This whole situation is so absurd, I can't even feel shy about the implications of us hiding out in here like this.

'Do you think people *actually* have sex in these?' I whisper.

Leon glances around. 'Well they *are* big enough. Look, there's even a mirror on the door. Kinky.'

I glance to my left to see the thin, full-length panel of mirror on the door just behind me – which is quite thoughtful decorating, given the limited facilities of an airport. I've seen hotel rooms with less. But Leon catches my eye and waggles his eyebrows, and I have to look away, shaking with silent laughter now.

Then he jokes, 'Do you think it counts as the mile high club, if it's just an airport?'

I can't contain myself then, but no sooner has a squeal of laughter left my mouth than he's pressing two fingers to my lips and shushing me.

Which works – a bit too well, because I'm startled into silence by the feeling of his calloused fingertips against my mouth, and I know the absolute absurdity of this situation has just gotten the better of us and he didn't mean anything by it, but it's so oddly intimate, even without the fact our bodies are still pressed up against each other, and I can only stare at him, my breathing suddenly so loud in the confined space, and his eyes are so impossibly dark and so impossibly intent on me that it feels like his gaze could swallow me whole.

As if catching himself, he moves his hand away.

I'm holding onto his sleeve, not quite sure when I reached for it.

267

I don't know which of us prompts it to happen, but his hand settles on the side of my neck, large and solid and warm, winding his fingers through some of my hair, and again, so oddly intimate – it's only my neck, but when was the last time someone touched me there, held me this tenderly? It's so much more intimate than a hug, or even maybe a kiss. My emotions all feel too close to the surface right now, and I'm absolutely powerless to resist the full-body shiver that ripples down my spine at the intensity of such a small, simple touch.

His breath fans across my face. Sweet, like blackcurrant, like apples.

We're both caught completely in the moment, barely breathing. Is his heart thundering the way mine is? Is he leaning in just a little, or is that me?

Are we really about to –?

Someone smacks the flat of their palm against the door right behind my head and I yelp, jolting away from it, stepping on Leon's feet. He stumbles back, falling almost onto the toilet and barely catching himself, a hand flung out to each wall of the stall.

His eyes are blown wide and his cheeks are bright pink, the blush spreading all the way down his neck from the embarrassment of being caught (as if it would be from anything else . . .) and he's stuck with his legs bent in front of him and arms akimbo, squatting barely above the toilet bowl.

He sets off the automatic flush. Some of the water splashes up onto the seat of his jeans.

'Excuse me!' shrills a posh voice on the other side of the door.

Leon cuts me a look, eyes narrowing and head angling as

if to say, *Don't you dare*, even as a hint of mischief tugs at the corners of his lips.

I stuff a fist into my mouth, unable to look away. His eyebrows tug lower as if to warn me to stay quiet, and I am barely holding it together anymore. Leon bites the inside of his cheek, shaking as he tries not to laugh too.

'Stop it,' he hisses, 'I'm gonna fall.'

Oh, he is, any moment – and he's at such an odd angle, I wouldn't be surprised if he drops right into the toilet rather than simply onto the seat. I take pity, trying to manoeuvre myself underneath one of his arms to help him up, which has us both staggering about in a bundle of flailing limbs, fighting to keep our balance. Leon trips forward, but when I fling my arm forward to try to catch him, he's already caught himself and instead his head collides right with my elbow.

I let out a strangled yelp at the judder that goes all the way up my arm from my funny bone, and Leon groans.

The woman outside our cubicle gives a scandalised cry. 'I don't know who's in there, but this is a *public space*! There are *children* around! You should *not* be fornicating in there! This is diabolical! You should be ashamed of yourselves, the pair of you! And in a *toilet*!'

Posh lady smacks the door a few more times before harrumphing.

'I should fetch security on the pair of you. This is absolutely shameless! And leaving your clothes strewn all about the floor, too!'

My denim jacket comes hurtling over the top of the door. I fumble to catch it, feeling suitably chastised even as the lady storms out before we can argue that we weren't doing anything wrong.

I don't *think* we were, anyway.

Although for a moment there . . .

For a moment, it did almost get quite close to . . . to *something* . . .

What am I doing? Crying over a man who's about to marry someone else, locked in an airport toilet with the bride's brother? What *has* my life come to? I'm sure this part wasn't in any of the romcom films building up to an epic grand gesture and a declaration of romance.

Defeated, and feeling less an idiot and more completely at sea, I unlock the door and say, 'Come on, I suppose we'd better go before she *does* go and get security.'

Time until 'I Do'

8 hours

Chapter Thirty-four

Gemma

I play the video again, watching Kayleigh snog the silver, nearly naked cowboy, waiting to feel something. *Anything*. A flicker of resentment. Just a little glimmer of jealousy. A tiny drop of bitterness.

But I don't feel any of that stuff, and my phone screen flashes up a reminder that my battery is down to ten per cent. I dismiss it and let the video play again.

I can't even conjure up the sweet, sweet mental image of the carnage it would unleash at the wedding if it played on the screen during my positively saccharine (but frankly hilarious) speech.

There's just . . .

Nothing.

There's just me, in this huge, empty, dark room, in the dead of night, with nothing to lose and . . . and *nothing*, period.

Just like I worried would happen if I ever tried to confront Kayleigh, she's already won our friends over to her side, tarnished my name with what I'm willing to bet are a thousand little white lies.

Oh, Gemma can't make it to drinks to celebrate my new job! She must be so upset she didn't get it, poor thing; let's not mention the fact I didn't invite her and she still doesn't know I got the promotion.

Gemma put work above coming to my wedding; poor little pushover Gemma trying so hard to make her best pal happy just to feel a scrap of love; selfish nasty stuck-up Gemma . . .

I bet I know exactly the story Kayleigh's been pushing. Selfish, selfish me.

It's the story Mum pushed for long enough. *Selfish Gemma, not everything's about you; selfish Gemma, so demanding and needy – if you were better behaved, if you weren't so much trouble, if you were quieter and if you weren't here at all, your dad wouldn't have left us, would he? Selfish, selfish Gemma, as if it's not hard enough to date as a forty-year-old divorcee? I've got you to deal with, too, and what man wants that?*

Adult me can recognise that the breakdown of my parents' relationship was not my fault. They argued non-stop about money and fought about both wanting to go out and live their lives, but they had this kid to look after instead, and my dad was constantly between jobs and my mum accused him of not being 'man enough' to look after his family instead of going to get a job herself.

Adult me knows, quite rationally, that Dad leaving and never showing up for me, even after he got his life together and built a new family, says more about him than it does about me. And Mum's constant exasperation and bad attitude preceded me by a country mile; it was never me that was the problem.

Except it always felt that way. Dad dropped us and Mum got saddled with me, and couldn't wait to wash her hands of me too. And Brittney was no better, when push came to shove. She lulled me into this feeling of security – of being loved, and wanted, and teased this lovely little future for the two of us that was so picture-perfect . . .

Until she got sick of me and walked out, too.

Kayleigh is the *only* person who hasn't.

I swipe the video off my screen, suddenly not so sure I have it in me to play it if it means risking our friendship for good. Our toxic, sickening, twisted friendship.

It's something, though, and isn't that better than nothing at all?

The door pushes open, and a beam of white light cuts through the darkness.

'Thank God,' I call over, relieved for the distraction from my own thoughts. 'I was starting to worry! Are you two all sorted now?'

A figure takes shape, silhouetted behind the torch. A man. I don't see Fran anywhere, and I swear to God, if Leon's left her bawling her eyes out in the loos, I'll be having *very* strong words with him. She strikes me as such a fragile soul, and she's so bloody *nice*, it's like kicking a puppy.

I mean, sure, he didn't say anything that wasn't *factually correct*, but still. The girl's going through it. Cut her some slack, you know?

But before I can tell Leon off, the shadow is barking, '*Qu'est que vous faisez ici? Mademoiselle, levez-vous, s'il vous plait.*'

'Oh! Er, sorry.' I scramble to my feet, holding my hands up in the very picture of innocence with the most polite smile I can muster when I am gradually losing my mind over the course of this layover. I respond in my very best French, 'So sorry. The door was unlocked, and my friends and I were looking for somewhere to sit. It's just *so* busy out there! Can't even hear yourself think, can you? Are we not allowed to be in here?'

The man lowers the torch a bit, and I see him scowling. It's a security guard with a big, bristly grey moustache. 'No, mademoiselle, you are not allowed to be in here. Where are your friends?'

'They went to the toilet. Gosh, I had *no* idea! So sorry, again. I'll just get our things and be out of your hair, shall I?'

He glares at me, unconvinced, and the torchlight sweeps over our collection of food, the suitcases, the bottle of whisky next to me. I suddenly panic that maybe I *am* going to be thrown in a French prison and forced to trade my bra for cigarettes like Bridget Jones. I don't even *smoke*.

I blather on about how hectic it is in the terminal and how simply *impossible* it is to find a seat anywhere, what a nightmare all these delayed flights are for everyone. I even thank my moustachioed security pal for letting me know this place is out of bounds, how I would *hate* to cause trouble when they have so much going on.

'. . . I mean, gosh, those Disney dads earlier! I saw them fighting. *So* terrible.'

He softens just a little bit, moustache bristling in a friendlier way this time. 'It is not the first time we have had a fistfight between Disney parents. The first time it was over who was the better Genie, though.'

I raise an eyebrow. 'Did they decide on a winner at least?'

'They were all equally terrible.'

Laughing, I try to wrangle all the bags and suitcases, but it's not as easy as Leon made it look earlier, especially now we have all the food, too.

Then I beam at the security guard. 'Could you help me with the bags, please?'

*

I'm sat on the floor – again – but at least this time I'm leaning against the end of a row of seats and have my phone plugged in to charge, so, silver linings and all that. And I've got a great view when a woman in a Barbour jacket and heels storms out of the loos muttering, 'Well, I never! Absolutely deplorable behaviour . . .!' and then mere moments later, Leon and Fran walk out looking decidedly rumpled, cheeks flushed, and furtive expressions on their faces. Fran's face is bright pink, and she looks all squirmy.

She spots me first, nudging Leon to point me out.

I'm hyper-aware of the fact that I'm pretty sure they should both despise and condemn me right now after I revealed my video 'mix-up' plans, but this is too good. How am I supposed to be busy feeling guilty and awful when they're going to show up, *together*, looking like this?

'Don't tell me that you two were party to some *deplorable behaviour* in those toilets,' I say, doing nothing to hide the giant grin on my face. It's all the more delightfully scandalous for it being meek Fran and awkward Leon. I would've thought a promenade through the gardens during a ball would be more scandal than either of them could handle – even in this day and age.

Will I get to be the maid of honour at their wedding? I *am* practically responsible for making this happen, I am sure of it. I mean, I did tell him to go after her.

I'm a total matchmaker. Emma Woodhouse, eat your heart out.

I say, 'Have you been shagging in the loos? Please say yes. Let me live vicariously through you.'

'We were not shag—' Fran cuts off, turning even brighter pink, realising how loud she was just being. She is doing precisely nothing to help her case, and I am fizzing with second-hand excitement. Who knew Leon had it in him? She clambers down next to me, cross-legged, and hisses, 'We were *not* shagging. We just – talked.'

'Oh, is that what the kids are calling it these days?'

I waggle my eyebrows at Leon, who glowers in response, and I hoot with laughter.

'What happened to your hide-out upstairs?' Leon asks me. He joins us on the floor; he starts to sit down next to Fran, then blushes, and moves to plop down on my other side instead. My, is the sexual tension so great they'll jump each other's bones if they're less than six inches apart? I almost crack a joke about it, but decide to spare them both. I'm not entirely sure if I'm forgiven, or if they're just distracted.

I wave a hand. 'Got kicked out by security. It's alright, though. He helped carry all our stuff downstairs, and I am not in a French prison, so I'd say that's a very good outcome all in all.'

Leon rolls his eyes and gives a soft chuckle, then opens up the last pizza box. My stomach growls, a booze-induced hunger hitting me at the smell of greasy cheese. I snatch up a slice, shoving it almost whole into my mouth.

Meanwhile, Leon waits for Fran to take a slice before getting one for himself. Oh my God, precious, they're like teenagers at the cinema too shy to let their hands touch as they grab for the popcorn.

It'd be perfect, if she weren't hopelessly in love with that douchebag Marcus.

As we chow down the pizza and dip into some crisps, too, the three of us sit in what I might call, dare I say it, *companionable silence.*

We're all just tired, really, I think. We've been drinking and it's been a hell of a day and we're all dealing with a lot.

So it's not that I'm forgiven, only that they don't have the energy to go on the attack and berate me. And it's not that they're choosing to stick with me; it's just that they don't really have anywhere else to go.

Another flight gets called to its boarding gate, and when I look around, distractedly people-watching, I realise the airport is getting pretty empty. The hubbub dies down, leaving it near-silent. Someone is snoring – great, big, rattling sounds that drift down from the food-court balcony. A kid is watching *Bluey* on an iPad, the volume low, and two women in the seats behind bop along to the title music, giggling quietly to themselves. The maybe-siblings/maybe-married ginger pair are sat side by side still; her head is on his shoulder as she snoozes, but that doesn't really prove anything either way . . . So annoying. I *need* to know. Is it rude to ask them outright? The messy gym-bro kid with the macarons and thong to woo his gal is sat on the stairs, rucksack hugged to him and fast asleep, a line of drool at the edge of his mouth.

I eye the Ladurée bag poking out the top of his rucksack, then root around our things for the three boxes I got at a steep end-of-day discount that we never got around to eating earlier.

As Fran opens her box to peruse, Leon only holds his in his lap and looks at me with an unnerving focus that makes my skin itch. He takes a deep breath before he speaks, and my spine goes stiff, my lungs squeezing tight.

'I don't think it's a good idea for you to play the video, Gem.'

I snort. 'You would say that. I'll cut the bit about your family, don't worry, but—'

'No, I mean it. Nobody's going to believe it was an accident, and it's going to make you look just as bad as Kay – worse, maybe. I'm not saying you shouldn't show it to Marcus, maybe he deserves to know, but—'

'So *what* if it makes me look bad? Who cares?' I should laugh, and roll my eyes, but I can't quite bring myself to do anything except pick a few flakes of blue off the Marie-Antoinette tea macaron in my box. I can't even look in Leon's direction, even as his gaze bores into my skull. 'You saw those messages, what she says about me. It's not like I've got anything left to lose. And Kayleigh . . .'

She's got so much to lose.

So much I want to *take from her*, like she's done to me over the years.

That thought swells in my chest, but it's not with the anger I'm used to. It's something heavy and wet and painful.

I close the box, my treasured French desserts suddenly losing all their appeal. I mutter something about being tired, and huddle down over my suitcase, arms folded under my head, where I can pretend to go to sleep, and they don't have to see me cry.

Chapter Thirty-five

Leon

I'm not so sure Gemma's *that* tired all of a sudden – exhausted, yes, but not sleepy – except Francesca clicks her tongue gently and unbundles her denim jacket, draping it over Gemma's shoulders like a blanket. She rests a hand on Gemma's back for a moment, almost like she's saying, *I'm here*, or, *We've got you*, and it makes me think again: *She's too good for Marcus.*

The thought sends me straight back to our interaction in the women's loos. Not the part where I told her I thought she was worth more, but the part where I freaked out and locked us both in a cubicle, and the soft graze of her mouth at my ear, the press of her body into mine, the way her pale eyes blew dark when I touched her neck.

The memory has my heart thudding hard in my chest, my stomach tightening.

Not that I was going to – I don't know, kiss her, or anything. We barely know each other. She's in love with someone else.

But . . . would she have wanted me to kiss her? The way her breath caught, the way she looked at me . . .

I try to shove the image away, because it's not like it's

going to happen anyway. All it's doing is making my head feel like the bloody Gordian Knot, except I don't have a sword to hack it apart with and try to make sense of.

Is this how Francesca feels about Marcus? A few looks, a kiss, a handful of flirty moments, and it's tangled her up into this great big mess where the only way through it is one drastic, unthinkable thing, like confessing her feelings before he makes it to the altar? If this is only an inkling of how she's feeling, I suddenly don't blame her for coming up with such an outrageous plan.

Francesca pulls away from Gemma to sit cross-legged, the green Ladurée box open on her lap as she browses the macarons. I don't think she's looked me in the eye once since our pseudo-walk of shame out of the toilets; but then again, I'm not so sure I haven't avoided meeting her gaze, too.

It was . . . a weird moment, back there.

Maybe fuelled by booze or proximity or that way she ticks her head to the side when she smiles. Probably nothing I should be dwelling on.

There's a little card inside the box listing the different flavours. I pick out a passionfruit one, offering it to Francesca.

'Want to trade?'

'Sorry?'

'For the pistachio one. You said earlier you don't like them.'

She jerks, blinking rapidly, and searches my face for a moment before accepting the orangey-yellow dessert and swapping it for a pale green one, and smiles brightly at me. 'Thanks.'

'Sure.'

282

She takes a bite of it, and I'm a beat too late in looking away, my eyes snagging on the way her teeth sink delicately into the biscuit, the drag of her lips wrapping around it.

Definitely the booze, and the fact we've been stuck here for hours. Maybe a bit of wedding fever, even, and my own lacklustre dating life.

Definitely *not* Francesca.

For a few minutes we sit quietly eating the macarons. She takes a tiny bite out of several, sampling them, and I watch her pull faces as she reacts to the tastes – the scrunch of her nose over the rose one, the appreciative way her eyes widen and she nods to herself at the matcha.

It's very different to how I pop the entire raspberry one into my mouth.

Francesca's been watching me too, though, because as soon as I bite into it I blurt, 'Oh my *God*,' and she laughs.

'It's like eating a whole berry, isn't it?'

I nod, savouring the taste now – which is so zingy and fresh, it's less like eating a biscuit and more . . . well, like she said, a whole raspberry. I've never known anything like it.

'The lemon one's good, too, if you liked that. The Marie Antoinette one's sort of . . . earthy? Like an Earl Grey.'

I follow her lead, taking a smaller bite of the blue macaron next. 'Huh, you're right. It is earthy.' It's not really my taste, and I regret not saving the raspberry one now. Francesca must read that on my face, because she laughs again, and snaps a bit off her raspberry macaron to hand me the half without a bite taken out of it.

I do the same with the Marie Antoinette one, and we make another trade.

'I've never been to France,' she murmurs. 'But I think this is mostly what I thought it'd be like. Sitting around eating macarons and being a bit liberal with alcohol and having deep conversations about life and love.'

'With almost twelve hours to kill, maybe we should've tried to get a train into Paris.'

I don't know what makes me say it, but suddenly I'm imagining the Eiffel Tower sparkling against a night sky, and a small, warm hand in mine at a little bistro by the Seine, and a smile so big her cheek is tucked all the way into her shoulder.

Francesca says, 'Oh, please, I don't think you even really wanted us to join you for a cup of tea after we sorted out the flight! There is no way you would've gone exploring Paris with me.'

I hum, conceding the point, but tell her, 'I'm sorry, for the record, if I . . . came across badly. I'm not usually so . . . confrontational.' I twist a macaron around between my fingers, cringing at my earlier attitude. 'I know it's not an excuse for being rude, but – I mean, it's not like I have a very high opinion of Marcus, and I was kind of wound up about talking to Kay before the wedding and worrying I wouldn't make it in time, and then . . . You know, you show up, all sunshine and with those big eyes, and all I knew about you was that you trail around after Marcus, you flirt with him and act too cosy and familiar, and that even if he laughs about it, it obviously bothers Kay a bit. I didn't know if this was all just an act, or . . .'

'Wait, if *what* was an act? My – my friendship with Marcus?'

'No, the . . .' I wave a hand at her in an all-encompassing

gesture, but she pulls a quizzical face. 'You know, *you*. Being nice. Not . . . I dunno, I guess I was expecting someone more like . . .' I glance at Gemma. 'More . . . assertive?'

'Someone who'd actively plot to steal someone else's man,' Francesca offers, with a self-deprecating smile now, and she nods. More seriously, she says, 'It's alright. I get it. If he has made me into a bit of a joke, even if it's just to try and clear his conscience or pretend there's nothing between us, I don't imagine I made a very good impression before you even met me.'

'I don't imagine I made a very good impression even *after* you met me,' I say, and when she catches my eye, we both break into grins.

And, because I didn't say it earlier when she asked, I nod in the direction of my bag – Dad's bag, covered in all his mementos, and tell her, 'I don't really travel much because I feel like I need to be around for my family. Because my dad's not well. It's hard to shake how responsible I feel, sometimes, for them. I guess I do it so much they all just rely on me by default, so then I feel even *worse* about . . . It's kind of a cycle. It's nobody's fault. And I don't mind it, really; I *want* to be there for them. But . . . yeah. Mostly I live vicariously through my dad's stories of all the places he visited when he was younger.' I turn a macaron in my hand. 'I think I thought this was pretty much what going to Paris would be like, too.'

Francesca smiles; I can sense it even before I look up to meet her eye again. She reaches over to put her hand on my arm, and . . . I kind of appreciate that she doesn't say anything. Doesn't tell me I need to get a grip, get a life, like some of the girls I've dated have done; doesn't tell me how

285

sad and pathetic that sounds. Just smiles, like she's thanking me for telling her. It's . . . kind of nice.

The two of us lapse into quiet again, picking through some more of our macarons. Gemma is fast asleep now – her breathing is slow and steady and even, and her face has tilted to one side a bit. She looks peaceful. Her glasses sit at an awkward angle where she's got her face pressed into her arms, so I gently pull them off to keep them from breaking, setting them down safe, before Francesca pipes up again.

'Leon? Can I . . . can I ask you something?'

I look over, and she flushes.

'You don't have to answer. I don't expect you to, I mean, and I know I don't have much right to ask, so you can tell me if I'm sticking my nose in . . .'

Is this about what happened in the toilets?

The almost-maybe-might've-been kiss?

I wait, apprehensive, but Francesca asks, 'Why do you feel so responsible for the rest of your family? I realise your dad's not well and you want to help, but this talk you want to have with Kayleigh, the stuff you said about it being okay if she cuts you off as long as the rest of your family don't have to go through that, too . . . That's so much to take on, so I guess I just wondered . . . Why?'

She's the first person who's ever actually asked me that; even before I answer, I can feel relief sinking into my bones, a gladness to open up about it.

'It's because I *am* responsible for them. Maybe that seems stupid because both my parents are still around, but . . . I was thirteen when Dad got diagnosed with MS. He'd been sick for a while, but it reached a point where he and Mum

286

were constantly going back and forth to all these appointments, trying to get answers, figure out medication and therapies and regimens that would help keep it under control and stuff, so I had to help take care of the girls a bit. Myleene was only a toddler, and Kay's world was basically plans with friends and hockey practice and new pencil cases and lip gloss, so she wasn't as aware of everything that was going on.

'We had Nana, of course. She was around a lot. And nobody asked me, but it was . . . it was like this unwritten rule, I guess. I was the oldest: I needed to step up, I needed to help out; so I did. And now we're pretty much all grown up . . . I mean, Myleene still lives at home, and Dad's still not well. He's okay,' I add quickly, when Francesca's face falls in sympathy, 'and he can still do most things, but when he does have an episode, it's – it's hard to see. It's tough on everyone. It takes him longer to recover these days than it used to, and that's only going to get worse as time goes on.'

It's why I never went away to uni. I got my qualifications from a local college and through online courses instead. It's why I haven't moved away, even now – so that Kay and Myleene are free to, and so someone is still there for Mum and Dad when they need help. It's why I find dating hard, because even though my family aren't a burden to me, it feels like I'd be burdening someone else who didn't choose it.

'Don't get me wrong,' I tell Francesca, 'I love my family, I'm happy to be there for them; I wouldn't have it any other way. But when my nana got sick . . . She always told me I'd need to look out for them, but it always felt like we were a team; now, it'd just be *me*. And I told you guys what it's like when Kay and Marcus visit: it really hurts my parents to see her pushing them away. Myleene absolutely idolises her, too, so she's willing to overlook it all just to feel like she's still got her cool big sister around.'

I can't help but glance at Gemma again. Maybe she's more like Myleene than she is like Kay; maybe I haven't been giving her enough credit, all these years.

'And this feels like something I can fix,' I tell Francesca, only realising how true it is now that I'm saying it out loud. 'Instead of just trying to hold it together or patch it up afterwards. I can't fix the fact Nana's gone, I can't fix my dad's MS, but – I thought at least I could fix this.'

I surprise myself when the words crack, and Francesca goes a bit blurry. I blink a few times, clearing the tears from my eyes. She makes a soft sound and sets her macarons aside to prop herself up on her knees, leaning forward. She clasps one of my hands in hers, and her other rests on my left knee.

And I blurt, 'Except maybe I can't fix it after all. And I've failed.'

'Oh, Leon.'

She shuffles around, and even though, sitting, I'm still a head taller than her, Francesca wraps an arm around me and pulls me into her side so my head rests on her shoulder. She smells like coconut, which I noticed in the bathroom, but this time it doesn't make me repress the urge to bury my nose in the crook of her neck – it just makes me sink into her side and close my eyes.

'I know that it's easy to say, but in case it's helpful to hear it: you can't be responsible for how Kayleigh acts, and you haven't let anybody down if she keeps pushing you all away – whether the wedding goes ahead or you talk to her or not. But for what it's worth, I don't think it counts as failing if you try. That's more than most people would do.'

Maybe she's got a point, I think.

But maybe it's still not enough.

Time Until 'I Do'

6 ½ hours

Chapter Thirty-six

Francesca

I must have dozed off, because the next thing I know, there's a sound that's half a shout and half a grunt, and my eyes are snapping open. They're bleary, crusted with sleep, and it takes me several seconds to get my bearings.

We're sat on the airport floor, an almost-empty pizza box and half-eaten tube of Pringles in front of us. Leon is leaning against me, snoring quietly in gentle little snuffling sounds, and I've been resting against him. On his other side, just across from me, Gemma has startled herself awake – she's the one who made that sound in her sleep, and blinks as she looks around.

It's only when she squints at me and pats the top of her head that I remember Leon took her glasses off for her. I hand them over, trying not to jostle too much so I don't wake him up.

'Thanks,' Gemma mumbles, voice thick and slow, and she smacks her lips before yawning widely. It sets me off, too. She looks up at the board and groans. 'How is it barely even four o'clock? We've still got *ages* till our flight leaves!'

'Oh, I don't know, an hour and a half is nothing when we've been here for ten already.'

And, God, do I *feel* like I've spent ten hours in an airport. My whole body is stiff and aching, there's a disgusting taste in my mouth – I can't have brushed my teeth since breakfast-time yesterday – and there's a slightly fuzzy, disconnected feeling between my brain and body that hints at either still being a little bit drunk or else the beginnings of a hangover.

I'd give anything to have a hot bath and then burrow down into a big, soft, lovely bed, wrapped up in a terrycloth robe.

The wedding is in a little over six hours.

In six hours, I will know whether Marcus has chosen me or not.

Will I know if I want him to choose me, by then?

Gemma is pulling faces, running her tongue over her teeth, massaging a crick in her neck, and lifting up an arm to shamelessly sniff her armpit.

'Reckon they've got any showers around here?'

'Chance would be a fine thing,' I say.

But she gets up anyway, groaning as she stretches. 'There's got to be a lounge or something around here somewhere . . .' She looks down at me. 'You coming? I've got some under-eye masks if you want to borrow them.'

Which, presumably, means I could do with using them. My face *does* feel puffy; I can only imagine the state I must be in. Even if I weren't planning a romantic confession to Marcus, I can hardly show up at the wedding smelling of stale booze and looking a mess.

I consider letting Gemma go to look and report back. I don't want to be caught snooping around the wrong part of an airport, where they're so tight on security. Although after the carnage of this overnight stay – the obstacle-course games, the fist-fighting dads, sneaking into a shut-up restaurant . . .

What the hell?

'What about Leon?' I ask.

'Oh, he's a big boy, he'll be fine.'

But Gemma helps me manoeuvre him gently around so that instead of leaning on me, he's curled up on his suitcase much like she just was. We pillow his head with his satchel – I'm not sure how comfy it is, but at least if someone tries to steal it, it will wake him up – and take our own bags into the bathroom. The food and drinks we leave behind with Leon.

'Minesweeping is a bold move at the best of times, but in an *airport*?' Gemma says, and sucks her teeth before saying, 'Oof, wouldn't want to chance it. Might be anything in those bottles. Could be some kind of chemical explosive.'

'Gemma!' I hiss, horrified, looking around as if a SWAT team is already sprinting our way to tackle us. 'You can't say things like that in an airport!'

She rolls her eyes, and I smother a giggle into my hand. The two of us scout out the nooks and crannies of the airport terminal, searching down corridors between closed-for-the-night shops, trying doors just in case.

A slightly rumpled man in a suit walks past us, carrying a briefcase, and Gemma's face lights up. 'The diplomats! Duh! They're *bound* to have better facilities where all the staff and ambassadors cut through, right?'

'Um . . .'

But as she chases off down the path where the man just came from, we come face to face with a burly, grey-haired security guard with a thick moustache. He's the very opposite of an Inspector Clouseau type: I'm intimidated enough to try to hide behind Gemma a little bit. But then he quirks an eyebrow at Gemma, as if not surprised to see her in the least, and she says something in rapid French. I only catch the word '*douche*', and the security guard laughs.

He replies, and although Gemma tries again, she obviously fails because she turns back to me with a sigh.

'Apparently I've used up my "free pass to sneak into prohibited areas" already. Whoops. Oh well, pit wash in the sink it is.'

When we get to the loos, it's instantly clear that while Gemma merely looks worn out and rumpled, I am an absolute *wreck*. There's mascara smeared all around my eyes and my hair is somehow equal parts matted and frizzy. There are huge, dark shadows under my eyes – which are *also* red and puffy, and that's quite the feat, even if it is also a bit of a disaster.

Just as well we won't board for at least another hour! It might take me the better part of a week to put myself back to rights.

We set up with our suitcases open on the floor. Gemma peels off her shirt to stand there in just her bra, using hand soap and splashing water over herself. I hesitate for a minute before following suit, deciding I'd rather be clean than modest – it's not *that* different to being in a changing room at the gym, I reason, just with a little bit less dignity.

When Gemma flings a scoop of water up to her arm, it splashes all over me and I yelp, jumping away.

'Oops,' she says, not sounding very sorry at all.

I splash her back.

'Oi!' she shouts. 'I didn't do it on purpose!'

I splash her again, and she tries to run for cover before doubling back to flick some more water over me. We're both laughing, though, and there's a childish abandon about the whole thing that has me still grinning to myself even after we both go back to our awkward sink-washes.

We dry off with bunched-up wads of rough toilet paper. Gemma borrows my little travel-bottle of body wash, and lends me her dry shampoo and a pack of eye masks, which she applies for me.

'It feels like a sleepover,' I say. 'Like we'll do sparkly eyeshadow and silly hairstyles next.'

She smiles. 'God, I miss a good sleepover like that. We didn't know what we had when we were kids, huh? Now, you stay over with a friend, and it's all about having the *good* guest towels and making those pretentious little baskets of travel-minis for them to use.'

I must look at her blankly, because then she adds, 'Well. Maybe that's a bit of a Kayleigh thing.'

'I can't say any of my friends do that,' I tell her carefully, 'but it sounds nice.'

She snorts, but says, 'So what *are* your friends like? Are they totally Team Marcus, supporting women's rights *and* wrongs when it comes to their delulu bestie chasing an engaged man?'

I cringe. 'Actually, they . . . They don't know. Nobody does, except you and Leon.'

Gemma's eyes bug wide. 'Shut the front door. As if!'

'Well I told them everything when he stayed the night and after I rejected him, and it was all so humiliating and upsetting that afterwards, I just . . . They'd tried to bolster me back up by saying he wasn't worth it, and I didn't know

297

how to tell them. They'd have only told me the truth, and I suppose I knew I didn't really want to hear it.'

'Oh, Fran.' Gemma's face crumples in sympathy, but that only makes me feel worse – *guilty*, suddenly, not because of Marcus, but because of all I've been keeping from my nearest and dearest. They'll forgive me, I know that, and we'll laugh about it later down the line – but I also know it'll hurt them to find out the whole truth.

Loving Marcus has made me selfish in a way I don't recognise, and don't like.

'They're not like your gang from school,' I say softly to Gemma. 'There's six of us. We all lived together through uni and completely bonded. We've been there for each other's milestone moments – new jobs, moving house, getting a dog or getting pregnant or getting engaged . . . We share everything with each other. We're always there for each other.'

'Except about Marcus.'

I nod.

'Wasn't that kind of a red flag? If your friends are so great, I mean, wasn't that a sign, that they'd disapprove of this whole thing?'

'Yes, but it's a running joke with us how I pick rubbish boyfriends and always get my heart broken. I think I just . . . needed to believe this time it was different.'

Her head cocks to the side as she studies my face, her eyes soft and serious all at once. Gemma sets a gentle hand on my shoulder. 'Do you still believe that?'

I don't know. I wish I did, but I've romanticised too much of my relationship with Marcus, and coupled with him leading me on and all the little white lies I've told my friends and family, all the horrible truths I've learned tonight . . .

298

Is it too late to turn back? Or is the only way out *through*?

When I don't answer, Gemma just gives me a small smile and squeezes my shoulder. 'Well, if anybody's got this, it's you. I believe in you, babe.'

My heart swells as she turns away. Whatever Gemma believes about herself, I really don't think she is a bad person.

I do think, maybe, it's something she's heard enough that it's the part she thinks she has to play, which is such a sad thought. I watch her bend awkwardly next to the sink to wash her feet and I say, 'You know, Leon said something to me earlier that I'm . . . It rang a bit true, and it's something I think maybe you need to hear as well.'

'Oh yeah?' It comes out blasé but there's tension in her shoulders.

'He said that he wished I could see I was worth more. And . . . tonight, I've realised maybe that's true. That I've been accepting the bare minimum and thinking it's enough, and not knowing that I'm worth more – and deserve more – than that.'

Gemma scoffs, and lifts a playful eyebrow at me. 'I could've told you that, Fran. I think I *did*, in fact, when I pointed out that he was breadcrumbing you with those texts.'

'Well, you deserve more, too. And you're worth more. Your so-called best friend took the apartment you found, manipulated you out of a job that you created, even swanned in and stole the boy you were messaging before you could meet him. I know your relationship with Kayleigh goes back a long time, and there's more to it than just those things – and maybe that used to be the case, but it doesn't sound like it is anymore. When you talk about her, you don't sound happy, or like you're talking about someone you love so you accept them, faults and all. I think you should see that you're worth more, too.'

I think, for a moment, that I've gone too far. Gemma's teeth are gritted, and she's refusing to look at me.

Then she sighs, and it all starts spilling out.

'Yeah,' she begins, 'but Fran, if I don't have Kayleigh, I don't have *anyone*.'

She tells me about how her dad walked out when she was little and her mum blamed her for it; how her mum was busier dating than looking after Gemma, so Kayleigh was her lifeline; how, when they left for uni, that was the end of her relationship with her mum and she and Kayleigh both had their sights set on a bigger, better, more glamorous future than the one they'd had growing up. She tells me that while she craved success because it meant *stability*, Kayleigh just wanted a swanky lifestyle, resentful of the 'small' life she'd had growing up – which Gemma always envied, and which Kayleigh was too materialistic to ever really appreciate.

'As if the latest trendy top in River Island or the cool new bag from Topshop that was in *Cosmo* that month was worth more than having your mum there to pick you up from netball practice, or a dad around to take you to the cinema on the weekend,' she snipes, wiping away a tear.

She tells me that she and Kayleigh built their glamorous new lives like they dreamed of and Kayleigh was always there with her, so did it really matter if they weren't good for each other? And she tells me about Brittney, the ex who said she wanted all the things Gemma did – a home, a partner, a life together with some cats or maybe a dog, and a nice holiday every now and then, and no kids . . . And called her 'exhausting' and 'clingy' and broke up with her, when Gemma thought it was going so well.

'I probably was exhausting and clingy,' she tells me with a crooked grin. 'I am *very* hard work. I'm kind of a lot, I know. And FYI, I do not need the psychoanalysis work of you telling me I don't want kids because my childhood was so rough, thank you very much.'

'Oh! I wasn't going to.' It hadn't even crossed my mind.

Gemma blinks in shock, and I can see a pre-prepared rant dying on her lips. 'Right. Okay. Well. Sorry, it's just – I'm used to . . .' She swallows. 'The girls always say I'll change my mind when I'm older or it's just that I haven't met the right person to make me want kids, and Kayleigh likes to point out it's my "childhood trauma" that prevents me from ever being a mother. Like it's a personal failing or whatever. And not like I just think kids are kind of gross and a lot of hard work and, like, you know, I'm hard enough work on my own, thanks. It's not for me.'

'They do have *very* sticky hands,' I say, and Gemma laughs.

'Right? Thank you! Why are they always *so* sticky? Why? What are they doing? I don't want to know.' She fidgets a bit. 'I, uh . . . I do realise that it's a toxic friendship. For the record. And I know the obvious answer is to walk away.'

'But it's not that easy. I know.'

I think it's about time to take off the eye masks; I peel them away to rub in the left-behind serum, and am astonished at how well they've worked. I look halfway human again. It's a miracle.

I study my reflection, and it's hard to recognise myself in it. I no longer look like I've been dragged through a hedge backwards, but I do look like I've been through *something* – in a way that's squared my shoulders, has me standing a little bit taller, steadies my gaze.

This girl – she's someone who looks like she's worth more, and knows it.

Time until 'I Do'

5 ½ hours

Chapter Thirty-seven

Gemma

It's a big question: *are you worth more?*

It's the sort of thinking that gets you down if you give in to it too much; the kind of thing that sends you spiralling into an existential crisis.

But sometimes, you have to give in.

You have to finally acknowledge how you've carried around the weight of your parents' failures, or the blind eye you turned to your girlfriend's non-committal nature in favour of her breezy, borderline flaky personality that you thought would balance out your own inherent need for control . . . Or your best friend treating you like dirt for most of your adult life, telling yourself that as long as you found petty ways to return the favour, it didn't matter in the end, because you were just as bad as each other.

Because deep down, you believe you're a bad person, and this is exactly what you deserve.

This kind of thinking will bury you if you're not careful.

It buries me now. Presses down like a physical weight on my shoulders, my chest. It's leaden and suffocating and inescapable and I know, *I know*, that I can't keep running away and pretending it's not going to ruin me in the end.

Fran and I end up fannying about in the loos for ages, primping and preening so we aren't immortalised forever in wedding photos looking like we spent the night getting drunk and crying in an airport. We run out of time before we're able to do our makeup; our boarding gate is finally announced.

I could almost cry – with relief, or dread, or mostly just the fact that *this endless night is so very nearly over at last*.

We wake up Leon and dig out our passports and boarding passes before we finally, *finally*, put the terminal behind us. We pass by the rotating tower of mirrors and move into uncharted territory: the passport-control queue beyond.

I look back over my shoulder.

Is this what it feels like for those kids putting Disneyland behind them? A weird and wonderful land full of all the things your wildest imagination could never dream up.

I feel like I was a different person when I landed here twelve hours ago.

It definitely feels like it was a lot fucking longer than twelve hours ago.

Ours must be the last of the delayed flights playing catch-up from the storm. I recognise other overnighters in the queue: the ginger couple/not-couple, the stag do attendees looking *very* worse for wear but happy all being together, and I even see the guy with the sparkly hair, who looks dead on his feet and in need of a strong coffee. The collective sense of relief and exhaustion is palpable.

Leon stands with his arm brushing against Fran's; she's facing me, chattering about the three pools at the hotel and the sunrise hike she read about on the website, laughing when I pull a face because there's no fucking way I'm leaving my bed before ten a.m. tomorrow, thank you, especially not with the hangover I fully intend to give myself. When she turns to Leon, he pretends to be *very* busy with his phone, apparently also not a morning person. She clicks her tongue and gives him a playful shove in the arm, and his façade cracks to show a smile.

And I can't find it in me to resent this layover or this night, not one bit.

We're through passport control quickly enough; I'm first out, and the gate is only a few metres away. Most of the seats there (not that there are very many) are already taken and I drift over to the huge windows, dropping down cross-legged on the floor to stare out of them.

It's still dark out. The sky is tinged pink with hints of dawn visible through breaks in the clouds. The airport runways are lit up below in neat rows of tiny orange lights. An aeroplane passes overhead, little more than a blinking light in the sky.

From here, with the runways stretching out and the sky coming to life, the world looks like it could go on forever. It feels . . . huge.

I tuck my arms around my knees, hugging them to my chest.

It makes me feel so small, and there's something oddly comforting about that. It eases the weight that's been threatening to crush me for hours – years. I am so small, a speck of life in the vast universe; there is so much more out there than I can fathom. What's a stolen wedding idea and a promotion snatched from under my nose, when I'm barely a scratch on the surface of everything that's going on, everyone else living their lives, all those planets and stars spinning through the sky? What do I matter, in the face of all that?

I don't.

And yet.

Here I am, anyway.

Someone comes to sit down next to me, close enough that her arm presses into mine. On my other side, someone else knocks their suitcase over and then practically falls onto his arse when he sits, graceless and uncoordinated.

Fran leans her head on my shoulder. Leon plants his hand behind me, his arm tucking around me.

So, so small. With nothing to lose.

And yet.

It hurts a little less, watching our plane come into land at last. It taxis down the runway all the way to our gate, and there's a flurry of activity outside as ground crew springs into action.

It makes a little more sense, watching the sky bleed amber and gold and lilac, with yesterday feeling so far behind me it might as well have been another lifetime, happened to someone else.

Because Leon and Fran were right, weren't they? I could just walk away from the job. I could apply to other places, rather than stick it out working for Kayleigh just to prove some self-destructive point. I could look for other house-shares, somewhere that isn't tarnished by Kayleigh having left – or ever having lived there at all.

I don't *have* to put up with those things.

I can . . . be worth more.

I tilt my head back and let my eyes slide shut, inhaling deeply.

And exhale.

Inhale.

And exhale.

It's a big question, and those kinds of thoughts can send you spiralling into an existential crisis if you're not careful, but I think I have an answer.

I've never relied on anybody else, had to be independent, had to build myself up when nobody else would. Why am I constantly waiting for them to tell me I'm enough? My boss, a partner, even – *especially* – Kayleigh?

I can be all I need. It's up to me to decide that I'm enough, and that I'm worth more.

I am. I am, I am, I am.

Fran squeezes my arm. 'Come on, they're starting boarding.'

Leon gives me a hand up, and I take it.

Time until 'I Do'

2 ½ hours

Chapter Thirty-eight

Leon

I get the aisle seat this time, able to stretch out a little more. Gemma spends most of the flight with her nose pressed to the window watching the sunrise and looking deep in thought, and Francesca is tucked into the middle seat between us, reading on her Kindle. Every so often she throws a hand over her mouth or gives a quiet squeal of delight over something the characters do, which is more endearing than I'd like to admit.

Given that she's on her way to tell another man she's in love with him, and all.

The unhappy redheaded honeymooners are in the row in front, and by unspoken agreement, we take turns sneaking a glance between the seats at them to try and settle our debate. I'm *sure* I see her kiss him on the cheek at one point.

This time on the flight to Barcelona, I pull down my tray table and open my notebook, pressing the pages flat. I flip past all my irate scribbles from earlier about what a prat Marcus is and start writing. I'm sure when she wakes up, Myleene is going to be frantic with the realisation that I never sent her my speech in case I don't make it in time, but she'll get over it.

I'll be there.

And, if I need it, if the wedding goes ahead . . . I'll have a speech.

The first time we met Marcus, we weren't sure he'd stick around. After all – meeting the family on Christmas Day? That could be make-or-break for most relationships. A far cry from a cup of tea and some polite small talk, everything hinged on whether he liked sprouts or if he complained about the turkey being too dry, and if he was willing to endure the Doctor Who *special. Just imagine, if he beat Nana at charades – that would've been the end of it . . .*

I write my speech, still not sure if I'll need it, and by the time the plane is coming into land around eight a.m., the whole thing feels totally surreal. Almost like I never actually *expected* to get here at all.

And, despite all the time I had to think about it in Orly Airport Terminal 3, after everything Gemma said about Kay, the stomach-churning WhatsApp group chat reveal, the damning video from the hen do . . . Even after all that, I still don't feel like I know what to do any better now than I did on the flight out yesterday.

Is it worth telling Kay we don't think Marcus is good for her? Is it going to make any difference? Should I tell her that she'll lose us all if she carries on like this, and is that *really* what she wants? Will I live in regret if I keep my mouth shut – like Francesca was scared of doing? It's driven her to pretty drastic measures. Maybe I should do the same?

It's easy for Francesca to say I'm not responsible for how Kay treats our family, and it's easy for me to acknowledge that she's right – but *accepting* it, feeling like I don't have that duty to our family . . . That's a different thing altogether.

Come on, Nana, send me a sign.

314

The moment the plane lands and the seatbelt signs are off, it's like someone flips a switch in all three of us – because we snatch up our things, leap to our feet, scramble to be the first ones off the plane.

'T-minus two hours, thirty minutes till the ceremony,' I tell the girls, but they're both so distracted I'm not sure they hear.

Gemma's turning her phone on and whispering curses, tugging at her hair and chewing her lip, frantically sending messages about the flowers and the caterers and the photographers to the 'new' group chat, trying to corral some sense of order to problems they're already haranguing her about.

Francesca, meanwhile, turns into a bundle of nervous energy – or maybe it's excitable, I can't quite tell. She bounces on the balls of her feet, her whole body practically vibrating as she clutches her passport and Kindle to her chest and fidgets with one of the pins on her jacket. She stares ahead, hardly seeing, and I wonder if she's daydreaming about the movie-perfect scene in which she declares her love to Marcus and he scoops her up in his arms and . . .

It's like an episode of *Love Island*. How long will they actually last, out there in the real world?

I glance over at Gemma, who's sending a too-chipper voice note saying, 'Joss, babe, the seafood paella is *for this evening*, can you just ask the hotel to make sure it's signposted? They did confirm with me three days ago the calligrapher sent all the labels over, I did tell you guys this, haha! There's a vegan risotto alternative and they're serving family-style anyway, so it's totally no big, we thought this might happen. But like, hilarious, who needs to flag their dietary restrictions on the RSVP like they're supposed to? *Soooo* typical. Also, Andi, hon, the hairdresser *does* speak English, she's an ex-pat, so you do not need to find a translator for Kayleigh to make sure it's all "bueno" . . .'

When she finishes, Francesca says to her, 'You even *sound* like a different person when you talk to them, Gemma.'

Gemma flinches, but she and Francesca share a weighted look, and her smile is small and sorry for herself when she shrugs it off.

There's a sinking feeling in my stomach, the ghost of a thought circling the edges of my sleep-deprived and hungover brain, a conversation I should've had with Gemma that's only just occurring to me and that we never got around to having.

Now's not the time, but I make a mental note that later, I'll catch her, and we'll get around to it.

My own phone is pinging like mad with messages from my family – Dad's gone on his flight-tracker app and seen I've landed, he's checked the traffic and it's very busy getting out of Barcelona right now – there's been an accident on the main road. Myleene, predictably, has sent me an all-caps demand for my speech, and several memes, and a selfie of her throwing up a peace sign I think is ironic, with half a pain au chocolat shoved into her gob. There are texts from Mum, a few from some of the cousins, aunties and uncles in a wider group chat, and . . .

Nothing from Kay.

I mean, she's probably busy. She's getting married in a couple of hours. She'll be with the girls getting her hair and makeup done, getting ready, having a glass of bubbly. Of course she's not on her phone wondering if I've landed and will get there in time.

She's busy, and what bride is spending the morning attached to her phone anyway?

But I remember how she sounded in those texts about Gemma, and in that video, and I have to wonder just how much she cares.

Whether Kayleigh cares or not, though, I have to get there – we all do, and we're on a *real* time crunch now we've got wheels down and feet on the ground. The three of us leg it to passport control, past the luggage carousels, and into yet another airport terminal.

It's big and bright with sunlight, and there's a humidity in the air we didn't experience in Paris. I'm bolting towards the nearest 'SALIDA' sign when the girls shout my name to call me back, and I realise they haven't followed.

'We have to go,' I tell them, 'we've only got—'

'Two hours and three minutes until the ceremony, *yes*, I know,' Gemma cuts me off. 'But *we* have to get changed. I'm the maid of honour, I can't show up in this, and I have zero plans to flash a taxi driver while I get changed in the back of a cab.'

'Why didn't you do that earlier?'

'Are you shitting me? As if I was going to risk getting my oh-so-stunning bridesmaid dress dirty and creased, or smearing lipstick all over my face if we hit turbulence? Not worth it. Besides, *you* need to change, too – and brush your teeth and comb your hair, while you're at it.'

'Oh. Right.' She does have a point. The three of us look pretty travel-worn – although the girls seem reasonably fresh, all things considered. You'd never know they'd spent a fair chunk of time last night drinking heavily or crying. They even *smell* fresh, which is more than can be said for me . . .

Yeah, Gemma's got a very good point.

'Alright. Back here in ten minutes, okay?'

We all dash off, on a mission. A spray of deodorant and cologne, a quick tidy-up of my beard; I wet my hair a bit in the sink and dry it under a hand-dryer before doing my best to style my curls into something a bit tidier and tamer, then it's into a cubicle to put on my suit. I try not to hurry that bit, worried that I might accidentally drop a trouser leg in the toilet bowl or something.

Francesca would laugh if I did.

She has a really nice laugh.

I hope Marcus knows what he's throwing away – or else treasures what he gets with her.

I'm ready within ten minutes, and the girls emerge only a couple of minutes later. Francesca's hair has been piled up into an updo with a few loose bits framing her face and neck and – God, I really need to stop thinking about that moment we had, or how soft her skin is, because it is *not* my place to reach out and brush some of that hair away, or think about touching the soft skin of her neck again and the way she leant into me.

Her dress is floaty and dainty, a pale green floral number that makes her look like she stepped out of a fairy tale, paired with strappy brown sandals and gold jewellery that makes her skin look a deeper shade of brown. Her eyes are smudged with kohl and her lips are painted a deep, bold shade of red that I must stare at for a beat too long, because it makes her blush.

'You look . . .' I clear my throat, a bit stunned at being left speechless. I didn't think that actually happened to people in real life. I flounder for a word that would do her justice, but eventually settle on, 'You're a knockout.'

She blushes deeper, but beams at me.

Gemma throws an arm around her shoulder. 'Like someone you'd leave your fiancée at the altar for, right? Come on! No time to waste! *Allons-y!* Oops, no, wrong country. ¡*Vámonos*!'

She sets off at a quick march towards the exit, heels clacking and that monstrosity of a turquoise dress billowing out behind her in a series of ruffles. Francesca giggles, but glances at me with a quick smile before hurrying after her, leaving me to keep up.

We pass by the joint stag do that we played games with. They're waiting with a holiday rep for a bus to their hotel, and we get waylaid by a hasty round of goodbyes: 'It was *so* fun to meet you! Have a brilliant time celebrating! Enjoy the wedding! Enjoy the stag! Yeah, God, never want to have a layover like that again, haha! And that *dress*, OMG, it's even worse than I remember! The bride must hate you, lol! Kidding, babe, you're killing it.'

Gemma gives them the bag with our leftover booze, which they take with a rousing chorus of cheers. As we walk off she tells us, 'Don't worry, I kept the limoncello. We *definitely* earned it, however this fucking wedding goes.'

Near the doors, we skirt past the unhappy honeymooners, and the girl throws her arms in the air. 'I *told* you Mum wasn't coming to pick us up! What do you *mean* you didn't book a taxi? I swear to God, I got all the brains *and* all the good looks in that womb—'

Francesca cries out and jumps at me, looping her arm through mine just as Gemma bursts into laughter. 'Called it!'

'You did. Guess I lose,' I say, grinning, not feeling like much of a loser.

At the taxi rank, Gemma strides right past the queue, saying loudly, 'Sorry, everyone, sorry, it's an emergency – my best friend's wedding, I'm not going to make it in time! Have a heart! This is desperate times! Maid of honour reporting for duty! Brother of the bride and groom's best friend in tow! Make way!'

I don't know what magic she has in her veins, or maybe it's just that she can be a little bit scary when she wants to be, but nobody seems to object when the three of us cut to the front of the queue.

A guy steps forward and opens the back door of a cab, and Gemma slides on in. Francesca follows, scooting by with a yelped, 'I'm so sorry! It really is a bit of an emergency!'

'What the hell!' the guy shouts.

I grab their abandoned suitcases from the kerb and the driver and I hurl them into the boot, along with my own bags.

Gemma is shouting, 'It's my best friend's wedding! She will literally *kill me* if I miss it!'

'You don't understand,' the guy yells, 'I have to get to—'

I nudge past him too, prising his hand off the top of the door so I can pull it closed behind me as I squeeze in beside the girls.

'Sorry, mate.'

It's only after I pull the door closed and Gemma all but screams at our driver to *vámonos*, giving him the address of the hotel and saying we'll pay extra if he can get us there quickly, that I realise the guy whose taxi we just stole is the kid with silver hair. He's got a sad-looking bouquet of tulips in hand, now.

Francesca notices too, and pulls a sympathetic face.

'Oh, I hope his girlfriend isn't annoyed he's late.'

'She'll be more annoyed at the absolute state of him,' Gemma says. 'At least *we* bothered to scrub up well. Now hold my phone up for the camera – I need to do my eyeshadow.'

Time until 'I Do'

32 minutes

Chapter Thirty-nine

Francesca

We breathe a collective sigh of relief as our taxi pulls up at the venue, all piling out of the car. I'm sweating, although I can't tell if that's because I just spent over an hour packed into the back of a car between Gemma and Leon on a sunny Spanish morning with barely adequate aircon, or if it's all the adrenalin for what I'm about to do.

The wedding venue is a massive villa sprawling over a beautiful cliffside overlooking the beach. It's all white stone walls and terracotta tiles, with manicured gardens full of brightly coloured flowers and palm trees swaying gently in the ocean breeze. Even out here on the circular tiled driveway in front of a fountain, it screams luxury.

It's the perfect place for a wedding. So completely, utterly gorgeous.

Gemma half falls out of the taxi, throws her handbag at me, and hoicks up her skirts to sprint into the hotel.

'I'll see you two later!' she hollers over her shoulder, vanishing inside.

The driver gets our bags out of the boot; there's a porter in a crisp white and gold uniform coming over to take them for us.

And this is all suddenly starting to feel very *real*.

My dress flutters around my legs and I can taste the salt in the air, feel the lovely heat of the morning sunshine on my skin that seems to soothe my aching muscles, and somewhere inside – somewhere on the other side of this villa . . . is Marcus.

About to marry the wrong girl. Having feelings for me he's tried to squash. Mistakenly rejected after the romantic night we spent together. My best friend at work, the great love of my life.

Those things all sound so . . . *hollow*, now.

But I'm here. I'll always regret it otherwise. I have to do this.

Don't I?

'Er . . .' I turn awkwardly to Leon, holding out Gemma's handbag. 'Can you make sure that gets up to Gemma's room for her, please? I have to . . .'

'Right. Yeah. Course.' He coughs, takes the bag, and then we both stand there awkwardly for several seconds. 'Uh, good luck.'

'Thanks. You . . . you too.'

'Sure.'

I'm not even sure he's planning to speak to Kayleigh anymore, after everything Gemma told us. We never got around to talking about it, and then it got too late to ask, and . . .

'I hope, whatever you decide to do, it goes alright,' I tell him. 'I hope it's not too painful.'

Leon blinks a couple of times, seeming to let the words sink in, and then gives me a small smile. 'You too. I hope . . . I hope you get what you're looking for. What you deserve.'

If he'd said that when we first met in the airport, I would've taken those words as a harsh insult – but I understand, now, what he means. That I deserve *more*, not less.

Looking unsure of himself, Leon makes an awkward move forward like he's going in for a hug, and then thrusts out his hand. I almost want to laugh. He was pressed up against me in a toilet stall a few hours ago, but now he's blushing and offering me his hand to shake.

I take it, but rather than shake it, I squeeze it tight and use it to duck in close so I can kiss his cheek. 'I'll see you later.'

I tell the porter that I'll check in properly later and cast one last look at Leon before I dash inside to do exactly what I came here to do, and tell Marcus how I feel before it's too late.

It's like something out of a painting, the kind of scene so breathtaking that it stops you in your tracks while you take it all in. The lush gardens full of greenery and flowerbeds and topiary, the huge white pavilion adorned in gold accents and flowering vines in the centre of it all, the rows of white chairs surrounded by garlands of peonies and lilac and euca-lyptus, the water features and fountains adding a decadent ambiance to the gentle sound of crashing waves from the sea.

There's already quite a crowd gathered around the pavilion ready for the ceremony, and I spot him. Down at the end, a drink in hand, surrounded by his groomsmen, laughing at something someone just said.

He looks so handsome, even from all the way over here. The crisp sandstone-colour linen suit, the turquoise pocket square, the fact he isn't wearing a tie but has a few shirt buttons undone. The sunlight gilds his dark hair in a halo of gold, and his laugh rings out, warm and rich and inviting.

I take a breath. My hand shakes as I set it on the stone banister and descend the steps from the hotel terrace to the pavilion.

I feel like Cinderella arriving at the ball, can almost imagine the music swelling and birds twittering prettily as I enter the party in my lovely new dress, with my eyes only for the man I've come to see, just waiting for him to glance over – the way the world will stop turning and I will catch my breath, sure he does the same, how he will leave the conversation with his friends to walk towards me, drawn as if by a magnetism he can't avoid but doesn't want to anyway, and he'll reach me as I get to the bottom of the steps, and . . .

Will he stare? Look bowled over, be speechless?

Say something like, *You're a knockout?*

There are butterflies in my tummy.

And – nothing happens. None of it happens.

This is not a movie; I am not the main character. Nobody pays me any attention and the world doesn't come to a stop for the two of us, and I get all the way up to Marcus and his friends before he even notices me.

'Fran! Shit, there you are! You made it!'

He slings an arm around me, kissing my cheek.

'I made it. I promised, didn't I?' The words feel like a script, though. 'Listen, I just wondered, could we maybe—'

'All alright? Leon and Gem get here okay, too?'

'Yes. Yeah, they're—'

'Great stuff. Damn, you look good for someone who spent the night at an airport! Give us a twirl, babe, go on.'

Marcus takes my hand, lifting it over my head to spin me around.

It doesn't feel like I'm the centre of his world, like this is flirty and sweet. It feels cheap, and like I am on display.

Can he tell I'm wearing the new underwear? Why was I stupid enough to believe Gemma when she said it was to make *me* feel confident, not for his benefit? Right now it feels like just another way I'm a joke.

He laughs. The others join in. A girl – one of his uni friends, someone I've met at the dinner parties and get-togethers Kayleigh hosts – compliments my lipstick. I wait for that familiar flutter when Marcus's eyes linger on me for a moment, but it's nowhere to be found.

There's only the sound of my pulse roaring in my ears like the ocean.

Can we talk? Can I just borrow you for a moment? Can I have a quick word, please?

And I'll take his arm and we'll step to one side, and . . .

He presses his empty beer glass into my hand. 'Couldn't get me another one, could you, babe? Peroni – you know me, can't resist.' He winks, and where my heart would normally be in freefall, I'm only numb.

There's another girl in the group, an old housemate. She's saying something to Marcus and the others, picking up a thread of conversation I missed.

Marcus throws his head back when he laughs. He winks at this other girl, says to her, 'Don't tempt me, babe. I'm not married yet, hey?'

It's not like being doused in a bucket of cold water. It's not like being woken roughly out of a deep sleep, either.

It's a cold, sickening trickle down my spine, a medley of

guilt and shame and stupidity and self-pity and fury bleeding through me in a great, tangled mess, and none of them quite win out because the dominant feeling is just *numbness*.

All that time I wasted loving him . . .

All those daydreams, the effort and energy and emotion, all the times I fretted over what I did wrong and should've done differently, the smiles and texts I read too much into . . .

I stand a little straighter, a little taller. I feel more sure of myself now than ever before.

How did it take an overnight layover with total strangers for me to finally see?

I interrupt to say, 'I hope you have a really great day, Marcus. Congratulations.'

And when I walk away, I set his beer glass down on a passing tray, and go wait quietly out of the way until it's time to take our seats for the ceremony.

Time until 'I Do'

22 minutes

Chapter Forty

Gemma

It's not hard to find which suite is Kayleigh's – there's laughter and chatter spilling out of the room and a flurry of activity. Someone passes me with an empty bottle of champagne upturned in an ice bucket, and a man who looks like a photographer's assistant is running in with some wires.

I catch the door before it swings shut behind him, chest puffed with pride that I've made it in the nick of time. And I don't even look too shabby, all things considered. No maid of honour has ever done more than me.

'I'm here!' I sing out, striding into the room. It smells like hairspray. The girls are piled onto a lilac-upholstered chaise beneath the window while Kayleigh has some final touch-ups done on her hair, the photographers capturing every moment.

There's a beat of silence in the wake of my arrival, and my heart seizes. There's a kernel of panic suddenly in the pit of my stomach, and every split second the silence stretches out makes another one burst until I feel like I'm going to explode in a ball of flame.

I remember the WhatsApp chat I was never meant to see.

How little they all think of me. How unashamedly they ripped me to pieces, and how Kayleigh encouraged it. How they would *all* like it far better if I hadn't shown up at all.

What will they say about me now? That I'm an attention-seeker trying to steal the limelight, showing up at the last minute, trying to undermine Kayleigh on her big day out of jealousy? That I'm late and clearly couldn't be bothered to make the effort, so should just leave?

But then the room is full of shrieks and all four of them hurtle out of their seats to run over and squash me into a group hug.

Kayleigh grabs me tightest of all, squealing, 'OMG, you made it! I can't believe it! I know the girls said you'd landed and you were on the way but . . . Ohmigod, Gem! You're here! Stop, I'm going to ruin my makeup, you'll make me cry.' She pushes me away to waft a hand at her bone-dry eyes, laughing.

'You look gorge,' I tell her. Now Fran's pointed it out, I can *hear* the way my voice changes, the affect it takes on, more of a drawl. I literally change my whole voice to fit the lifestyle Kayleigh wants. How have I never noticed I do that before? 'Totally stunning.'

'Don't I?' She spins, just enough to swish the many layers of skirt. The dress is all beaded ivory and boned bodice and expensive silk. The skirt will detach later so that instead of the fuller, princess-style, she'll be left with a simpler shift look for the evening. Her hair – honey blonde with recently touched-up highlights, rather than the sandy, brownish colour of Leon's and Myleene's – is in soft, shiny waves that cascade over one shoulder, pinned with a glittering hair comb. She really does look beautiful.

'Let's get you in the chair, quick!' Kayleigh grabs my shoulders to propel me across the room, then touches my hair. 'Savannah will sort you out; she can fix this bird's nest right up . . .'

Oh, it doesn't look *that bad*.

Well. Maybe next to the rest of them with glossy, sleek styles, it does.

As hairdresser Savannah takes a pair of curling tongs and several hairpins to me, the girls all chatter at a hundred miles an hour.

Andi says, 'So much for a relaxing evening before the wedding, we were running around like headless chickens. It was such a pain you weren't here, Gem. You've been like Kayleigh's wedding planner! We were scrambling to try to fix things last minute.'

'You would not believe the nightmare we had with the flowers yesterday,' Joss tells me. 'Lavender, instead of lilacs! Luckily we got it sorted, though. You probably mis-typed it in one of your emails to them.'

'Bit of a waste of time planning a backup speech!' Laura says with a laugh. 'We were all ready to step up when you weren't going to make it. But I'm sure you'll smash it, Gem.'

'Ooh, no!' Kayleigh says. 'You girls should do yours anyway! After Gemma's. All the effort you put in for me yesterday and today . . . It's really the least I can do. And it would be *so* nice! You don't mind, do you, Gem?'

It doesn't sound like I've got much choice. I give a toothy smile in the mirror. *Surely they can see how fake it is? What the fuck are we all doing, pretending like this with each other?*

'Ohmigod no you guys *have* to! That'll be so fun,' I chirp. I'm sure they can't wait to upstage me.

There's a tiny voice in the back of my mind saying, *Good luck upstaging that video with the stripper*. But it drifts away as soon as it arrives, a wisp of smoke in the wind.

I listen with a sense of detachment as the girls continue to chatter. Joss, Andi and Laura tell me dramatic stories about yesterday and manage to throw some back-handed compliments in there to bruise my ego – which is familiar, but I don't snipe back the way I normally would, and we don't all laugh about it like it's some affectionate in-joke we're all in on together. Kayleigh needles me for gossip about Fran, making snide remarks and saying, 'I bet she shows up wearing white,' and, 'I can't wait to see the crushed look on her prissy little face when she realises *I* got the guy in the end.'

I end up telling her, 'You know, I didn't really see much of her in the airport,' just to shut her up.

With my hair done – curls revived and slicked with argan oil, a few pieces twisted back to frame my face – I pose for photos with the girls, and it feels like I'm watching it all happen *to* me, like an out-of-body experience. I watch my arms hug Kayleigh and our faces smush side-by-side, beaming for the camera. I watch my mouth open in a bright laugh as I squash into the middle of the chaise with them and hold up the glass of champagne I'm given as a prop.

When someone arrives to tell us it's time to go downstairs, I end up walking near Kayleigh while the others fall behind.

'I'm *so* relieved you finally know about the job,' she tells me in a breathy rush. 'It was killing me not to tell you! You're not upset, though, are you? I mean, you *know* it would've been way too much for you to take on. And I'm just better suited for it, at the end of the day.'

Snippets of that video from the hen do burn themselves into my brain.

I take a breath; I think about sitting by the window in the airport, and my resolve hardening on the flight.

'Totally,' I tell her. 'You know, I just don't think it's right for me.'

She squeezes my arm. It feels more like a pinch. 'I knew you'd understand.'

In that moment, I make up my mind.

While the photographer gets some solo shots of Kayleigh in the gardens on her way down to the pavilion, the girls and I go ahead.

'You know, Gem, it was really crap of you to leave us in the lurch like that,' says Joss. Her voice is arch and sharp, but there's a glint in her eye: she's absolutely *revelling* in my fuck-up.

Andi adds, 'It's her *wedding*. You couldn't make the effort for this one day?'

'You're so lucky to have Kayleigh,' Laura tells me. 'Nobody else would put up with that kind of bullshit from their "best friend".'

'You're so right,' I say. 'They wouldn't. But you know what else they wouldn't put up with? Getting kicked out of the group chat the night before the wedding so the rest of you can slag me off, when you're all too stupid to notice I had two different phones connected to the chat. But you're right. I'm *so* lucky.'

337

Joss turns bright red; Andi gasps. Laura goes deathly pale and her jaw hits the floor.

I smile serenely, and leave them behind. Most of the guests are seated now; Marcus is standing front and centre and gives me a smile and a nod. His groomsmen are lined up behind him. I can't see Leon anywhere, but Fran is dithering around like she's not sure exactly where to sit.

She spots me and honestly, she has the *most* expressive face. Her eyes widen a fraction, her eyebrows twist upwards in the middle, and she has this sorry little half-smile on her face that all seem to say, *Are you okay? You look nice.*

I give her an eye-roll and shrug one shoulder then smile, which I hope she takes to mean, *Eh, could be worse. I'm okay.* Then I jerk my head towards Marcus and mouth, 'What happened?'

Fran blushes and shakes her head. Intriguing! I will get the full story later. Did she think better of it? She looks way too calm and collected for someone who got rejected by the guy whose wedding she came to stop.

Then she mouths, 'Where's Leon?'

I shrug again.

Her face bunches into something full of concern, and I don't blame her. I really thought I'd gotten through to him about writing Kayleigh off as a lost cause, but if he's not here, he must have tried to corner her at the last minute . . .

It won't go well. Poor Leon, she'll tear him to pieces. He'll be too heartbroken at letting his family down to show his face. I should probably try to mediate, if nothing else, or – or I don't know. Do *something*.

Before I can decide whether to set off to look for him,

though, there's a man's voice screaming, 'Kayleigh! *KAY-LEIGH!* I'm here! Kayleigh, stop the wedding, I'm here!'

The entire congregation turns, people standing up to get a better look, and I hear the collective intake of breath as a guy comes running down the staircase, and—

'Oh my God,' I blurt. 'Holy shit.'

And careening towards the pavilion in a very rumpled, days-old T-shirt, a backpack knocking against him as he runs, sunlight glinting off the remnants of silver glitter in his hair, with limp tulips in hand and a green Ladurée bag . . . is the kid from the airport.

The one who bought the sparkly thong, whose taxi we stole.

Here, yelling for Kayleigh like a man possessed.

What the fuck is going on?

I'm too stunned to do anything but gawp.

Someone comes up next to me. 'Is that . . .?'

I tilt my head towards Fran, but can't take my eyes off the scene. The guy is breathing hard as he comes to a stop, eyes searching wildly. The guests are all murmuring and whispering behind us. A little way off, the bridesmaids are looking aghast, conspiring about what the best course of action is.

'That's the boy from the airport,' Fran says. 'What's he doing here?'

He shouts at us all, 'Am I too late? Has it started? Where is Kayleigh?'

I tell Fran, 'Looking for Kayleigh, apparently.'

And then Leon is appearing out of nowhere from a garden path, and he really does scrub up well in that navy suit. He spots us both immediately, but keeps his eyes on the inter-loper, scrutinising him.

'Wait. Wait, I know him.'

'Yeah, from the airport. He was almost as clumsy as you.'

'No, that's not . . . I think he's—'

And then Kayleigh arrives at the top of the stairs for her grand entrance. Except the band hasn't begun to play like they were supposed to, and we don't all stand up as one with a reverent gasp, and her eyes blow wide as she sees what all the commotion is about. She grabs her skirt in one hand, bouquet clenched in the other, and we all hear her saying, 'David, *what* are you doing here?'

I let out an actual shriek when he throws himself down on one knee, arms flung to the sides. I'm not the only one.

Leon says, 'It's the fucking stripper from the video.'

NOOOOOO.

Oh my God. Oh my God, it is. It's the silver cowboy!

'It is *not*,' Fran gasps.

'I didn't recognise him with all his clothes on!' I say, maybe a bit too loudly.

'I'm not too late! Thank God! I've been trying to get hold of you for ages! You stopped replying to my messages yesterday. I can't let you go through with this, Kayleigh. What we have is special. It's something worth fighting for, I just know it. I think you're the woman I want to spend the rest of my life with. That kiss rocked my world, baby. Didn't you feel the same way?'

Next to me, Fran cringes. She presses her face into my shoulder and groans quietly.

'Oh, God, I just heard it. Please tell me I didn't sound that pathetic.'

Leon and I exchange looks, biting back laughs. She groans again.

The bridesmaids have hurried forward, and Kayleigh is hissing at the stripper, her face contorted into something furious and ugly. Marcus has walked over, too.

'I know you felt it!' cowboy guy crows. 'I know we met on your hen do and it's only been a couple of weeks but it's you, baby. It's you. You're all I can think about. We're meant to be together, I just know it.'

I am screaming. Internally, obviously. This is pure fucking gold.

'Mate, who *are* you? Kay, who is this guy?' Marcus asks.

The stripper – David, apparently – stands up. He's all thick neck and beefy arms, which apart from the fact he can't be a day over twenty-two, does make Marcus look a bit like he's facing off against The Rock.

'I'm the guy she's meant to be with,' he declares, chest puffed up.

Kayleigh presses the heel of her wrist to her forehead, exasperated – angry at the disruption more than she is embarrassed. After all, this is not how she (we, I) planned this moment. David's spectacle is eating into her post-ceremony photo time.

She huffs, 'No, you're not. He's no one. He's a stripper we met on the hen do.'

Marcus laughs, pointing at him. 'What, the cowboy? As if!'

'We have something special!' David insists. '*We kissed.*'

There's a collective inhale from the congregation. Leon cringes, and on my other side Fran is clutching my arm tight and whispering, 'Don't you dare let me try to tell a man I

341

love him ever again. I cannot believe I was actually going to do *this*.'

Leon leans around me to look at her, wide-eyed. 'You didn't tell him?'

'No! I couldn't—'

I have to cut them off. 'I'm not being funny, you two, but save it for your next *deplorable* toilet trip. There is peak reality show-level drama unfolding here.'

Kayleigh gives Marcus a long-suffering look while he laughs, and the mood shifts so sharply I almost feel the wind change with it. There's no outrage from Marcus that his bride snogged another man only weeks ago; he thinks it's *funny*, and she is clearly only annoyed by this interruption in her otherwise perfect day – not humiliated, or even sorry. And Marcus just . . . *doesn't care*.

It's not even like he's trying to save face. He genuinely thinks this is going to be a funny story they tell about the day later, not something that would spoil it, or get between them.

Marcus claps David on the shoulder. 'Alright, mate, time to go. Unless you want to wait for them to ask if anyone objects?'

'*Don't* give him ideas,' Kayleigh snaps. 'David, get out.'

'But—'

'One kiss and a bit of harmless flirting doesn't mean I want you to fly halfway across Europe and ruin my wedding, for God's sake. Get a grip!' she sneers at him, then snatches the Ladurée bag out of his hands, passing it to Andi. I don't blame her; they are *really* good macarons, and would probably be wasted on David. 'Now take your pathetic flowers and sad attitude and go home.'

342

'I really hope she kept the thong,' I whisper to Fran, who snorts a laugh and draws a few glowers from guests. Even Leon has to choke down a chuckle, fighting to keep his face neutral.

David stands shocked for a moment, before stumbling back a few steps and fleeing the scene. I feel kind of bad for him, getting shot down like that – but you know, he did bring this humiliation on himself.

Marcus tells Kayleigh, 'You look gorgeous, babe.'

She beams. 'I know.'

'Ready to do this?'

'Well, I've got to do my entrance again. He ruined it.'

'Wouldn't have it any other way.' Marcus winks at her, and Kayleigh looks a little happier as she goes back up the stairs to have her big moment for the crowd and cameras, and an uneasy mutter sweeps through the guests. Marcus notices and calls to them, 'Nothing to see here, folks! Show's back on!'

He takes his spot back at the altar.

There's a lot of sidelong glances and hastily whispered conversations, but I hardly pay them any attention. Kayleigh's true colours got a reveal after all, and – shocker – nobody even cares that much. Especially not Marcus.

She really is the most like herself around him.

They're made for each other.

'I have to go,' I tell the other two. 'Catch you later? Cocktail hour?'

They both nod. Leon puts a hand on Fran's back, saying, 'Do you want to sit by us?'

'Oh! Yes, please.'

I leave them to it and go join the other bridesmaids. The

343

music starts up, and one by one, we make our way down the aisle as Kayleigh descends to the pavilion once more, with all eyes on her.

She wouldn't have it any other way.

I'm sure the only person who notices me smiling to myself is one of the photographers, busy capturing every inch of the wedding, but that's okay.

This will be the last thing I ever do for Kayleigh. I suppose I should do it well.

Time after 'I Do'

2 ½ hours

Chapter Forty-one

Leon

Cocktail hour is a blur after the ceremony. Mum and Myleene are aghast about the arrival of David the stripper, although Kay convinces them quickly enough to see the funny side, and Dad merely rolls his eyes when I catch his gaze.

None of us exactly say it, but I can feel the sadness in the air when my family watch Kay interacting with her other friends and Marcus's family. That withering, trembling, fragile scrap of hope that we won't lose her for good, this isn't the end – even if she hardly bothers to come speak to us for more than a minute or two, all the while looking for someone else to spend time with.

Mum and Dad go off to mingle with some of our extended family. I have to track down a chair to bring out for Dad – I don't know how many times we reminded Kay about it, could it really have been that difficult? – but they seem to be having a good enough time, in spite of it.

Myleene's been sticking to my side ever since the ceremony ended. Francesca vanished to chat to some work friends, which I think was really just an excuse to give me some time alone with my family.

'I wish you'd been here sooner,' Myleene tells me. 'I

kind of needed you. Mum keeps trying to find out if they're coming for Christmas, and I don't know what to say. Kay said she didn't know what their plans were, but . . . Well, Joss told me they've all booked to go skiing. So obviously Kay's lying, she's just trying to find a way to break it to us that she won't be home, and – do you think I should say something? She always comes home for Christmas. It's . . . it's like, the only time we *see* her, it feels like. But now, she's . . .'

'I'll talk to her,' I promise. There might not be anything I can do about the person Kay really is, but I'm still her big brother – and I can still tell her that if she won't tell Mum and Dad about the skiing trip, I will. 'That's not for you to worry about, My, okay? I'll handle it.'

Her relief is palpable. 'Thanks, Leon. God, I cannot *tell* you how much it was stressing me out. I don't like keeping secrets from Mum and Dad. We're not that sort of family.'

'No,' I agree. We aren't, but Kay's personality isn't a secret I'll be keeping. It's just a fact I have to let the rest of my family see for themselves. I so very nearly confronted Kay before the ceremony, but seeing her pose for a few solo shots in the gardens and order the photographer around – I knew it wouldn't make a difference. It didn't feel so much like chickening out or giving up as simply accepting a fact.

And I think I haven't been giving Myleene enough credit. She's more tuned in to Kay's attitude than I have been.

'It's not *fair*,' she whines now. 'I get that she's got this awesome new life that doesn't include us, but sometimes it feels like she doesn't want to bother with us *at all*. You should've seen the way she talked to Mum yesterday. All the olds were up dancing like I told you about, and Kay

348

went over and told Mum she was *embarrassing* her. It was horrible. And I thought maybe I should say something, but I didn't want to make it worse . . .'

'I'm sorry I wasn't here.'

'Oh, that's not your fault!' She elbows my side. 'But . . . would've been nice if you were. I thought, *Leon'd know how to handle it*. You always do. Like Nana.'

Maybe it's all the exhaustion and adrenalin and the sheer madness of the last twenty-four hours, but Myleene's words make emotion swell in my chest, and I give her a one-armed hug. She holds on tight, and then informs me that I smell like hangover, and offers me her sunglasses. They're shaped like hearts. I take them, strike a pose, and we both crack up laughing before she grabs a selfie.

'I know it's rough,' I tell her. 'But Kay's her own person, with or without Marcus around. I guess we just have to accept we're not always going to fit into her life these days. We'll be there if she ever wants to come back home, though.'

'It just *sucks*. I hate that this feels like goodbye.'

'I know, My.'

'I miss Nana,' she says.

'Yeah. Yeah, me too.'

But then Myleene snorts and adds, 'She'd have bloody hated this, mind. Can you imagine her face when that David showed up? Then again, she probably would've paid him to stay and give a performance at the reception, just to piss off Marcus.'

I crack up at the mental image. 'Maybe I should've done that. Reckon he's already on a flight back home, or can we still catch him?'

*

'Hi, everybody. Thanks all for being here today to celebrate Kay and Marcus,' I say, standing at the front of the packed dining tables arranged around the terrace with all eyes on me. 'For those of you who don't know me, I'm Kay's older brother, Leon. In lieu of a father-of-the-bride speech, this is a bit of a family-of-the-bride speech instead, on behalf of all of us.'

I talk about Kay's childhood, how she always wanted to play dress-up and made me play Barbies with her where they were doing impressive, girl-bossy jobs like she has now, and what a romantic at heart Kay's always been . . . How the way she and Marcus looked at each other lit up the room, you could tell they were meant to be . . .

I say all the bland empty pleasantries that I'm supposed to, and the crowd make all the right noises in all the right places. Kay and Marcus sit holding hands at the top table, smiling at each other.

I talk about the Christmas she brought him home to meet us for the first time and how the two of them are made for each other, and I couldn't imagine a couple better suited. I wish them every happiness in the life they are building together.

'Kay,' I wrap up, 'we love you, and even if you're moving on to make your own family, you'll always have a place at home with us.'

I mean it. But I also know what Myleene means: it feels like goodbye, more than anything else. And I feel like I've said all I can, if that is the case.

We all toast the happy couple, and I sit back down, a weight off my chest.

Francesca catches my eye from her table and gives me a warm smile that makes me feel like – yes, I got this right.

Gemma's speech is great. It's short and sweet, about the journey of Kay and Marcus's relationship and with a couple of funny stories from the wedding planning that get everybody laughing. The compilation video she made rolls in the background on a screen and there's not even a hint of David and the strip club in it.

'Kayleigh and I were fast friends at school, and inseparable ever since. We did everything together – we always have. People talk a lot about the impact romantic love has on their lives, but sometimes we forget about how monumentally the love between you and a good friend can change your life. And like all good love stories, there's a beginning, a middle, and an end. Kayleigh – I wish you all the best in this next chapter of your life.'

People coo, and raise their glasses as Gemma leads the toast, but I notice the sharp look Kayleigh cuts her, and I hear the words Gemma's not exactly saying.

I don't manage to catch her alone until a little while later – the speeches are done, coffees have been served, and she's leaning against a wall, tapping furiously away at her phone. I wonder if it's another wedding-related crisis.

'Good speech,' I tell her.

'Huh? Oh, thanks. You, too. Very restrained, minimal Marcus-bashing. Good job.'

'Everything okay?' I nod in the direction of her phone. It's an email, I can see now. Quite a long one.

Gemma takes a long, slow breath. She types out, *Regards, Gemma*, then hits send without so much as a quick proofread, and lowers her phone. 'Everything is *very* okay, actually. I just quit my job. Well – I'm sure I'll have to deal with some long, annoying conversations with HR on Tuesday morning

351

when they actually read my email, since it's bank holiday weekend and all, but.'

'But,' I repeat, and smile. 'You quit. Good for you. That's . . . I'm really proud of you, Gem. That sounds like a good move.'

'Yeah. Yeah, it does, doesn't it?' She nods with conviction now, and grins at me. 'I mean, it's kind of unhinged behaviour, I'm well aware, but – once this weekend is done, I'm *out*. Kaput. Finito. I am *away*. I've got enough of an emergency fund saved up to see me through till I find another job, but *anywhere* has got to be better than that place. Anywhere so long as I'm not working for a girl who stabs me in the back and cheats me out of things I've earned and deserve. And when I'm back, I'll start looking for another house-share. Maybe even leave London? I mean, there's nothing keeping me there. I could go to Bristol, maybe. Or Manchester. Edinburgh! Belfast! *Paris!* As long as I never have to see the inside of Orly fucking Airport ever again in my life . . . It's a clean slate, Leon. I could go anywhere. Do anything. Be . . .' She finally falters, her breath hitching and eyes shining. But she keeps smiling at me, shoulders squared, looking so completely sure of herself. 'Be someone else.'

'Be yourself,' I say, and she nods. A couple of rogue tears drop off the ends of her eyelashes, and I think I've seen her cry more in the last twenty-four hours than our whole lives put together.

'Yeah,' she says in a shaky voice. 'Myself. I like that.'

Just as we lapse into quiet and I'm trying to figure out how to say what I probably should've told her a while ago, Gemma laughs. 'Who knows? Maybe Fran's looking for a new flatmate. If she could put up with me for twelve hours in a Parisian airport, maybe she won't mind spending a bit more time with me. At least then I won't be totally alone and starting from scratch. Oh, God, *starting from scratch*. Isn't that a midlife crisis sort of thing? I'm only twenty-five!'

I wait for her to stop laughing, and tell her, 'You know you don't have to be alone, Gem, right? You've got us.'

She cuts me a dry look. 'What part of clean slate did you miss? I'm cutting Kayleigh out of my life. I don't—'

'Yeah, but . . . I mean, she's cutting *us* out, too, so it's not like you'd be running into each other constantly if you came to visit. Mum'd like it if you did, you know. She's always liked you. And you were always hanging around the house like you were part of the family anyway.'

'This better not be you trying to replace your sister with me. Although, admittedly, I am a *significant* upgrade.' She pauses for a moment. 'And I *do* really love your mum's roast dinners. She makes the best lamb.'

I grin and knock my shoulder against hers. 'Of course that's not what I'm doing, you muppet. I just . . . I want you to know, that's all. You're welcome any time. You always have been. You send each of us a bloody birthday card every year.'

'Of course I do! It's only a birthday card, though, it's not that deep.'

It's more than Kay has remembered lately, but I don't point that out. I just roll my eyes, and when Gemma sniffles and throws her arms around me, I give her a hug back, and don't let go until she's ready.

It's not replacing Kay, because I really do mean it – Gemma's been like part of the family since Kay met her, too entwined in Kay's life for her not to become part of ours, too. And besides, if Kayleigh can move on and build her own sort of family, shouldn't Gemma be allowed to as well?

'Thanks, Leon. I'll take you up on that.'

'You'd better.'

She kisses my cheek before swanning off to pull up a chair by my parents. They light up when they see her, even though they've spoken a few times already over the course of the day. Dad laughs at something she says, and Mum's getting her phone out to show her photos of something while Gemma responds animatedly.

I catch Myleene's eye across the room, and she jerks a head in their direction quizzically. I shrug, she shrugs back, we end up caught in an elaborate, silent shrug-off until Myleene is too busy laughing to keep it up, and gives me the middle finger before heading off to chat to some of Marcus's work friends. I'm a bit worried she's got a mind to chat them *up*, but we'll deal with that later.

On the other side of the room, Kayleigh has a glass of champagne in her hand and is showing her rings off to some people I don't recognise. She looks totally in her element. She's hardly stopped smiling all day; she's glowing.

I really am glad she's happy.

But it's nice to finally accept that her happiness doesn't have to be at the expense of ours, and I head over to join my family with a smile on my face and a lightness in my chest.

I pass by the table with the couple of photos commemorating the loved ones who couldn't be here. There's one of Nana on her seventieth birthday at the *Mamma Mia* experience she went to with some friends, draped in a bright blue feather boa and wearing a giant badge and plastic heart-shaped sunglasses that match Myleene's, her wrinkled face beaming out of the photo at me.

Nana, I hope I did you proud.

A warm breeze skitters along the terrace, ruffling my hair. I decide to take it as a sign.

Time after 'I Do'

10 hours

Chapter Forty-two

Francesca

It really is a beautiful wedding, and Kayleigh has such immaculate taste. The venue is made soft and romantic with flower garlands and lanterns and candles, the turquoise accents tasteful and understated (with perhaps the lone, garish exception of Gemma's dress . . .) and the band play acoustic covers of love songs. It's pleasantly warm without being swelteringly hot, a nice breeze rolling in off the sea. The signature cocktails are delicious, the cake is to die for, and the food is some of the best I've ever tasted.

It is such a perfect day.

Apart from the fact that . . . I would rather be anywhere else.

It feels like I've stumbled into the wrong place – the wrong life, wrong body – and I'm just waiting for someone to notice that I'm a fraud and I don't belong. I can't believe I was *ever* planning to try to break off the wedding. I can't believe I ever thought it was a good idea to come here at all, or that Marcus thought it was even halfway acceptable to invite me in the first place.

It's a beautiful wedding, but I shouldn't be here.

The main subject of discussion at our table throughout

dinner is the arrival of David the stripper. I find myself blurting out that we saw him in the airport, which causes a riot of laughter as everyone wants to know more, even though I haven't got much to say. I don't mention the sparkly thong; it doesn't seem very fair to humiliate him further, even if he's long gone.

As if I didn't already feel silly enough for the feelings I was clinging to for Marcus, the entire embarrassing display David made proclaiming his love for Kayleigh was sobering, to say the least. A wake-up call that yesterday's version of me desperately needed.

Every time I look over at Marcus, it's like I'm seeing a stranger. Did I really find that smarmy smile so charming? His coiffed hair is always styled so pristinely and he frequently jokes about how long Kayleigh takes to get ready, but he surely can't be much better. And he *does* constantly interrupt; his voice is the loudest in the room, most people can hardly get a word in edgeways. Did I really find him so endearing?

Not just endearing, but so *everything* that I was willing to put my dignity, my heart, my soul on the line to see if he returned my feelings?

I keep looking over at him as the day goes on, trying to find a hint of those emotions, remember that spark – but there's *nothing*. And I breathe a sigh of relief each time I don't find it, glad that it seems to have vanished without a trace.

I've wasted more than enough of my time and my feelings on Marcus. I don't need to waste even more in getting over him.

Even the crowd from work have lost their usual lustre:

I'm normally so happy to be included and feel part of the cool, popular gang that I get swept away in their bawdy jokes and heavy drinking, but throughout the day I can't help but realise that I'm not truly having any fun *with* them.

The girl from Marcus's uni days is lovely, though, and her husband is really interesting, so I spend a lot of time chatting to them. And Kayleigh's family are brilliant, all good-humoured and smiley, so I spend a while with some of her cousins and aunts. I catch Gemma a couple of times, but always only briefly because she's so busy tending to an endless stream of wedding tasks for Kayleigh, and . . .

Well, I'm not sure if I'm avoiding Leon, or if it's only right to give him some space. He seems to be enjoying himself so I assume that, whether or not he spoke to Kayleigh, he's made his peace with it.

I just feel like such an intruder.

I came here for Marcus, to steal him away and break up the wedding. Leon wouldn't have even given me the time of day if we hadn't been stuck in that airport. We wouldn't even have met if . . .

There's a distant little whisper of a thought that says, *Maybe that's fate.*

But I'm being ridiculous. If there's one thing I have learned about myself in the last twenty-four hours, it is that I am *very* ridiculous. Especially when it comes to romance.

As the evening draws in, the tables are moved away to clear space on the terrace for a dance floor. The band is replaced by a DJ and the drinks flow more liberally. The first dance will be coming up soon; I wonder if I'll be able to sneak off to bed a bit early once the party has started.

I nip inside to check into my room, which I never got

around to this morning, and after collecting my key and being told my things will be taken up for me, I stop by the loos on my way back out to touch up my lipstick.

Gemma was right; it is my colour.

I'm not sure if it's the lipstick or the lingerie nobody but me knows I'm wearing or the release of finally letting go of Marcus, but I *feel* rejuvenated. Like a better version of myself, someone I was too scared to be before now.

Someone a bit bolder, and a bit more confident.

When I come out into the corridor outside the toilets, I collide with someone leaving the men's.

'Oof!'

'Sorry, sorry, I – oh,' Leon says. He's caught my elbow to keep me from toppling over in my heels when he bumped into me, and doesn't let go. 'It's you.'

'Fancy seeing you here,' I joke.

He pulls a face before laughing. 'Come on, let's get back out before we're accused of fornicating again.'

He says this just as Marcus's grandmother rounds the corner. She yelps, startled, and rushes past us. I lift a hand to my face, trying not to laugh as Leon flushes with embarrassment. He tugs on my elbow, leading us back to safer ground.

'Are you alright?' I ask him. 'About . . . Did you speak to Kayleigh, in the end? I didn't know whether to come and ask you earlier, or if . . . I didn't want to intrude, or put my foot in it at all.'

'You came out here to break up a wedding, and you're worried about putting your foot in it?'

'Oh, shut up. You know what I mean.'

He grins, but it fades quickly. 'I didn't speak to her. I was

362

going to, but . . . I don't know. Felt like a losing battle. I figured she'll come around on her own if she wants to, and I don't need to sacrifice my peace and happiness for her sake. I didn't need to put my neck on the line just to end up making things worse, you know?'

He's not holding onto me anymore, but I slip my arm through his. 'I'm glad. You're worth more than that, too, Leon.'

'Thanks, Francesca.' He looks at me earnestly and his voice is low, and slow, and the way he says my name sends a pleasant shiver down my spine; it makes me think of the almost-might-have-been kiss. I wonder if it makes him think about it, too, because suddenly he clears his throat and looks away, focusing on the ground in front of us as we walk back to the party. 'So, um . . . Marcus. You didn't . . .?'

'I didn't.'

'Oh. I thought . . .?'

'I was going to, but . . . At some point last night it stopped feeling like this grand romantic gesture and more like ripping off a plaster – like I was too far in to back out now, and like I owed it to myself to be honest with him and see how he felt, but . . . I didn't need to put my neck on the line, either.' Leon glances at me from the corner of his eye, and I smile. 'It doesn't matter how he feels – if he ever did feel anything for me.'

I don't need to know; I won't carry that uncertainty and regret around with me.

Because I finally know my own worth, and that's more than enough.

'It's not . . . going to be weird for you at work? Seeing him all the time?'

'Believe me, that office is more than big enough that our paths don't have to cross if I don't want them to. I think it's about time I found some different work friends, anyway. They're really not my sort of people. I only hung out with them for Marcus's sake; I'm sure they won't miss me too much.'

'Speak of the devil,' Leon mutters, snatching his arm away from mine, and I look up to see Marcus jogging away from the terrace to go to the loo.

'Alright, you two? Leon, how's it going?' Marcus gives him one of those bro-hugs, smacking him on the back, then winks at me with his usual grin. 'Keeping this one out of trouble?'

Oh, God, did I *really* fall for lines like that?

I need to get out more.

'Aren't you supposed to be having the first dance any minute?' Leon replies instead.

'Yeah, but you know how it goes. One too many beers, lethal. And I don't think this lot would be best pleased with me if I took a whiz in the shrubbery.' He laughs, and I grimace, and wonder yet again why I thought this man was so perfect. His hand rests on my arm when he moves past and he says, in a quieter voice, but one Leon must surely still hear clearly enough, 'Real shame you didn't make it here last night, babe. Save me a dance later, yeah?'

His hand is sweaty, and I push it off, unable to stop myself from pulling a face.

'No, I don't think I will,' I tell him curtly.

His face is a picture – a blank, slack look of shock.

I wonder how long it will take him to notice I've blocked his number and unfollowed him on socials. Probably quite a while. He'll get over it, I don't doubt.

It's only after we walk away that Leon stops, laughing so hard he has to hug a stitch in his side.

'I don't think that man's ever been told "no"' for anything in his life! Did you see his face? Oh, man. Wish Gemma had seen that, too. You're something else, Francesca, you know that?'

When he straightens up and catches my eye, I find myself throwing him a cheeky smile in response.

'Some might even call me a knockout.'

'They'd be absolutely right.'

This time, his arm loops around my waist on the way back into the party, and he turns to face me when we stop near the bar. 'So is it all dancing that's off-limits for you, or just a dance with the groom?'

'Is that you asking me for a dance, Leon?'

His eyes glitter. 'It's me hoping you'll say yes.'

'Then, yes.'

Which is how, half an hour later, when a slow song plays, I end up on the dance floor with Leon's arms around me and our bodies pressed close together, and I could just sink into his embrace. He's a terrible dancer and keeps tripping over his own feet, but he holds me so gently that when he spins me around, it feels like my feet hardly even touch the ground.

At one point, I notice Kayleigh glaring daggers at me, and faintly wonder what sort of story she will paint of me – first stealing her man, and now her brother.

I decide that I really don't care. I am not going to allow her or Marcus to take up any more space in my life.

I rest my head on Leon's shoulder and his arms curve around my waist. The dance feels so strangely intimate, especially when we haven't even shared a kiss, but I let my eyes slide closed as I relish the moment, my heart fluttering in my chest.

Maybe romance doesn't have to be dramatic grand gestures that put everything on the line.

Maybe it can just be like this.

I think, in hindsight, I know which I'd rather choose.

When Leon speaks, his voice rumbles through his chest, and I feel it against the palm of my hand pressed there. He says, 'Do you think maybe when we get back home, I could take you out on a date?'

I lift my head to smile at him. He's so close that our noses brush, our breath mingles. I can feel his own heart thudding hard against his chest, too.

'I'd really like that.'

'I can't promise any fornicating in toilets,' he jokes, all mock-seriousness.

'And I can't promise any deplorable behaviour.'

'Or pizza on the floor of an airport.'

'Or drinking games fuelled by duty-free booze.'

'Or taxis stolen from lovelorn strippers,' he says, and then, more earnestly, 'And I can't promise that sometimes I won't have to cancel because my family need me, or—'

'Leon,' I interrupt, and I press two fingers to his lips to shut him up just like he did to me last night, and it really is unerringly effective. His eyes widen a little, and darken. I lower my hand back to his chest, and go up on my tiptoes to press a feather-light kiss to his lips instead.

It's hardly a kiss at all.

But, God, is it so much more than anything I've ever felt before.

It's dizzying and grounding all at once. It feels like a promise, and a homecoming, and we both inhale sharply at the same time before I move away.

'I'd really like to go on a date with you,' I repeat.

He breaks into a smile so wide that my heart skips a beat, and I'm grinning back at him.

The music changes – moving all too abruptly from a classic John Legend ballad into an upbeat, catchy new Dua Lipa song. Some of the crowd around us cheer as they start singing and dancing along, and before I can quite catch my breath from the finally-kiss, someone hurls an arm around my shoulder, and around Leon's, making my forehead smack into his chin and both of us yelp.

Gemma, a little bit tipsy, with an open bottle of last night's limoncello in her hand, shouts, 'I love you guys so much. Can I be your maid of honour too?'

I'm not sure if it's me or Leon who's blushing more, but I wrap an arm around Gemma to hug her back.

'Do you guys want to get out of here and go drink on the beach? I've got macarons, too.' She moves her arm away from Leon to reveal a Ladurée bag. 'I stole the ones David brought Kayleigh; I feel like he'd really want *us* to have them.'

'Absolutely yes,' I say, unable to imagine anything better than spending the rest of the wedding – well, not at the wedding, but with these two instead. Gemma and I have already made plans to meet up when we get home, and to hang out tomorrow, too, before we have to leave. I take the bag from her. 'Macarons sound perfect. When in France, right?'

'Dibs on the pistachio,' Leon says.

Which maybe isn't a grand romantic gesture, but it sure feels like one.

He slips an arm around my waist and Gemma links her elbow with mine, and the three of us leave the wedding behind.

Acknowledgements

Firstly, a big thank you to my friend Katie for being my research buddy for this book, and for being so game when I messaged you saying 'Do you want to come to Paris with me? My only condition is that we spend a couple of extra hours at Orly Airport before we fly back home.' While rowing (mainly in circles or directly into some low-flying ducks) down the canal in Versailles and a late-night hike up to the Sacré Coeur didn't make it in, the macarons sure did.

A shoutout to the rest of the Physics gang (love you guys! Stay awesome), to Amy and Aimee for always lifting my spirits with a good story and a laugh, and the ever-epic Cluster for being such brilliant champions of my books across the Pond. Big thanks as usual to The hivE (née Gobble Gals, née Cactus Updates) for answering my nonsense questions and forever being such wonderful friends and supporters-slash-groupies coming to Waterstones with me so you can buy my book. Also to Rachael and Ellie – I feel like you guys in particular might enjoy a book full of 'ehpowt' shenanigans!

And thanks to Lauren – you get all my brain bees, but occasionally there's a nugget of something good in there to use in a book. Like when I said, 'This toilet cubicle is big enough to bring your suitcase and get changed in. It's probably big enough to shag in, too, but you would probably set off the automatic flush,' which you dubbed a 'wonderful medley of thought', so enjoy that scene playing out. Thanks for always being there and being you!

(Also, Lauren and Ellie – I hope you enjoy the ACOTAR reference. It's especially for you!)

Thanks to my family for all your continued support with my books – and occasionally being my photography assistants on mini book tours! Kat, hopefully this one's another winner for you!

And, last but never least, a MASSIVE thank you as always to my brilliant team behind the scenes, bringing this one to bookshelves! My phenomenal agent Clare, my editor Bec, and all the rest of the team at Sphere: Zoe, Alison and Lucie. Thanks for all you do!

Also by Beth Reekles from Sphere...

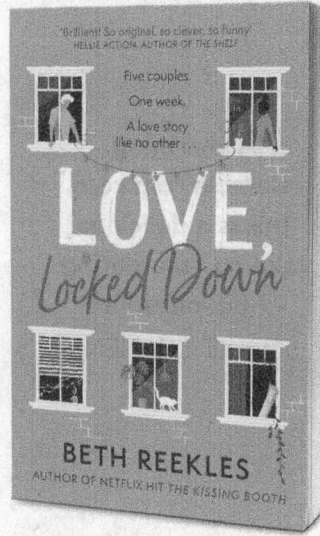

Five couples. One week. A love story like no other...

When an apartment block is put on lockdown, its residents are in
for a whirlwind week. In Flat 14, wild and reckless **Imogen** is stuck
living with a one-night-stand whose name she can't remember.

Upstairs, **Isla** and **Danny** are still in the honeymoon period, but a warts-and-all
week together so early in the relationship could make or break their romance.
Meanwhile, **Zach** and **Serena's** steady relationship is on tenterhooks,
and pineapple on pizza might actually be the last straw.

In Flat 22, **Olivia's** Maid of Honour duties are pushing her to the edge as
a wedding-planning weekend has turned into an entire (nightmarish) week...
And speaking of weddings, this whole thing has made Ethan realise he wants
to spend the rest of his life with **Charlotte**, if only he can surprise her with
the perfect proposal – and find a way to sneak her into the building...

OUT NOW

Can you fall in love if you're only ever pretending?

Sophie, 25. Looking for: a plus one

Perfect first date: At my sister's wedding pretending we're already dating ...

Lifelong singleton, Sophie, is looking for love. With her friends settling down and her family piling on the pressure, it seems that her anonymous column about relationships is more successful than her actual dating life. But now, with her sister's wedding approaching, she's determined not to turn up alone – and if she can't find her soulmate in time, she'll just have to fake one.

Enter Harry. Charming, attractive and seeking a post-break-up distraction, he answers Sophie's plea on a dating app, promising an all-expenses-paid weekend to anyone crazy enough to go along with her charade. And with the wedding a hit and a calendar full of 'couple' events on the horizon, the pair realise the only way they'll survive the next few months is with each other – and a little white lie . . .

But as their love deception deepens and the pair grow closer, Sophie realises their charade may be holding them back from facing the truth. After all, when you're pretending to be in love, how is it possible to find the real thing?

OUT NOW

SIX OLD FRIENDS.

TEN YEARS LATER.

IS IT TOO LATE TO LEARN A LESSON IN LOVE?

Ten years after graduating, the class of 2014 are back at Tisdale Comprehensive for the reunion, packed into a school gym full of familiar faces – and plenty of new secrets.

MOST LIKELY TO END UP TOGETHER: **Shaun** and **Steph** were each other's first love. Now, they're settled and planning the perfect wedding – to other people. Could reconnecting spark a new romance?

MOST LIKELY TO BECOME FAMOUS: **Bryony** was supposed to travel the world, rule the West End, have a dazzling career as a TV actress . . . Now, she's a drama teacher who's exaggerated her whole life on Instagram, and is desperate to save face.

MOST LIKELY TO SUCCEED: **Hayden** was told he'd achieve great things, like be on the cover of *TIME*, win a Nobel prize . . . or, the accolade his daughters just awarded him: World's Best Dad. Is it too late for him to turn things around, and more importantly, does he even want to?

MOST LIKELY TO KILL EACH OTHER: **Ashleigh** was an A* student, and **Ryan** the star of the school rugby team. After years of putting each other down, they left school each convinced they would have the better life. Now, that old rivalry finds them drawn back together in a new, intoxicating way – one they're both determined to hide.

With an evening of power cuts, fire alarms, sneaking off to explore classrooms in the dark, stolen kisses and heated fights – it's like they never left at all.

With enemies-to-lovers, forced proximity and second-chance romance, *THE REUNION* is the ultimate romantic read.